THE HAUNTING OF SOLOMON HOUSE

THE BLAIR GRAVES FILES

MARNIE VINGE

For Dad, wherever you are

ONE

SEEING my father's face front and center as the headlining story on a tabloid should be more surprising. This would come as a shock to anyone with anything resembling a normal childhood. Or a normal father. But I'm not just anyone and neither is my father.

Or *was*.

It's a moment in which any other person might find themselves speechless.

Confronted with their father's face on the cover of a publication that was also featuring a story about someone called Bat Kid marrying worldwide pop phenomenon Ainsley Gold.

You know the kind. They run stories about current or former politicians and world leaders being reptilians sent from another galaxy to take over our world.

I've never been able to get behind that or any theory resembling it.

My father had absolutely no problem getting behind such ideas. He also provided an amplified stage for anyone who ever had similar thoughts. My dad, Graham Graves, was the host of one of the most popular AM talk radio shows, and he's been missing for seven years today.

I unload my cart onto the conveyor belt, but my eyes remain glued to the tabloid. The girl at the register scans and bags, neither of us exchanging more than a stiff smile throughout the ordeal. Unloading the last of my items, several bottles of cheap wine, I push my cart around for her to place the bags back in it. As I fish for my wallet, the guy behind me says something. "Hey," he says. I turn, expecting him to ask me where I found something I'm purchasing.

"You're his daughter, aren't you?" he asks. I take in the man's appearance: plaid pearl snap shirt, fitted Wranglers, cowboy boots, and a smile.

The kind of smile that you only get when you run into a celebrity. He looks star-struck.

But I have news for him: I'm no celebrity and I have absolutely no desire to follow in my errant father's footsteps.

"I am," I confirm cautiously.

"I used to listen to him every single night," the man says wistfully. He's older. The thought strikes me that he's my dad's age. Current age. How old my dad would be. The phrasing is strange and I roll it around in my mind. It occurs to me that I haven't done a lot of thinking about the implications of that phrasing. That my father might *not* be of a certain age, that he may not exist anymore *at all*.

For a split second, the wall I've erected against such thoughts comes down.

A flood of emotion threatens to overrun me. It's momentary, but it feels worryingly like something resembling emotion in my gut. It's a sinking feeling in my chest.

"Oh," I say. It's all I can manage.

"That'll be $103 even." The teen behind the register reminds me where I am. I snap my attention back to her and away from the man. The far more familiar man on the cover of the tabloid. I slip my debit card out of my wallet and swipe it quickly in the reader. It chirps happily, letting me know the transaction went through. I start to stick my card back into my wallet and my eyes momentarily go to the tabloid. Without thinking, I reach out and grab it.

"And this," I tell the girl. She rings me up once more. I swipe my card again. I smile at the man who knew my father in the loosest way possible, and I head for the parking lot.

AFTER I LOAD my groceries and lock my doors, I get my phone out and check my notifications like a well-trained dog. Somewhat surprisingly, two names are missing from the screen that I expected to see there. The first is my best friend, Noelle. The other is my twin brother, Blake. I expect to hear from both of them today for entirely different reasons. One pleasant or slightly so, the other likely unpleasant and more than slightly so.

I plug my phone into the port that makes it display itself on my car stereo screen. I press the button on my steering wheel that allows for voice control. Play my station, I tell it.

"Here's some music picked just for you," Siri chirps back quickly. Immediately, Ainsley Gold, the same pop star that was featured as a smaller image on the cover of the tabloid about my father's disappearance, starts to sing.

I pull out of the parking lot and, at a stoplight, I check my phone again, making sure I haven't missed anything.

And I haven't. I think about calling Noelle, just to make sure that we're still on for tonight. I can't imagine she'd cancel. Not tonight.

Not on our annual thing.

But the thought that she might creeps in and makes me face the idea that I might have to spend the night alone. Or worse: on the phone with Blake as my only company.

I banish the thoughts and head home.

I blast the Ainsley Gold music. She's always been one of my favorites.

She's the kind of pop star that captured the zeitgeist of a generation. She can do no wrong.

She's America's golden girl. Much like Princess Diana was for the UK. I find myself staying up late at night reading articles about her latest romance all the time. It's an escape from the life I'm living. It's December and people are scurrying around Christmas shopping. The only person I ever shop for anymore is Noelle. It's been a long time since Blake and I exchanged anything warmer than a *fuck you*.

I hit a second stoplight. I catch movement in the corner of my eye. I glanced at the minivan beside me and see two kids in the backseat fighting with each other. They're laughing. The mom in the front seat reaches back to break it up. But before the light turns green, she's laughing and dad in the driver's seat eventually gets involved, too. They're happy. It's a family dynamic I'm not that familiar with. It's the family unit I should have had.

That everyone should have.

The person behind me honks, letting me know the turn light is green. I shake myself out of my little daydream and hit the gas. I peel out of the stoplight, leaving the happy family in the other lane behind, and I also leave behind the chance that I can ever make my childhood right. Today is a special marker of that.

The house that I live in—my father's house, legally still until today—is just outside of town. Oklahoma City has become somewhat of a booming metropolis in the last ten years. A development I'm not sure any of us saw coming back in the 90s, but now it's packed. There are breweries and bars, coffee shops and bakeries, restaurants and shopping centers. Even a resort coming soon, the likes of which I don't think I could have imagined as a kid. And there's still enough of a rural patch in the city that provides for properties like the one my dad bought when Blake and I were seventeen and his radio career had really taken off.

I slow down just before I get to my driveway. A giant truck that looks like a substitute for healthy masculinity whips around me and the gust of air from it shakes my SUV.

"Jesus!" I shout, as if the guy in the pickup can hear me. A little shaken, and a lot annoyed, I head down the winding driveway that leads to the Graves' property.

My dad, because of his moderate fame, had chosen a piece of land that was isolated on all sides by the woods. Trees still line every edge of it and even hide the house from the main road. People know this is his house, though. Sometimes teenagers will get up the courage to do a little trespassing, though it's grown more infrequent with the passing of each year since his disappearance. It's strange to think that my father—my family—has become the stuff of urban legend.

It's amazing to me that the guy in the grocery store recognized me. Probably from a photo shoot that Blake and I did with our father years ago. A feature about Graham Graves and his family, or what remained of it.

My mother wasn't in the picture. She died when Blake and I were very young.

My mind goes back to the trespassers.

The thought that they've become fewer and further between hits me with unexpected sadness.

As I wind my way through the trees along the gravel drive, I spot a red sports car outside the garage, and a smile creeps across my face. Noelle. I guess I hadn't realized how much it might have depressed me if she had chosen to spend her night some other way than as my sad and lonely company tonight.

But there's her Mustang that she just purchased. Prior to that, she had driven a Mazda Miata that she had owned since she turned twenty-one. The wheels were ready to fall off when she bought the Mustang. That thing was a coffin on wheels waiting for the opportunity to take its owner, and any passenger she might have, straight to hell.

I smile as I pull into the garage, thinking about the time the brakes went out while we were on the highway. We'd screamed, and I'd seen my life flash before my eyes. But we lucked out. It happened on a straight stretch of road in the middle of a weeknight. We were practically alone on the highway.

Noelle and I have many such stories. Close brushes

with death that I never shared with my father. Lest he keep me from ever hanging out with her again.

I'm sure she kept our near-death-experiences from her parents as well.

Especially considering that her family had its own brushes with the dark side of the world. Noelle has a cousin that went to prison for attempted murder.

I guess we all have our dark things.

I shut the garage door and head for the back of the SUV. I groan as I carry the groceries, straining under the weight of all of them. The plastic sacks dig into my wrists, but I'll be damned if I need to make two trips. I'd rather throw my back out. I reach for the doorknob, but the door opens before I can even give it a twist.

"Hello, gorgeous!" Noelle chirps, her cheeks flushed with either cold or wine. It isn't until she embraces me and I catch the scent of her flammable breath that I'm sure which. Her freckled face is flush with drink and her strawberry blonde hair is tucked up in a messy bun that always looks better on her than on me. I end up looking bald in pictures if my hair isn't down, and she looks like she just rolled out of a Pinterest ad, despite her tipsy state. Her light green eyes are bright.

"Someone started early," I say in return. I stand there for a moment, holding the groceries.

"Oh, shit. Here. Give me those!" She takes part of them with her free hand and helps me into the house. We walk down the darkened hallway that leads into the kitchen. It's so dark that only the lights beneath the cabinets are on, the fading winter daylight outside casting the house in a gloomy blue grey. We place the sacks on the island and get to work unloading them. It's not much, but her help is invaluable.

I hate unpacking groceries by myself. There's something lonely about it.

I remember when I was a teenager, my dad and I would go grocery shopping together. Blake usually stayed home. When we got back, we unloaded the groceries and my dad would usually put on some music, some golden oldies from his day.

We'd have a good time. He'd tell me jokes. He'd be a regular dad. It was one of the few times that he did that.

The rest of the time, he was buried in his work and dedicated to the pursuit of something other than the pursuit of a relationship with his children in the next room.

Noelle knows all about the importance of certain dates. She's got one in her own life, with just as grim an overtone as what today holds for me.

"How are you doing?" She asks as we finish up. I turned to see her holding a glass of white wine out for me. I take it.

"I'm fine." A brittle laugh comes out unexpectedly. It sounds breakable even to me. And I told myself the reason for that is that today marks uncertainty.

Nothing else. Just a little question mark about the future.

For Blake and I.

"It's okay if you're not, Blair," she says.

"Why don't you drink some more wine?" I say in a snippy tone.

"Why don't *you* drink some *period*," she quips in return.

I can't help but smile.

"Sorry," I say. "You know that's not directed at you." My smile falters, becoming something sad.

"I know," Noelle says, returning the expression. Though I know she's not sad for herself. She's sad for me. And that's worse somehow.

I think in any of our lifetimes we're gifted once, maybe twice, with a human being who truly and utterly understands us. For some people that comes in the shape of a romantic partner. For me, that came in the shape of Noelle.

I raise my glass to hers and we clink our delicate drink ware together.

"To the future," she says.

"To the future," I echo.

And we drink. Even though the future for both of us is a murky cloud of uncertainty.

At least tonight we have each other.

TWO

WITH ENOUGH WINE in my veins, the concrete of the patio doesn't feel too cold. Noelle and I lay head to head, our legs stretched out in either direction and our eyes cast upward into the stars. I killed the patio lights that hang from the pergola, giving us a better view of the celestial bodies above.

"Do you think he really believed?" Noelle asks. She doesn't have to specify who or what she's inquiring about. It's a question that comes up every year, usually prompted by her and resented by me, even though I don't show that. I'm silent for a long moment, rolling the question over in my mind.

I don't know what I think the truth is, and it's one of the many points of contention I have with my missing father.

"I don't think he did," I say.

I feel Noelle roll over onto her forearms, her hair

brushing against mine. I look backward, meeting her upside-down face.

"You really think he could do that radio show all those years and not believe in any of that stuff?" she asks. Her words are slightly slurred and her eyes are bloodshot. I imagine I look and sound much the same.

"I think people will do a lot of things for money," I tell her.

The sentiment comes out more bitterly than I intended and the implications cast my thoughts to my brother and the meaning of this day.

Blake and I haven't seen each other in years. We barely talk anymore. Maybe on the phone a couple of times throughout the year, mostly on holidays. Those calls have gotten fewer and further between over the last couple of years.

I feel like I needed to talk to him today. No, I know I need to talk to him today.

It's kind of strange that he hasn't called yet.

We're going to be talking about something that affects me strongly.

I don't think my father believed in the things he claimed to believe in.

I think he saw a market, and he tapped into it, which is what any good businessman would do. I shouldn't fault him for that.

But I do because he was taking advantage of the people he talked to. Wasn't he?

I listened to his show as a kid and into my early

teens. As I got older, I got the vibe that maybe those people would have been better off seeking professional help rather than talking to my father.

"Have you heard from Blake?" Noelle asks. She's asked once already, but I imagine she's forgotten at this point. I reach for my cell phone, fishing it out of my pocket. I look through the notifications, searching for one I might have missed, but I turn up empty-handed. There's nothing from Blake. No sign of him.

"No," I tell her.

"I'm kind of surprised," she says. "I figured he'd be beating down the door today."

I thoroughly expected to hear from him today on the seventh year anniversary of our dad's disappearance.

It will mean that I need to sell the house. Something that I've known was coming for a long time. Blake has financial problems. He's got a gambling addiction. And it's not something that he's ever been able to address over the years. I'm sure he's just waiting for the right moment to come in and pounce. I guess calling this evening seemed in poor taste, even to him.

Though knowing when things were in poor taste wasn't a strong suit of his or my father's. I'm sure I'll hear from him soon.

The two of us are silent for a moment.

"What about you?" I ask her. "Have you heard from Jenna lately?"

Noelle is silent. It occurs to me that she might not

have enough alcohol in her system yet for such questions. We rarely, if ever, talk about her cousin Jenna.

That's the darkness that her family has known. When we do talk about Jenna, Noelle is the one to bring her up. Usually after we split a few bottles of wine. I'm not sure we've reached the requisite alcohol threshold to talk about this subject.

"Not lately," she says.

I glance backward at her, and she's still resting on her forearms. She looks down at me and reaches out a single finger.

"Boop." She touches my nose.

A big smile spreads across Noelle's face, and I find myself unable to resist the contagion. I smile right back at her and we leave the conversation there.

FINALLY, numb to our toes, we decide to go inside. The gust of warm air that hits me on the way in is a welcome respite from the numbness I've developed along the backside of my body. It's almost as pleasant as slipping into a hot tub after swimming in a frigid late fall pool.

We go into the kitchen and I pour both of us another glass of wine. We start working our way through another bottle.

I know I'm drinking entirely too much tonight. Noelle seems to be along for the ride. She always is when all other coping mechanisms have been exhausted.

She's been with me through at least one breakup, lost jobs, and all sorts of things over the years.

Noelle plants herself firmly on one end of the green velvet couch, and I sit across from her in a matching chair. I grab the remote and turn on the television. I find the YouTube app and open it.

One of our drinking rituals involves watching cooking videos on the internet or food tours of different cities. Vlogs that people have made of restaurants in places that we would like to go someday. We're forever doing that: planning trips that we might not ever take.

But I'd rather spend the time planning them with her, even if we don't go.

"What kind of video?" I ask.

"Cooking," she says.

I nod and navigate to the search bar.

"Cashew chicken," she adds.

"Sounds good to me," I tell her.

I pull my phone out of my pocket and place it on the table beside me. I'll need it handy once we watch several and realize we need take out. I start typing cashew into the search bar.

C-A-S-H

"Hey, wait!" Noelle shouts.

I look over at her, unsure what she's excited about.

"That guy!" She points with more animation than she's had all night. "Cash Kelly!"

"Who?" I ask.

She gestures at the television in the recommended search terms that have auto populated. *Cash Kelly* is first.

"What about him?" I ask.

"He's like your dad," she says.

"What?"

"He does videos about weird shit. He lives here, actually. He interviews people about Bigfoot and UFOs and ghosts and stuff."

I believe that all of our lives can be boiled down to a few moments that set our course one way or another. And I believe that right now I'm unaware that such a moment exists in front of me.

Out of sheer curiosity and a bit of irritation, I click on the name and a host of videos pop up. Each of them has a title more outlandish and click-baity than the last.

Aliens real! Final proof of ET life?

Real ghosts caught on tape?!

We're living in a simulation! Proof!

The irritation flares into a full-blown inferno of disgust. This guy isn't like my dad. He's worse.

"Well, you're right about that," I say, referencing Noelle's assertion that this idiot is putting out the same kind of crap that my dad did. Only this guy's doing it in video format. Somehow that's worse. More easily consumable, shorter pieces of content. Titles that make you think you *might* get a definitive answer about things. Not a four hour long radio show every night primarily only listened to by older American men. Kids are probably watching these. People with still undeveloped brains trying to form their ideas about the world.

I wonder what makes up his audience. What demographics? What kind of people?

"Should we watch one?" Noelle asks.

I glance over at her. I know the answer. Without a doubt, we should not watch one. My blood pressure will skyrocket. No one will have a good time. Except Cash Kelly, who will be glad for the minutes added to his monthly viewing calculations.

I'm sure he'd love those ad dollars.

"Come on, Blair," Noelle prods me. I wonder if it's because of the alcohol in her system. Normally, I don't think she would encourage me to do something like this. It feels self destructive. Like picking at a wound that won't heal.

"Fine," I bite off the word.

I want to tell myself that it's because I want her to shut up. But part of me knows that it's because I'm curious to know.

I click on the first recommended video, the alien one.

As soon as it starts and we're watching the intro, I realize one thing. Cash Kelly is incredibly attractive. Ridiculously so. He's blond with blue eyes and a nice tan. His shoulders are wide enough to show a movie on. He looks like an ex Special Forces guy. He's got the look about him that makes me think the tan is real. And he's not the product for a tanning bed.

He probably spends time outside, adventuring. That sort of thing. Somehow, it makes him feel more genuine.

He almost looks like the kind of guy that would be most at home hanging ten in Hawaii or hiking the four-teeners in Colorado.

"Hey guys, welcome back," he says after the intro finishes. "It's me, Cash Kelly, and tonight we're going to talk about aliens."

The introduction makes me snort out a laugh. His voice is serious, heavy, even. Like he's an investigative journalist about to lay some uncomfortable truth on you. The guy takes himself seriously. It's another thing he has in common with my father.

I can't help but return to his attractiveness.

His buttoned up shirt is just a little too tight, show-casing his physique just a little too much. It's definitely intentional. It's something that makes me dislike him almost instantly. I wonder how many girls watch him thinking, *He's so hot.*

Probably a lot and most of them are probably minors. It makes me roll my eyes.

"Hey," Noel says.

I snap out of my daydream about Cash Kelly's muscles and teenager audience, and come back to reality.

Noelle points at the screen. I look back at it. One of

the recommended videos has been updated. The title sends a shock through my system that sobers me up instantly. In the little column beside the YouTube video that we're watching, the first suggested video is titled *Graham Graves: radio host that disappeared seven years ago today* by Cash Kelly. The video was posted only minutes ago. The algorithm just grabbed it. My heart thunders in my chest and blood rushes to my ears. I can't believe what I'm seeing.

It should seem logical. The leap that someone making this kind of content might cover my father's disappearance. But somehow it feels like an invasion of privacy. The magazine was one thing.

This feels worse somehow.

I click on it, unable to help myself. At this point. I'm not just picking at the wound. I'm pouring salt into it.

"Hey guys, Cash Kelly here." He leans forward into the camera. His elbows are braced on his knees, bent forward in his chair. He looks like a dad about to give you some bad news. There's a seriousness in his face that I doubt is sincere. "Today is a sad day in the UFO community. In the *entire* paranormal community, actually." He goes on. "Seven years ago today, Graham Graves went missing. As all of you know, I took his disappearance particularly hard. Graham was not only an idol of mine, but someone I considered a mentor."

I bark out a laugh. Who the fuck does this guy think he is?

Noelle hisses. Cash goes on, uninterrupted by me.

And it irritates me.

"There are a lot of theories about what happened to Graham, and I have my own thoughts. We're going to dissect a few of those theories here tonight and talk about his legacy," Cash says. I feel blood rush to my head.

I feel a primal protectiveness that I didn't think myself capable of. I don't want him talking about my dad. I knew that people would, especially today, especially tonight, but there's something about hearing a stranger say his name out loud that unsettles me. I feel territorial. That's *my* dad. That's *our* story.

Cash goes on to outline several theories. Each and every one I've heard before. Aliens got him. The government got him. Bigfoot got him. Some other thing he was searching for got him. Cash concludes the video solemnly and says something I'm not expecting. Something that sends me right on over the edge.

"Tonight, my thoughts are with his family. With his kids." He glances down, then back at the camera. "To Blake and Blair. I hope that you find peace."

"Oh, fuck you!" Before I realize exactly what I'm doing, the remote is flying through the air. It collides with the television screen and a huge lightning strike crack issues from one corner to the other, making the picture have something of a seizure.

The screen flickers and then it goes black.

THREE

I WAKE in the early hours of the morning the way you only do when you're over thirty and you've had way too much to drink. My head pounds like it always does when I over indulge in white wine. A lesson you'd think I'd have learned by now.

It's the kind of headache that you can't get rid of. Advil, Aleve, Tylenol. None of it helps. When I arrive in the kitchen, I see wine bottles everywhere.

A grim reminder of how Noelle and I spent the evening before. Little dead soldiers reminding me that I'm at war. Maybe just with myself, maybe with memories, maybe with my father, or what happened to him.

It's not the sign of a mind that's in a good place. I tip each of them over into the sink, hoping that there might be some left just to prove to myself that I don't have a binge drinking problem.

Alas, they're all empty.

A deep snore emanates from the couch. Noelle crashed there, I assume. I made it to my own bed. Though everything between the moment I cracked the television screen and now is a blur. I walk into the living room and walk up to the television. The crack is deep. I run a finger along it. It sweeps from one corner to the other. In the center is the center of impact, with little spiderwebs blossoming out from it.

I see my reflection on the TV. Something I'm not expecting. I look like hell.

So that *did* happen. Unfortunately.

I turn around and see Noelle draped along the length of the velvet couch. One arm tucked beneath her and the other outstretched toward the floor. Her cell phone is just out of reach on the rug below.

I wonder if she messaged anyone she shouldn't have last night. Hopefully, just Hooper if anyone. I'm sure he'd be glad to hear from a drunk Noelle. The thought makes me smirk and the motion of my facial muscles sends a fresh thudding through my skull.

Immediately, I drop the expression, returning my face to something neutral. I reach for my temples and rub them in an attempt to stop it. But it doesn't. The ache is deep.

Golden hour sunlight blankets the living room and kitchen. On any other morning, it might feel hopeful. I've always thought the sunrise did. Even after the worst night, the sun would be there in the morning.

Ernest Hemingway even titled a book after the idea. Today it doesn't feel that way.

There's a heaviness leftover from last night. A residue of the events that led me here.

My father is legally dead. I don't think it's something that I was quite prepared for.

It feels like a death sentence. Like the way a sunrise might feel in the morning of an execution.

I know that today will probably bring an unwanted call from Blake. A call that I've been dreading for some time now, even though I've known it was coming.

Blake needs money.

This property is worth a lot.

We both got the same amount when my father disappeared. Dispersed through a trust in case of his disappearance. But Blake couldn't manage his. It's something that's broken my heart for him over the years as I've watched him struggle.

And he's resented me because I didn't.

I did what I was told by the financial advisors and I was able to live a nice lifestyle, maintaining the house, maintaining the property, and still being able to do some of the things I wanted to do.

It occurs to me that I silenced my cell phone last night. If he has called. I wouldn't have heard it, though I doubt he would do it this early. At any rate, I need my cell phone's alert audible so that when the time comes, I might hear it.

Still in my pocket, I fish it out, and when I wake it

I'm met with a barrage of notifications, almost every one of them a comment reply on YouTube. A few of the messages. Also on YouTube. I've never posted a video on YouTube. I've never so much as commented on a video. I don't even think I've gone as far as to subscribe to anyone's channel.

"Oh," I say out loud. My stomach sinks. "Oh, no." Please, God, tell me I didn't do that.

But after a quick swipe to open the app, I see that. Oh yes, I absolutely *did* do that.

I commented on Cash Kelly's video about my dad.

My finger hesitantly opens the replies. I cringe, waiting for the worst. I have no idea what I said, but just from the little pop up previews of the comments I've gotten back, it wasn't good.

After reading several heated threats to my life, several defenses of Cash Kelly, and several invitations for me to kill myself, I find my original comment. Jesus Christ.

Ur a fucking idiot who preys on people just like he did and I hope you go missing too

My God.
My God, Blair. How old are you?

I go through more of the replies. Although now with my own comment as context. I don't blame any of them for their epithets. Who wishes for another human being to go missing?

For just the tiniest split second, I know exactly who does: someone hurting really bad.

At least there's solace in the fact that my handle is only bg1987bb. It would take some logical leaps for anyone to connect the screen name with my actual identity. There are probably a lot of people born in 1987 with the initials BG. Although I don't give myself very high marks for creativity, or protection of my own privacy. On the other hand, it's likely that Cash's fans would put it together with the context of what I said in my comment.

We are dealing with an audience who thrives on conspiracy, conspiracy theories. They'd love to sink their teeth into this little mystery.

I hear Noelle behind me and I turn. She shields her eyes with her free hand and uses the one trapped beneath her to hoist herself up into the sitting position. The grunts and groans make me think the entire action takes a lot of effort. And I can relate. Being hungover after thirty is no joke. It's no longer a matter of getting the local diner to fill your tummy with carbs. It's more a matter of hoping that when you sneeze, you don't shit yourself somewhere in public. A diner is the last place you want to be.

"I think I'm dying," she says as she leans back into the couch, one hand still shielding her eyes from the golden hour sunlight. It pours through her strawberry blonde hair, making it glow champagne pink. The thought of the drink makes my stomach turn. I think we even had some of that last night.

"You're not," I assure her. "You just wish you were."

"Yes. Yes, I do wish that," she confirms. "Why did you make me drink so much?"

"I was going to ask you the same thing," I tell her.

"I think I'm gonna barf." Noelle brings her hand down and her glassy eyes focus on me. Her face flinches, and she stands abruptly. She stumbles, probably still a little drunk from last night, and rushes for my bathroom.

The thought occurs to me that now, even after all this time, Noelle uses *my* bathroom. It's nestled inside the junior master bedroom. There's another bathroom specifically for guests in the hallway just before my bedroom door. But Noelle has known me the entire time I've lived here, way back when Blake did, too, in the other junior master bedroom. And when we were teenagers, Noelle and I spent most of our time locked in my bedroom. Using my bathroom is logical even now that we're over thirty. I have a sad thought that all of this will change soon.

I know in my gut that the call from Blake is coming.

All of that is accompanied by the notion that this house isn't going to be mine for much longer.

At least not after the messy sorting out of Dad's

estate. I can't imagine Blake being reasonable about any of it. Dad hurt him, too.

Two things happen at once. I hear Noelle vomiting loudly from the bathroom and my cell phone rings. It's before eight in the morning.

My television is broken. Noelle is vomiting and Blake is on the other end of the phone.

I sigh and know I have to take the call.

I THINK for a moment about how long it's been since Blake and I had anything resembling a real conversation. Given the significance of yesterday, I imagine this is going to be the longest conversation I've had with him in years.

And it's going to be an unpleasant one.

Blake always had it in his head that it was me and Dad against him. That I was the favorite, which was absolutely absurd. The reason he and dad didn't get along had a lot more to do with the fact that they're exactly alike. In so many ways. Blake accuses me of the same thing and insists that it's the reason that I was dad's favorite.

Neither of them knows how to take advice or listen to any outside source. Once they get an idea, it's set in stone. They're like dogs with bones.

There's a little part of me that acknowledges I might be the same.

Understandably, it made it difficult for the three of us to cohabitate beneath the same roof, and it made it even more difficult for Dad and Blake. I look at Blake's name, the slider taunting me and asking me to pick up the phone. Finally, I do.

"Hello," I say after a moment. It's not a question so much as a long-awaited statement.

"Hello, Blair."

Blake's voice is just as I remember it, though a little older now. A little more gravelly?

The conversation feels like it's taking place elevated on stilts. Walking through eggshells, like one wrong move and it'll be crashing down, and we haven't even started to cover anything of substance yet.

"I imagine I know what you're calling about," I go on cautiously, advising myself to tread lightly. The silent tension between us is a stark reminder of how fucked up our childhood probably was, without either of us really knowing it until we were older.

It's a reminder that Blake perceives it as much more fucked up than I do. Finally he sighs.

"Blair, you need to sell that house," he says, the words coming out combative.

I don't want to be on the defensive this soon. I promised myself for years that I wouldn't be when the day finally came when we had to have this conversation.

Blake seems to be weighing his words in the silence.

"Dad's dead," he says.

"You say that like you're sure," I retort, venom leaking onto my lips.

I know as well as anyone that he's dead.

But having to admit that to Blake isn't something I'm willing to do.

"Blair, he left seven years ago and never came back. No one's heard from him. He hasn't been seen. He's dead."

I have very little problem with the idea our father might be dead. He was barely present when he was alive, so the situation feels the same. It lacks the vacuum power that death should have, sucking the air from your lungs when it comes to pass. I feel like I've been suffocating for seven years now. This isn't something new. It doesn't have the power of a fresh wound, merely the dull and persistent ache of one that's been there for years.

There's a part of me, though, that thinks he might not be.

It kind of wouldn't surprise me if he was holed up somewhere working on something that amounts to little more than an unhinged conspiracy theory. And he just happened to lose track of time entirely. And the fact that he has a set of twins, a son and a daughter that he left behind to clean up his mess as usual.

My silence is met with a sigh on Blake's end.

"You were always his favorite," he starts.

I bark out a laugh.

"Here we go," I mutter.

"Just let me finish, okay?" Blake says. I sigh, resigning myself to silence long enough to let him spew whatever bullshit he's got on his mind. "Things weren't the same with me and Dad." Here we go, indeed.

"Look, Blake," I say.

"Blair. Let me finish," he says, his voice taking on a sharper edge.

"I don't care what slights you think I dealt you or Dad dealt you. What the hell does that have to do with the house?"

Blake sighs. I hear crackling silence on the other end. Letting me know he's still there. Just not speaking.

"Oh my god," I say, even though I'm not shocked. "You need money."

"I wouldn't ask if it wasn't an emergency," Blake says, sounding resigned, defeated, and humiliated.

I know my reaction is wrong. Probably only serving to make Blake feel ashamed and more isolated. The words came out before I meant them to. Before I had a chance to filter them through what might be appropriate. One of the many things that Blake and Dad have in common is a propensity for gambling. Dad liked to gamble with wild ideas and Blake likes to gamble with money, especially money he doesn't have. Usually other people's money.

"I thought you gave that up," I say, my tone is accusatory without me meaning for it to be.

Blake sighs. He takes on the air of a child,

explaining to a parent how he fucked up and he'll never do it again. Even though we both know that's crap.

"I will," he says. "This is different."

"It's always different, Blake." I think about all the times I bailed him out.

"Please, Blair," he says. There's a brokenness in his voice. A sound that calls to something deep inside of me. That twin connection that people talk about. No matter what he's put me through, Blake is the only person left that shares my DNA.

I roll my eyes back into my head. I keep them closed for a moment, then open them up, and look around the kitchen that we sat in a decade ago. A good time. The three of us laughing. A good day, maybe. A good memory.

Everything is so broken.

"Okay," I say.

FOUR

NOELLE LEAVES a little worse for the wear after our night of drinking. She looks like a disheveled college student after an all-nighter when she climbs into the driver's seat of her car. Her hair stands on end and giant Jackie O style shades prevent too much sunlight from increasing the pounding inside her skull. Once again, I'm struck by the way her strawberry blonde hair looks in the warm morning sunlight.

Her hair is standing on end and little pink strands reach out towards the roof of her car. The thought makes me smirk. And once again, my head pounds. I go back inside and start cleaning things up. My conversation with Blake rumbles around in the back of my mind.

"Fuck!" I shout the word, my frustration reaching a boiling point as I scrub the counters down in the kitchen. Alcohol has made them sticky, reminding me of times when my dad went out of town and Blake and I would have friends over. Jesus, the parties we had. Mad Dog 20/20. The kind of drinks that populate a lot of millennial teenage memories.

I remember a particular party. Noelle was there. So was Hooper.

I think again about the possibility of Noelle texting him while she was drunk. It's a welcome respite from thinking about Blake for a moment.

Hooper is a good guy, and he'd give anything to be with Noelle.

At that particular party, Hooper did a keg stand. He threw up before he was even done, and Noelle took care of him for the rest of the night. I think it might have been when he fell in love with her. After that, he followed her around like a puppy. This was after Noelle's cousin went to prison.

All those parties and Dad never knew.

I pause and stare out the huge picture window that looks out over the backyard, patio, hot tub, and the pool.

Maybe he did know. A thought occurs to me. It's bleak. Maybe he knew, and he didn't care.

I feel hollowed out by the notion, cut down to the bone.

Maybe Blake's always been right about him.

And I think on some level I know that Dad is dead.

Who could go seven years without contacting anyone from their former life? Who could leave two young adults to fend for themselves without having given them any of the tools to do so?

Who could do that?

Could my father do that?

I don't want to think so.

The thought fills me with sadness. I return to scrubbing the counters and clean the rest of the house, fueled by the discomfort I feel from the conversation I just had with my brother.

What does it matter?

The quiet voice poses the question that accompanies me in moments when I'm alone for a little too long.

It doesn't matter, does it? This house was never truly a home. Was it?

I think about the nights Noelle spent here with me. Two of us in my bed. Her reaching for my hand sometimes in the night when things were hard for her at home. This place was a comfort to her, and she was a comfort to me. And just by her being inside these walls, she filled this house with goodness. Maybe my own family couldn't do that consistently, but Noelle could. And the thought of leaving behind a place that houses memories of that goodness is painful.

These ideas circulate, whirling in my head like a dust devil kicking up uncomfortable emotions. I bury myself in cleaning for the rest of the morning.

I END up taking a less than satisfying nap in the afternoon. Something about drinking too much seems to ruin the following forty-eight hours for me now. Maybe even more sometimes. It's probably a side effect of aging, reaching the crest of thirty and going over it.

Your body is still that of a creature that used to die around that time in the Middle Ages. It's hard to convince it otherwise when all you're feeding it is alcohol and fast food.

A text from Blake waits for me on my phone screen. I chuckle bitterly. Years without much talking and now that I can help him out, he's barking up my tree.

> What is the house worth?

Jesus Christ, Blake. Let the dust settle.

I ignore the text message, and message Noelle instead, checking in to see if she survived her hangover with the same grace as me. But it looks like she already sent me a text that I missed.

> Apparently I sexted Hooper last night.

There's a little emoji with wide eyes next to her message. My own eyes widen, reflecting it.

God knows the guy wants to nail Noelle like the lid

of a coffin. He's been in love with her since we were in high school. But Noelle can't see it. I feel a tinge of sadness for Hooper, wondering how much false hope their interaction gave him. I feel a little sadness for myself. I'd love to see them together.

He's such a good guy. Not that creepy, I'm a nice guy way, but like a person who's actually a decent human being. He's a teacher and a coach at the high school that we went to. Single, never married. Our age. No kids. And if he's ever going to change any of that, I guarantee you that Noelle is the one he imagines doing it with. Even if she's oblivious to the whole thing.

I roll my eyes, not ready to deal with that kind of crisis this early in the morning. At least not today. Not on the heels of dealing with Blake. I send a Dr. Phil gif with my question.

How's that working out for you?

She takes longer to reply than I'm willing to wait. So I jump in the shower, wanting to wash away the remnants of an unsettling twenty-four hours. I stand under the scalding hot water, trying to focus on the sensation of the heat on my body. And not the reality that's waiting for me when I get out.

The one where I'm going to sell Dad's house to bail my brother out once again.

The reality where internet celebrities are making

click-bait content about my dad's very real disappearance

I have a half a mind to send Cash Kelly an email
and tell him to take that shit down. I'm not sure I have a
legal leg to stand on, but it would do a lot to make me
feel better. I imagine Cash Kelly operates on the
currency of his attractiveness. I also imagine his DMs
are flooded with thirsty women and likely teenage girls.
I hope he ignores the latter.

But at this point, I'm not feeling generous enough
to give him credit for being a decent person.

I hop out of the shower, dry off, throw some
product into my hair, and let it start to air dry. I look at
myself in the mirror. My wavy brown hair falls limp,
wet from the shower and weighed down by the gel I
just put in it. My blue eyes are still bloodshot. An unin-
vited memory comes to me: my dad, years ago, one
afternoon when I just washed my hair. It was late
December. He was on the back patio, sitting and
staring into the woods, lost in thought and unreachable
as he so often was. He was here and not here all the
time.

He noticed my presence and glanced at me, smil-
ing. "You'll catch your death coming out here with a
wet head," he said.

I can't even begin to chronicle all the articles I've
read that have supported the assertion that there's
little to no connection between a wet head in the
winter air and sickness. Even so, I can exist in the

winter with a wet head without thinking of that particular day.

Without thinking of my father sharing that bit of
wisdom with me.

It's sad how good that memory feels.

How important it seems. It really is the little
things.

I think my father never realized that it was those
things that mattered the most.

Today that memory seems more vivid, the edges of
his face harsher.

What parts of Dad did I not see? What parts of me
did I keep from him?

I guess there was a part of me that thought there
would always be time. Time to fix our relationship.
Time to get to know him. Time for him to get to
know me.

And then he vanished into thin air.

Just like that, all of those *somedays* were shattered.

I SPEND the remainder of the week looking into
selling the house. I go through the motions, unfeeling
and partially glad to be rid of it. As the week closes in
on the weekend, I realize even more how this has never
felt like home. Aside from my memories with Noelle.

Once I'm out of here, I'll be able to pick the place
where I'll live. I won't have to be constantly shadowed

by memories. The bad ones, at least, are of a house that was built on a series of fractured relationships my dad left in his wake. It'll be a new beginning. Friday, a realtor comes and we get the selling of the house in motion.

Later that evening, a glass of wine in hand, I surreptitiously go in and delete my comment from Cash Kelly's video, figuring it does little to better my situation and will only keep the bile coming from his legion of fans.

I don't need that, especially not right now. I need peace. I scan through his videos once again on Friday. Looking at the absurd titles and realizing just how much like my dad he sounds, which is probably a huge part of why I find him irritating. It makes sense that he would cover my dad's disappearance. Although I think back on his comment that Dad was a mentor to him. I never heard my dad mention Cash Kelly.

But I also never heard my dad mention many people.

I watch one of his videos, a piece about Bigfoot in Oklahoma. I roll my eyes with such force my skull aches. This is the same drivel my dad put out into the world, chasing shadows and his tail for money. I'm not even sure that either of them really believe in what they're chasing. And something tells me that Cash mainly chases clicks and ad dollars, not monsters.

A sickening sensation hits me as I realize one more time just how alike he and my father are. Dad had sponsors for his program, and he had anonymous donors who wanted him to investigate certain things. Usually people who believe they've been abducted by aliens.

Taking their money was gross. I always thought it belonged to a therapist or back in their hands to do with what they wished. Cash strikes me the same way, coming across just genuine enough for the most susceptible in his audience to believe every word coming out of his mouth. Just genuine enough to be dangerous. I hate watch about six of the videos and realize I've spent my evening with someone I loathe. I finish the glass of wine, the last from that bottle, and decide to go to bed.

The house is officially on the market, and Dad is legally dead.

And I'm spending a drunken Friday night alone with Cash Kelly's pixelated face. I reach up to slam my laptop shut, but a notification stops me short. An email.

Sender: Cash Kelly
Subject: Hi.

My hand pauses mid-slam. I stare at the notification in the top right corner of my MacBook screen until it slides away into the background. My heart thuds with anticipation. Maybe it's the wine in my veins or maybe it's the bitterness about how everything is shaken down, but I'm spoiling for a fight.

As I open the email, I hope I'm about to get one, but instead I get this:

Miss Graves,

Jesus fucking Christ.

I noticed you deleted your dazzling comment on my video about your father. I realized it's likely you might have been drinking when you made it. I gather you don't have much appreciation for what I do, but I wanted to see if you'd be willing to give an interview for my channel about Graham Graves's disappearance. Your father meant a lot to me.
Thank you for your time.
Cash Kelly

Oh my fucking god, this *guy*.

I realize that we live in an era where everything is content, but Jesus fucking Christ.

My palms sweat and my hands tremble as I begin to type out a scathing response. I want to douse him in verbal gasoline and light a match at his feet. Pure rage comes over me. Protectiveness of the legacy of the man I don't even know, the man that I'm not even sure I respect. I want to tell Cash Kelly to get fucked. My heart pounds in my chest. I guess I was right about thinking that he or one of his cronies would figure out the username. Not my brightest moment.

I take a pause to weigh my options and decide to leave it alone. Just then, a notification, delayed by my ancient computer, pops up and asks if I'd like to send Mr. Kelly a read receipt on the email.

My lip snarls up and pettiness descends into the index finger on my right hand as I click the button that indicates *Yes*.

Yes, I would.

FIVE

THE HOUSE SELLS ALMOST INSTANTLY. 5000 square feet, a pool, and a lovely wooded surrounding help with that. And the couple who buy it can totally afford it. He's a surgeon. She's a lawyer. And neither of them strikes me as the kind of person who has any idea who my dad is, which probably helps in solidifying the sale so quickly.

I don't think you have to disclose that a property belonged to a missing person, or that said missing person enjoyed spending time with people who believed they'd been abducted by aliens, had a spiritual communion with Bigfoot in a Las Vegas motel, or swam with the Loch Ness Monster, all of whom were regular callers on my dad's show.

When my first serious post-high school boyfriend found out what my dad did, he had a lot of questions.

"He doesn't really believe them, though?" he asked,

laughing nervously. "Right?" He prodded me for an affirmative answer, but I just gave him an awkward smile as I watched our relationship slip through my fingers.

His name was Colson, and he came from a respectable family. A family whose money hadn't been milked out of vulnerable members of society. His dad was a doctor.

But when Colson asked me the question, there was a tone of incredulity in his voice. Like he couldn't imagine the type of person my dad would have to be to entertain such ideas, and I remember how his words cut me.

It was painful. It was one of the times when I was a young adult that I was embarrassed by my dad. It was probably the first time that I really realized we were different. Our lifestyle was different, and there was nothing I could do about it.

I blushed, looked down. At my feet, I can still see the Converse sneakers I was wearing.

"I honestly have no idea," I told him. My tone was empty, void of emotion.

It was also one of the first times I learned to put a wall up between me and other people.

Sitting here now at the breakfast table, thinking about it. It dawns on me how little I truly did know about my father. Boxes of his things are piled in the attic. Things that I moved about a year after he officially became a missing person. Things I couldn't stand to look at because they reminded me of the fact that he was gone. But I kept them in the attic, ever hopeful that one day he might need them.

Boxes full of photographs, boxes of journals, boxes of day planners, boxes of things that my dad had kept from his journey as a radio personality. Awards, certificates, books—a host of books—by fringe scientists and conspiracy theorists.

I'll never forget the way Colson made me feel when he found out what my dad did for a living. The way his reaction made it all feel *dirty* and *illegitimate*.

Not only was my dad an illegitimate radio personality, Colson made me feel like he was illegitimate as a person. And I felt like I didn't even know my dad well enough to defend him, but still had the piercing instinct that I should.

It was one of the most confusing situations I've ever encountered in my life. That relationship fell apart quickly. Colson moved on to a sorority girl with a pedigree and I buried myself in grief, sleeping with randoms I met at bars. Randoms who had no idea who I was, and who I'd never introduced to my father.

Sometimes, I google Colson. He's married now. Two kids, white picket fence. They even have a golden retriever.

It's a life that I tell myself sometimes I could have had, even though I know that's untrue.

Graham Graves lived his life on the run, quite literally traveling from place to place to avoid the reality that was our family. My dad's disappearance wasn't the first tragedy to befall the Graves family. First, there was my mother's untimely death. She passed before Blake and I could form memories of her. It seems that tragedy has always been destined for the family Graves.

IT TAKES the movers three days to get everything in the house moved to a storage unit. The place becomes a carcass being picked clean by scavengers. It occurs to me then to extend the metaphor, realizing that this place has been dead for a while, rotting from the festering father wound, turning green, bloating and decaying over the course of years. Finally, desiccating, drying out and becoming a hollow void where something resembling a family once had been.

The house represents so many bad memories, all of them blunted at the edges because there was never any maliciousness. Never any violence, just neglect. I sit on the hardwood floor of the living room. After the movers get the last of everything, I stare out into the backyard. The woods make a pretty perimeter. I gasp as a tear sneaks out and I swipe it quickly, making sure that no one sees me cry.

Hollowness aches in my chest. Grief, unfelt for years, creeps up on me and I tamp it down, pushing it further and further and further until it melds with the foundation of my soul.

I'm doing what I've always done: denying it.

I swallow it, and I stand up. I take one last look around the house. It sold. It's not mine anymore. It's not his. It's not ours. It's someone else's now. New memories will be made. That hollow ache returns as I imagine just how happy those memories will be.

BEFORE THE HOUSE SOLD, it dawned quickly on me that I needed to find somewhere to stay, and Noelle promptly offered up her place. Couch-surfing with my best friend would be slightly less shameful if I wasn't over thirty, not that I haven't done it before. There have been times in the past when I just couldn't bring myself to stay in that big empty house. Sometimes Noelle would come and stay with me, but other times I would want to go to her house. Somewhere else. Somewhere that felt more like a home.

"It's no big deal, Blair," she assures me as I haul my only suitcase out of the car, sitting it in her driveway. Noelle owns a house in town. And there's some comfort in the fact that Noelle knows about the legacy of family secrets. Hers has its own. We don't dip into that territory often, and it usually requires an excessive amount of alcohol and some sort of trigger that sends her down that path. We have a mutual respect for the things that neither of us really wants to speak of. And there's some safety in that, even if it mirrors the way my father held me at a distance.

I try not to acknowledge that part.

The idea that my relationship with him could have any effect on any relationships I might have now.

My phone rings and I roll my eyes, fully aware of who it'll be, and I'm right.

"What?" I snap as I answer it.

"Blair, it's Blake."

"I'm going to send you a check today," I tell him.

He quiets on the other end, the silent sound of shame. I regret my words almost instantly. There's something uniquely horrific about embarrassing someone you love, and I do love him. Even if I don't like him now.

"Look, I'm really busy right now and I'll text you when it's done. Okay?" I try to soften my tone and indicate therein that I don't think he's a complete piece of shit.

"No worries," he says hastily. Though, as I hang up, I'm fairly certain Blake has nothing but worries at the moment.

There's really no other reason that he could be pressing so hard for the money. I wonder for a second just how deep he's gotten himself into something bad. I'm sure it's really bad. I'm not sure I want to know how bad. Ignorance is bliss, especially when it comes to members of your own family.

"Come on," Noelle says, taking my suitcase by the

handle. "Welcome to your new home!" She smiles and ushers me up the steps and into her modern two-bedroom home that I'm already familiar with. When we enter, the smell of apple cider hits me. It's instantly comforting, instantly warm. Two things I was never able to associate with my own house. My dad's house. There's always been an emptiness I couldn't put my finger on, even when the three of us still lived there.

Noelle's house has never had that.

"Go get settled and I'll get you some," she nods toward the kitchen, indicating the cider. "I just made it."

I smile and take my things to the second bedroom. Inside, she's prepared an air mattress. The space is small, usually functioning as a craft room for her. A desk sits in the corner with a large light on top, perfect for illuminating intricate projects. Bookshelves line one wall full of Noelle's overflow of reading material. The rest of the house is jam-packed with shelves as well. I can remember her telling me when we were teenagers that a house full of books was never lonely.

Maybe she was onto something. Maybe that's why my dad had so many.

I don't unpack, but return quickly to the kitchen. She has a cup ready for me and I take it, my hands absorbing the heat eagerly. She sips hers and I do the same.

"Have you looked at houses?" she asks. I meet her eyes. Something passes unspoken between us. "Oh,

God! I didn't mean it like that," she says. "You just got here. You're welcome to stay forever."

I laugh.

"No, I haven't," I say.

"It might be fun," she suggests.

I hadn't really made the mental leap to the fact that I'm about to have to buy a house or at least rent one. That I'm embarking on a truly new chapter of my life. Selling my dad's house was the closing of another one that he was still a part of. He's legally dead now.

Maybe holding on to the house had been a way of keeping him with me, keeping him alive.

"Let's do that. I always love looking at listings and pretending I might live in one of them someday," she says with an eager smile. For Noelle, the idea of me buying a house is exciting. It isn't wrapped up in anything else. I feel the excitement, too, but there's an edge to it. The knowledge that this certainly means moving on. And I don't know how ready I am for that. It's a thought that hadn't occurred to me. Blake asking me to sell the house forced my hand and propelled me into an unknown future. And even though I don't know where my dad is, or if he even *is*, staying in the house made it feel like, in a way, there was a good chance he'd come back.

I kept the light on for over a decade and he never showed up on my porch.

SIX

CHRISTMAS LOOMS on the horizon at Noelle's house. I guess it looms large everywhere by mid-December. The holidays have always been weird for my family.

As kids, my dad did everything he could to make sure that Blake and I had all we could ever have asked for. Every toy, every electronic, everything. The one thing we didn't have was him.

There were a couple of years when he left Christmas celebrations to the nanny. He had to be somewhere for a story. The two of us open presents with Sheryl, and she was nice enough. We left his gifts under the tree for when he returned.

But there were some years that even when he did come back, he left the gifts unopened. Like he was a ghost living in our house.

Sometimes, as a child, it made me doubt his existence. I thought of him that way, as some sort of specter that drifted in and out of our lives.

After he disappeared, Christmas became non-existent for me, aside from doing an exchange of gifts with Noelle. Blake was long gone by that point.

And I didn't really have anyone else to celebrate with. Both sets of my grandparents were gone.

Turns out money can't buy everything, least of all the presence of a parent.

But as the holidays approach this year, I feel a different sense of dread and an extra hollowness encroaches on me.

Noelle and I sit in the living room, watching the latest corny Christmas movie released by Netflix, both of us sipping hot chocolate with caramel Bailey's. The tree stands in the corner, casting a red, green, and yellow glow across the carpet. I snuggle under a blanket on one end of the couch and Noelle does the same on the other.

I watch in silence as she nods off and her hot chocolate begins to tip, growing dangerously close to spilling. My hand darts out quickly and I save it. She wakes.

"Oh shit," she murmurs. I place it back on the coffee table. "I think I might go to bed," she says.

"I'm not tired yet," I tell her.

She gets up and takes the remainder of her drink to the kitchen. I stay on the couch after she goes to bed. Just me, this atrocious movie, the Christmas tree, and everything whirling around in my head. All sorts of unwelcome thoughts. Thoughts about my dad. Thoughts about my brother. Thoughts about Cash Kelly.

I'm alone and somehow Noelle's house is warmer and more welcoming than the house I just sold. Somehow, this feels more like home than that ever did. There's a warmth here, a lived-in-ness. Even with all the thoughts that are swirling in my mind, somehow they seem easier to bear here.

My memories of that house are cold like December. Like the day my dad disappeared.

I LICK and seal the envelope containing the check for Blake, pressing the paper firmly against itself. Noelle drives us to the post office and I hand it off to her. She tosses it in the letterbox and we turn out of the post office onto the main road.

"So have you looked at houses?" she asks.

There's an air of excitement in her voice that I know I should feel.

I don't.

Part of me doesn't want to leave Noelle's place. It feels safer than the prospect of truly embracing the fact that I'm starting over. I feel like a middle-aged divorcee faced with the prospect of rebuilding my life from scratch.

I sigh.

"I haven't," I say.

"Well, I have," Noelle says. When she stops at a red light, she looks over at me.

"Is that your not-so-gentle way of telling me I need to get a job and get out of your house?" I tease. She laughs.

"Of course not. You can stay forever if you want," she says. "I just saw a place, and I think it might be good for you."

"Good for me?" I ask. There's an edge of something in my voice. I don't need to be saved.

"That's not what I meant," she corrects. "I just think you might do well with a project."

"Do I look like someone who wants a project?" I halfway tease.

"You look like someone who *needs* a project," she says tersely.

I stare at her for a moment, waiting for the laughter, but it doesn't come.

It's not a joke.

She's serious. And she might be right. I might be nearing a point where there's no return.

I feel like I've become this scooped out version of a person. Like the outer skin of an avocado after you make guacamole. Like I don't even know who I am anymore. Like my adult life, up to this point, has been defined entirely by my dad's non-existence.

Maybe I need to start over.

Maybe I *do* need a project.

I lean my head against my hand, resting my arm on the closed window of the passenger seat. Noelle drives, taking us out of the suburbs and into Oklahoma City. We hit the northern edge of town and enter a semi-rural area much like the one where my current house is, or rather, the house I just sold. The houses are old here, like turn-of-the-twentieth-century old.

They're separated by fields, large acreages. I make a mental note that at least out here, I'd be a long way from any people. That's one thing I did love about the old house.

We drive down to the end of the road, passing a few old barns and other structures that look like they haven't been used in decades.

There's something very Carpathian about the property when we arrive. Trees line the edge and create a canopy over the narrow drive. I feel like I'm either traveling back in time or straight into a horror novel. I sit up straighter and when we emerge from the canopy drive, the house reveals itself.

Three stories stand like a monolith. The siding is aged, charred by time and weather. It's a dingy gray color now, the paint almost entirely stripped. I notice at least two cracked windows on the second floor, which has a large covered balcony. Noelle's car creeps along the gravel drive in front of the place. A wraparound porch on the first floor yawns wide to encompass the whole first floor.

The house is huge.

The stones in the walls look expensive. There's stained glass in a window downstairs, a matching one on the other side. Both of them somehow standing the test of time.

But the house itself seems rundown.

"Well?" she asks as she puts the car in park. I look at her wide eyed.

"Well, what?" I snap.

"What do you think?" she urges.

I can tell she's pleased with herself and her discovery. I struggled to find the words to tell Noelle that I have absolutely no desire to buy a dilapidated turn of the century house that probably needs tens of thousands of dollars' worth of work.

She must see it written on my face.

"At least look around," she says. She kills the engine, determined to make me get out of the car. So we do. I stare up at the towering house. She walks along beside me as the cold nips at my cheeks. I tuck my hands into my coat pockets. "It's not like you don't have the money," she says. "Or the time," she murmurs.

She's not wrong. It's no secret that my dad's money has provided me with a nice living and a cushy existence.

The same kind of living that Blake could have had. If he didn't gamble it all away.

I wonder where he's staying now. If he can afford a house. If he's living with someone else.

To imagine him struggling turns my stomach. It's usually something I'm pretty good at not thinking about. I don't have much affection for my brother. But I do love him. I do care about him and I don't want him to go hungry or be out on the street.

And the urgency with which he seems to need this money makes me think that's going to become a reality for him sooner rather than later.

We step up on to the porch. I get closer to one of the windows and peer into the interior of the house. The window is so dusty, it's almost impossible to make out what's inside. Buying the house wouldn't be a problem. Neither would the cost of work needed to restore it. And thinking about Blake has me realizing I probably need to make a move on this soon.

But just as I'm starting to entertain the idea, something slams against the glass and I shriek.

"What the fuck is that?!" I shout.

Noelle grabs my arm, jumping just as much as I did.

The pair of us look at each other and silently decide to creep forward to make a better observation of my would-be assailant. A small furry hand reaches up and snatches something.

"Oh my God, Noelle," I say. "There's a goddamned raccoon in that house."

She presses her lips together.

"Okay, so maybe it needs *a lot* of work."

"Or an exterminator!" I shriek. "You cannot be serious."

"It's just a raccoon," she says. "I mean—it could be worse."

"Worse? How?"

"It could be—I don't know—an armadillo?" she offers. "They carry leprosy."

"You're literally standing here telling me that this place is a viable choice because instead of a leprosy-ridden armadillo trying to attack us, it was a raccoon, who at worst, might have rabies."

"Well," she says with a shrug.

We stand there in silence for a moment.

"Can raccoons carry leprosy?" I ask quietly.

WE WALK around the back of the house and find a large, beautiful, if somewhat weed-infested patio area. It looks like the kind of place where whoever lived here previously might have hosted fancy parties. There's also a kidney-shaped pool. Beautiful if somewhat faded, art déco style tiles line it. Some are cracked, others have broken entirely. Some of them are missing at the bottom of the pool. I spot something.

"Well," I say cautiously.

"What?" Noelle asks carefully, peering into the back windows. "This kitchen is huge," she says.

I point when she turns around. She walks up to the pool and looks at the bottom of it.

"Oh, my God," she says.

The two of us peer down at the bottom of the pool.

A puddle of dirty water lined with dead leaves sits in the center, and sticking up out of it is a half-decayed animal.

"What the hell is that?" she asks.

"It looks like a coyote," I say. The animal looks so strange—almost half-preserved.

"It's definitely been dead for quite a while."

"Lovely," I say with heavy sarcasm. I cast a glare at her. She shrugs with a sheepish smile. "Remind me again when you thought this was a good idea," I tease her.

She says nothing and the two of us keep walking the property. We arrive at a small gated area. A little spiked fence lines it and several blank rectangular stones rest in the grass, eroded by time and weather. There are numbers and letters, but they're hardly legible.

"Looks like a cemetery," she says.

"Good. We can bury the coyote here once we clean out the pool," I say.

On the gate leading into the little cemetery, I spot the Egyptian symbol of life.

I reach out and touch it, a memory coming to me. My father showed me this symbol once as a child. In something he was researching, it was quite important, and apparently they would put it on sarcophagi because death wasn't the end. "Life continued after death," he told me. Sitting in his lap, I reached up and touched the old tube style computer monitor to trace the symbol as electricity hugged my finger as I drew it along the shape of the symbol. How strange it is that an ancient Egyptian symbol might find itself on an iron gate in Oklahoma. People are strange. But I remind myself this place was probably built in the Victorian era.

Things were different then. Symbolism mattered.

Noelle and I head back to the car and I can't shake the ankh or the memory it triggered as we turn out of the driveway. Noelle is entirely resigned to the fact that she misjudged an opportunity with the house.

"Stop," I say before she pulls completely back out onto the road. I pull my cell phone from my pocket and snap a picture of the realtor's sign. "Okay," I say.

Noelle smirks at me. But I give her a look, telling her not to say anything. She just nods and raises her hands in surrender. And then we leave.

SEVEN

BENEATH THE CHRISTMAS LIGHT AMBIANCE, Noelle and I digest another romantic comedy while I do some digging on my phone. It takes a while. The listing for the house out on the north side of Oklahoma City isn't easily found.

And once I do find it, I start combing through the pictures.

Shockingly, my little raccoon friend doesn't make an appearance in any of them.

The house has five bedrooms, three baths, and a host of other spaces.

There's a room that looks like its original purpose might have been as a ballroom. Another room strikes me as the kind of space where the gentlemen of the house might have retired after dinner for a cigar and conversations that the little women wouldn't understand.

The kitchen and dining room are antiquated. The whole place needs a ton of work, and the price is right for that.

I look at the listing history and see something unusual for a house that seems not to have had much love in a long time. It's been on and off the market over and over.

I wonder if there's mold or some extreme problem with the plumbing. But once I get into the description, it appears that the electrical and plumbing were recently updated. Also, the house has been inspected for things like mold and gotten the all clear.

I stare at the house, puzzled as to why anyone would go through the trouble of repairing the plumbing and electrical features without sticking with it. It has broken windows. That seems like the most costly and daunting prospect of buying a house this old. But those could have happened after the last owner vacated. Maybe trespassing teenagers did it.

"Whatcha doin'?" Noelle hovers over my shoulder behind the couch. I gasp, startled, not having realized she got up from the other end of it.

"Jesus Christ," I breathe and lock my phone.

"You're gonna buy it, aren't you?" she asks with a Cheshire Cat smile.

"I didn't say that," I tell her. A silence hangs between us that reveals the answer.

"It's okay to admit I was right," she tells me. "There's no shame in being wrong, Blair," she teases as she saunters to the kitchen and I whip around on the couch.

"Do you think I could restore it?" I ask her. My heart flutters in my chest. Excitement suddenly seizes me. The idea of taking this old house and making it my own is a bit intoxicating. I have the money. I have the time. And I've always wanted a place of my own. This could be it. This could be a new beginning.

This could be a fresh start, free from all the things in the old house that hung like relics, reminding me of worse times gone by.

"I absolutely think you can do it," she tells me as she grabs a snack from the pantry.

"It'll be a lot of work," I start. "But I think you're right. I think it'll be worth it."

"I'm just thrilled to not have dragged you out there for nothing," she chirps as she settles back on her end of the couch. I unlock my phone and keep looking at the listing. The number listed for the agent matches the one I took a picture of on my phone. I'll call tomorrow.

AN ANXIOUSNESS DESCENDS on me as I dial the realtor. After a long period of ringing, someone picks up the phone, a woman.

"Diana here, may I ask who's calling?" Her voice is

that of a woman who spent most of the late eighties chain smoking. I can almost smell it.

"Hi, my name is Blair Graves, and I wanted to ask you about a listing you've got," I say.

"Well, I'm your woman, then," Diana says. "Which house?"

I read her the address I've written down. Diana is silent on the other end for a moment.

"Hello?" I say, afraid that I've just lost her.

"Sorry," she says. "It's just been a moment since anyone's been interested in the Solomon house."

The Solomon house.

Something about the idea that the house holds its own name feels glamorous, recalling the art déco glory days that wall must have seen.

"Is it still available?" I ask.

She barks out a laugh.

"Oh, yes," she says.

"I don't imagine many people are interested in such a renovation project," I tell her.

"You could say that," she mutters. I hear the clicking of long nails tap against the keyboard. "When would you like to see it?" she asks.

"I'm free pretty much anytime," I tell her.

"How about this afternoon?" she asks.

"That works," I say. We set a time and I get off the phone and shoot a message to Noelle letting her know that I'm going to see the house.

She texts back immediately.

This is going to be such a good thing for you, Blair.

God, I hope she's right.

I GET THERE BEFORE DIANA.

I pull up out front of the house, exactly as we left it. But now that I'm actually meeting with someone about buying it, it seems all the more intimidating.

I hear gravel crunching under tires and the low whining hum of an engine that sounds like it's about to commit suicide. I turn and see Diana—who I assume to be Diana—pulling up in an ancient Toyota.

When she gets out, smoke pours out of her car and she makes a show of stomping out a cigarette. I smirk thinking about her driving all the way up here. Getting the best she can out of her nicotine with the windows rolled up. That takes true dedication.

"You must be Blair," she says. She smiles, revealing two rows of slightly crooked teeth, yellowed by years of smoking. She extends a bony hand and I take it for a handshake.

"That's me," I tell her. "Nice to meet you."

"So, let's get inside," she says without further ado. I follow her up the staircase that leads to the porch and I look at the window where I encountered the raccoon.

"Oh," I hesitate, searching for the words. "I think there might be a visitor inside."

"You're referring to the beaver?" she asks.

I stare at her, puzzled.

"A raccoon, actually," I say.

"Oh, dear," she says. She unlocks the front door. "I was aware of a beaver, but not a raccoon." Jesus Christ. I follow her into the entryway. The front door leads into a small enclosed room that features another door that Diana unlocks, and that door leads us into the house proper.

Dust clings to everything.

As I look down the hallway, I can see various pieces of furniture covered in moth-eaten sheets as well.

"The house comes with the furniture," she says, making note of my roving eyes. "Though not sure how much of it you'll want to keep. I understand quite a bit of it has seen better days. Moths, you know?" She reaches for a light switch and illuminates the place.

Despite the rickety furniture and dust everywhere, the lighting is magnificent. Old fixtures line the walls of the living room that stands off to the side of the entry hallway. A chandelier hangs over the staircase leading up to the second floor.

"Those are gorgeous," I remark.

"Quite," Diana confirms. "Additions made by the house's last owner."

"I understand they repaired the plumbing and electrical stuff," I say.

"That's true," Diana says. She moves further into the house and I follow her. She turns and gives me a wink over one bony shoulder. "You've done your homework."

I smile. I like Diana.

We walk into the dining room adjacent to the kitchen. The doorways are narrow. A throwback to another time. The wood-paneled walls are dark, beautiful, and timeless, if a little dusty.

It looks like the last time any of the interior was updated was during the art déco period other than the lighting, but the last owner did their best to make it match the rest of the updated features of the house.

An antique refrigerator sits in the corner of the kitchen. A basin sink stands beside it. There's an island and windows that provide ample daylight to see by.

"I suppose you know a little of the house history," Diana says.

"No, actually," I answer her.

"Well, it belonged to Andrew Solomon," she says. "Robber baron, he was, but not quite as skilled as those for whom significant parts of Oklahoma City are named. No, he wasn't quite as prolific at acquiring land. His passions lay elsewhere."

She leads us out of the kitchen through the dining room, which features another chandelier and back down the hallway where the living room sits on one side and another equally large living room sits on the other.

"The house was a funeral home for a while," Diana remarks. "But that was after Solomon owned it."

The revelation startles me. I glance back into the parlor opposite the living room.

"That bay window there," Diana points. "Those windows open. They would place caskets in that corner. The floral arrangements helped with the smell."

The thought that multiple dead people rested here unsettles me. It's nothing I can't handle, I tell myself. I think of the little cemetery outside.

She leads us past the other living room and down the hallway. Another room is nestled off to the side, its narrow doorway almost hiding it under the staircase.

"The conservatory or sunroom," Diana says, ushering us inside. Glass walls and a glass ceiling encase the room. "One of Mr. Solomon's favorite rooms, I'm told," Diana says.

"Tell me more about him," I prod her as we make our way out of the room and upstairs. The second floor hosts all the bedrooms and two of the bathrooms. She shows me each in turn as she chronicles the life of the former homeowner.

"Oh, there's not much to tell," she says. "His wife had a stroke when she was quite young, died tragically by drowning in the pool one evening during a party. Their son drowned as well. Mr. Solomon was so grief stricken that he lost his senses, becoming a recluse and eventually moving out of state."

"That's horrible," I tell her.

"Oh, quite. The boy was just a toddler. It's thought

that he jumped into the pool after his mother to save her. Unfortunately, they both perished."

"I can't imagine what that was like for Mr. Solomon. Jesus," I whisper. I thought my house was marked by tragedy.

"Indeed," Diana confirms, almost like she's reading my mind. "Mr. Solomon sold the house and moved away in the early part of the 20th century. It belonged to the family who made it a funeral home after that. But when neither of Mr. Horn's boys wanted to take up the mortuary arts, the Horn family sold it as well. And it's been through a host of other masters since then."

There's a mural in the master bathroom and I stop and stare at it when we arrive.

"That was painted for Mrs. Solomon," Diana says. The mural features a nude woman and a nude man standing on either side of a mountain. Above them, a heavenly being seems to be looking down. They both cast their eyes upwards. Roses line the outside edges. It's the sixth card of the Tarot. The lovers.

"Did Mrs. Solomon enjoy Tarot?" I ask.

"Oh, she enjoyed a number of occult things," Diana assures me. She begins to make her way back to the second story landing. I cast a glance back at the mural, faded and peeling. It's still beautiful, it could easily be restored. "She dabbled in table rapping seances. That sort of thing was very common near the turn of the century. Victorian spiritualism was quite in vogue."

We head up to the third floor.

"This space was mainly used as storage by the Horn family," Diana says. The giant attic-like room hosts a number of objects, all covered in the same moth-eaten white sheets that we found downstairs. A musty smell accompanies it. I feel an itch in my nose and promptly sneeze. "There's also a basement," Diana says. "I should note that it was used by the Horns for embalming," she adds hesitantly. I imagine this is the sort of information that served as a deal breaker for other prospective buyers.

There's a bit of comfort in knowing that the saddest things that ever happened in this house had nothing to do with me, Blake, or my father. It's a strange perspective, but I welcome it. We head back downstairs to the first floor.

"I imagine you have a husband with whom you might discuss the purchase," Diana says.

"No," I say. "It's just me."

"Any children?" she asked with an arched eyebrow.

"None of those, either."

"No husband and no children," she clucks. "Smart girl." Diana winks at me.

I take in the house one more time before we step outside.

As Diana turns to head to her car after giving me her card, I call out to her.

"Diana," I say. "Wait."

She raises her eyebrows and looks as if she might want to ask me why I've stalled her getting back to the office. Like this was a fool's errand, and she needs to go.

I inhale deeply and look back at the house once more. I leap entirely on faith.

"I'll take it, but be sure an exterminator comes first."

EIGHT

"I FEEL like I may have led you astray," Noelle says cautiously as we pull up outside the Solomon house. She puts her car in park. A moving van sits out front, waiting for me to unlock the house.

"You cannot be serious." I say.

She kills the engine and looks up at the house. Irritation flares for a moment as I try to figure out if Noelle is kidding. Her hesitation makes me think she isn't. That she thinks I've possibly bitten off more than I can chew.

I start into a downward spiral, thinking that maybe I've lost my mind. Buying a fixer upper like this probably wasn't the most intelligent thing to do with my father's money. Have I lost my mind? Is this a bad idea? It could be.

I cock my head, staring at her and waiting for her to say something.

"I just can't believe you really did it," she finally turns from the house. Her face breaks into a wide smile. Excitement bleeds through her trepidation.

I'd be lying if I didn't say I'd lost about a week of sleep, mulling over the intelligence of my choice to buy the house. Ultimately, I decided I hadn't made a colossal mistake.

We get out of the car and one of the movers waves at me, a young guy probably in his early twenties, working his way through college. He offers me a clipboard and a pen.

"Sign here," he says. "And here." He flips the page once I give him my signature. "We'll get started. The other van is headed this way now." I nod. He stares at me for a second. "And we'll need the—"

"Key!" I say, having forgotten the most basic thing I walked up here to do: let him in the house. I run back to the car and return up the steps. I notice a crack in the concrete of the wraparound porch.

The house seems less glamorous today. And the thought that I've made a mistake washes over me once more. Noelle steps up after me and the movers start their work. We get out of the way.

"Any specific instructions?" the young guy asks me as he tucks his hat tighter onto his head, ready to get to work.

"Basically, if it looks like it goes in a bedroom, put it in the master upstairs. If it's a couch or a dining table, put it down here." I gesture vaguely at the living room and dining room. My arm stops mid swing as I'm about to point to the other front room. The viewing room from when the Horns had the place. The casket bay window.

"Yeah..." I look back at the room opposite the former state room. "Just put the living room stuff in this room."

He nods and they get to work.

THE DECISION TO move in before actually renovating was my own. The house is well off enough that I can live here, and in the last week, the windows have been fixed. There's running water, electricity, heat and air. All the good stuff. Most of the things that I want to fix are cosmetic. Noelle tried to keep me at her place longer, but I didn't want to become an imposition. We're best friends, but I'd hate to overstay my welcome. It's possible in even the best relationships.

The movers place the dining table from my dad's house in its new home beneath the sparkling chandelier. The beautiful chandelier and pristine dining table look a little strange in a room that clearly needs some love. The carpet is worn and could use an update. The wood needs polishing, even though the panels are beautiful. The rest of the house is much the same. And it's toward the end of the day when I finally wander upstairs to check out the state of things in the master bedroom.

Noelle remains downstairs overseeing the placement of several other things in the living room. One of the guys is walking out of the master bedroom when I hit the second story landing. We bump into each other and he turns to face me, his cheeks pale, eyes wide. He rushes past me to the staircase and jogs down, taking them two at a time. I watch him and then look back at the open doorway of my new bedroom.

An eerie feeling settles over me in the quiet of the upstairs. Suddenly, it seems thick. Like I could run my fingers through it in the air. I can hear the faint sounds of movement and Noelle's voice below.

Up here, it's silent as I start walking toward the open doorway. The floorboards creak beneath me, giving me pause. I've never lived in an old house like this. The house I shared with my dad was new, built in the early 2000s. It didn't have the groaning propensities of one-hundred-year-old walls and floors.

Suddenly I'm brought back to wondering if I've bitten off more than I can chew.

Do I want to stay here alone?

Even if it's technically safe. It's a big house. Bigger than my dad's. I'm not sure that I want to be here in the middle of the night when the strange noises of the house settling fill my ears.

Have I made a mistake? Should I have waited longer? Should I have weighed my options?

Panic begins to seize me as I realize that I bought the first house I looked at. A nervous laugh bubbles up in my chest.

I shake the silly ideas and questions out of my head and I walk into the bedroom.

It's a house like any other, it's just older.

And it used to be a funeral home.

And had a tragic death in the swimming pool.

Two tragic deaths.

Fuck, I'm creeping myself out.

I place a hand on the double doorway that leads into the master suite. The room is huge and the windows overlook the back of the property. That was one of the things I liked most about it. It also opens to the balcony that stretches around the back of the house on the second story.

In a way, it reminds me of my dad's bedroom at the old house.

My bed, a queen, seems way too small in the space. Moth-eaten drapes hang on the sides of the huge window. I make a mental note to shop for curtains later. Or maybe I'll get blinds. A little surge of excitement hits me again, realizing that this place is mine and that I get to make it however I see fit, however I'd most enjoy it. A reflection of myself, something that I've never been able to have in my entire life.

There was no true reason that I couldn't after my dad was gone. But emotionally, I don't think I could handle it. Keeping the house the same as he left it felt like some sort of offering to the gods. Like if I moved any of his furniture or changed things around, it might curse him and he might not come back.

When I finally moved my dad's files and journals out of his office and started to use it myself, I was stricken with guilt. I thought for sure I had damned him to some unimaginable fate. That I had tempted the gods.

My dresser sits on the opposite wall. Something that looks like a couch sits against another wall. One of the pieces of furniture left behind by the Horns.

I reached for the sheet blanketing it. It's stiff, has holes in it, and hasn't been moved in ages. As I pull it off the piece of furniture, it crumbles in places, giving in to the forces of time. The quickly deteriorating sheet reveals an antique fainting couch.

I cast the sheet—what's left of it—aside and kick the other remnants away from the clawed feet of the couch. The upholstery is torn in places, holes eaten by more moths, but the wood frame is beautiful. The fabric on it is velvet and worn by time. It's a piece that I might restore. It's too beautiful to get rid of. It deserves to see its former glory again.

I glance over at my modern bed and a light bulb goes off in my mind.

The attic. The furniture. I head upstairs.

THE NARROW ATTIC door creaks as I open it and sunlight pours in through two windows on opposite walls. Various pieces of furniture sit beneath crusty old sheets, treasures to be revealed.

I spot what I think might be the treasure I'm seeking in the corner that looks promising. As I pass through the maze of covered furniture and belongings, something brushes my leg.

"Shit!" I yell.

I spin, looking down quickly enough to see my fat little friend from the other day.

The raccoon hisses at me and disappears into a hole in the far wall.

"Jesus Christ," I mutter, shaken and fully aware that I won't be staying here alone. At least not until I get an exterminator out here.

I refocus on my search. I reach for the sheet covering the item in the corner and I'm not disappointed.

I gasp when I see it. A large bed frame that has to have a birthdate somewhere between 1910 and 1930.

Cobra heads enshrine each of the spires marking the corners. Green jeweled eyes rest in their faces. Intricate hand carved designs line the headboard, more snakes, and in the center is the symbol I saw in the graveyard. An ankh. Above it is a face that I recognize from Greek mythology. It probably didn't belong to the Horns.

This probably belonged to the Solomons.

What tales could this bed tell?

"Hey," I holler for Noelle. I call for her twice more. And finally, I hear footsteps ascending the staircase to the third floor.

"What?!" she gasps, out of breath, probably hurrying, thinking I had gotten myself stuck beneath some piece of ancient, faulty architecture.

"Get the movers, would you please?" I ask her. She stands there for a moment looking around, taking in the attic. She looks at me and nods silently. She fetches the guy who had me sign for everything. "Could you take this to the master bedroom?" I ask.

He looks at the bed frame for a moment. I wonder how much antique furniture he sees. Probably a lot. Still, he seems disconcerted.

"Sure," he says. He turns to go back downstairs and Noelle comes over to inspect the bed.

"Oh, my God," she says.

I glance back at her. I can't tell if she's taken aback by the beauty of the piece or the fact that it's a little disturbing as she pauses, leaning closer to inspect the face in the center of the headboard.

"Medusa," I say.

"How pleasant," she remarks. Her lip turns up slightly.

"I wonder what other creepy shit is up here. I like it." I assert.

"You've always liked dark shit like this," she says.

"What?" I ask, unsure of what she means.

"I think it's because of your dad," she says. "He liked all that weird stuff, too." She says it so casually. It stings. I'm silent. The past tense still catching me off guard. "Sorry," she says quickly.

"No, he's gone," I tell her, my voice emotionless as I shove it all down.

"I think you get a lot of things from him," she goes on.

The movers get upstairs and start for the corner. The pallid-face-guy that I ran into downstairs looks just as uneasy to be up here.

Noelle and I head downstairs, letting them have some space to do what they do.

I look at Noelle when we get downstairs and I say with a bubbling disgust, "You're wrong."

"What?" she asks, genuinely confused.

I glance back upstairs. A rage I wasn't expecting uses my mouth to speak.

"I'm nothing like him." I spit out the words like something nasty I want off my tongue and her eyes widen. She presses her lips together in a way that tells me she doesn't agree.

Not even a little bit.

NINE

EVENING FALLS FASTER than I'd prefer.

Partially, I think it seems that way because Noelle and I didn't get to the house until around 2pm. The afternoon was eaten up by a mind-numbing amount of choices as to where certain furniture should go. I think it also has to do with my distaste for the fall and winter.

I'm making my bed as Noelle tucks some of my belongings into the dresser and hangs up other pieces of clothing more suitable for the closet.

"Once upon a time," I say à propos of nothing. "A therapist told me that trauma leaves a thumbprint on your brain."

I glance over at Noelle.

She doesn't look up from her task. I continue.

"Things like temperature, light, barometric pressure... They all get to be part of the thumbprint. It's like your brain takes a snapshot of data surrounding the traumatic event so that you can forever be prepared to avoid it if it ever comes back." Noelle is staring at me now. "But that's hard when all of those events, time, daylight, temperature, barometric pressure are tied to the seasons."

Her expression softens.

I realize it's the most I've said to her in a long time about how I feel. The most I've admitted in a long time, even to myself, about how I really feel.

I saw a therapist briefly after Dad disappeared.

I couldn't bring myself to go back after the fourth or fifth session because I knew deep down inside of myself that there was a good chance I was never going to get better. The only thing that could make it better was impossible. And that was for my dad to go back in time and right the wrong of how he left us.

"That's the most you've ever let on about any of that in a while," Noelle says after a beat. I keep working on the bed.

"I guess I never really admitted to myself how much this time of year bothers me," I say.

"You think?" Noelle says quickly.

As we work in my bedroom, I think about the night he disappeared.

He packed his bag. He was going by the radio station before heading out of town for a road trip to meet some source for something.

At the time, I had lost just about all my patience with him. So my memories about where he said he was going are fuzzy at best. And he didn't leave a note or an itinerary. He never did.

It's almost like—if something was going to happen —he didn't want anyone to know where to look for him.

Those last moments between us were so casual.

I was in the living room watching TV. He told me he was leaving. Maybe even where he was going. None of it registered. All I could think was I couldn't wait for him to shut up so I could hear my TV show.

And then, just like that, he walked out the front door and he was gone forever.

I know a lot of people talk about that. How they'd give anything for those moments of irritation. Just to have them back again.

I finish smoothing the comforter. I walk over to the king size bed frame in the corner. The one that we had them bring down from the attic.

I trace the finger over one spired corner.

"You gonna get a new mattress?" Noelle asks. She shoves the drawer closed, and it groans in defiance. She bumps it with her hip and it slams shut. I say nothing, still staring at the piece of furniture. "You should," she says. "You should get all new furniture. You should make that your winter project. Renovating this place, decorating it, and making it your own."

I turn and look at her.

"A fresh start, Blair," she says gently.

I inhale sharply.

"Probably not a bad idea," I say. I want this to be a fresh start.

NOELLE LEAVES, giving me a hug at the door. I stand on the porch as she turns on her headlights, backs up, and turns around, headed for the main road. It isn't until her taillights disappear into the trees that I finally step back inside.

The rush of warmth is welcome. The air got a lot chillier after sunset.

I close the second door, the one that leads from the house proper into the small entry space, and I lean against the glass.

I close my eyes for a moment and inhale.

There's a mustiness to the house still, I should make an appointment with a company that can do a deep clean. Maybe I rushed moving in.

I open my eyes and glance around, taking the place in, alone here for the first time.

The realization washes over me with an unexpected force, like the wave of a tsunami crashing back inland after being sucked out into the ocean in the wake of a falling meteorite.

It's like I'm only just feeling the repercussions of everything.

My dad being legally dead.

Him being missing seven years. No one having heard from him.

And me buying this stupid house thinking that Noelle was right that I needed a project

I feel my heart pounding in my chest. Harder, harder, faster, faster, until I feel the blood rushing to my head. I gasp and a sob follows. There's a squeezing in my chest. Like someone is wrapping a fist around my heart. And all I can think of is all the PSAs I've ever seen in my life, about how heart attacks are different for women.

My heartbeat resounds in my ears. I feel like my chest is caving in, that my heart might explode, but it doesn't. I throw the door back open and open the other to the porch. Even though the warmth was welcome only moments ago, now I'm grateful for the icy air on my cheeks.

I ride the crest of the anxiety wave until it reaches its apex. I feel myself starting to come back down. I feel my pulse slowing. My adrenaline has dumped everything it's got into my bloodstream.

My hands shake as I hold them out in front of me.

I inhale deeply, trying to calm myself.

Jesus, it's been years since I had a panic attack. The first one happened the day I had to talk to police officers about my dad's disappearance. It made it real. It made it serious.

It was all so much more than any young person should have to deal with.

For so long, I assumed he was just off on one of his trips. He would leave home sporadically and come back with just as little announcement. Sometimes he'd drag in late and not greet me until the morning.

But this was different. When the police showed up, I knew that.

Blake spared himself a lot of that grief by moving out before dad went missing.

By the time that happened, it was just me and dad in the house.

A team, for better or worse.

Twilight envelops the property. And the trees, though stripped by winter, are dense enough to obscure whatever portion of the sunset I might be able to see at this hour. A lavender light coats the dead grass in front of the house. The realization that I really bought this monstrosity settles over me. The last few weeks have been a whirlwind.

Dad's legal death. Blake's gambling problem. Selling the only house I've known as an adult and buying another that I'm starting to have a sinking feeling is going to be nothing but a money pit.

And I'm alone for all of it.

Barely over thirty and entirely alone in this big house.

I inhale sharply, the way you do after your body settles down from a good cry. I turn, grabbing the doorknob, ready to face the interior of my new home once more.

BACK INSIDE AND drained of adrenaline, things seemed slightly more manageable, the way they always do after a good sob. My breath hitches a few times and hiccups follow, making me feel like a little kid as I wander the house taking in the chaotic surroundings.

My furniture, at least the pieces my dad picked out, is the kind of stuff you'd find in a luxurious log cabin. Masculine, big, dark, and leather other than the green velvet couch that I helped him pick out. Those pieces stand out as those that a man would have in his home. They don't feel like me. They feel like my dad.

Those pieces combined with the few antique pieces I picked out of the attic and kept downstairs make it seem in more disarray, like nothing matches in a bad way.

It needs a little love and attention.

The wood floors are in decent enough shape. I imagine restoring them won't be difficult. Same for the walls.

My phone buzzes in my back pocket, and I draw it out, eager for a distraction. But when I see that it's another email from none other than Cash Kelly, I groan and roll my eyes. I dismiss the notification and slide my phone back into my pocket. I continue on my rounds.

I survey things and take note of who needs to be called: a flooring specialist, a furniture and upholstery specialist, and a host of other experts, not to mention cleaners. By the time I'm done, I find myself in the kitchen.

My fridge looks weird in here.

A giant black monolith next to a basin sink. I'm unsure how much it would be to get one that had a retro vibe about it. Something that wouldn't look so out of place.

I wonder if I look out of place in here.

Not that there are any neighbors to care.

It's then that I hear scurrying, but not the tiny scurrying of mouse feet. The lumbering of something bigger.

My dear old friend the raccoon.

I creep over to the wall where I hear him. I press my ear against it. Silence. I wonder if he knows I'm listening. It occurs to me at that moment that I'm speculating on whether a raccoon is aware of my presence in my own house. Maybe it's not so absurd. He's been squatting here a lot longer than I've even been aware it existed.

Maybe I'm the interloper.

I still my breathing and strain my ears.

Finally, I hear the little guy start moving once again.

I follow him going along the wall of the kitchen. I wait for him to emerge on the other side of the fridge and track him until we reach the door to the basement and the trail goes cold.

I wonder if he's got himself a hole down there. He's got to have a way in and out of the house, and that might be it.

I grab the knob and open the basement door.

A dark staircase looms ahead of me.

I flip the light switch and bathe the little dank little downstairs room in a flickering light. I make a note to get light bulbs. The effect is downright Hitchcockian.

The light bulb is on its last legs in the unused basement. There are more shredded sheets, eaten by moths and other vermin, draped over various pieces of furniture from decades and eras past, and the place smells musty. It smells old. It smells like no one has given a shit about it in a long time. And somehow that's comforting to me.

Somehow I relate to it.

That little negative realization bolsters my spirits in my quest to renew the energy of the house.

Maybe I can find new life too.

I creep down the staircase, each step protesting my weight and making me feel glad that I have health insurance. I stop midway, listening for my furry friend. I press my ear to the wall and remain still for almost a minute. Finally, I hear the scritch-scratch of his little feet traversing the innards of the house.

I wait a bit and continue down the stairs. When I get to the bottom, I sit, arms resting on my knees, and I wait.

The basement looks much like the attic. But there

is a line of cabinets on the far wall. One of those chemical emergency shower stations and giant tanks with tubes running out of them. They look as old, yellowed, and brittle as the sheets on the furniture.

After a few minutes pass and I fail to hear the raccoon, I get up and walk over to the cabinets.

I meander through various pieces of furniture and emerge in front of a casket.

"Shit," I gasp.

The thing is old and, hopefully, unused. It looks as pristine as a casket can look if it's been sitting in a basement for a few decades. It's wooden and looks expensive. I stare at it for a moment. My mind wanders.

Dad was declared dead, but there was no memorial. There was no funeral. Nobody. No cremains, no nothing, no closure.

My hand reaches out for the lid.

I tell myself not to think about every single horror movie I've ever watched.

Telling myself this is not a good idea. But the thought of returning upstairs without at least looking inside to make sure a serial killer or a zombie isn't lying in wait is too stressful.

I pop the lid slowly. It creaks and groans, much like the aged staircase.

Inside is something I wasn't expecting.

Candy wrappers, broken beer bottles, and various pieces of food-related trash. Then, with a quickness I don't anticipate, a grubby, little, furred paw reaches out from the bottom of the casket—the end where someone's legs might be—and snatches one of the half-empty bags of chips. I hear a hiss, and I step back with a gasp, my heart thundering.

"Well, fuck," I say. After thinking I spotted him earlier, and now confirming that, I guess the exterminator didn't relocate this little guy.

And this is his hiding place.

I debate opening the casket completely to reveal my raccoon roommate, but ultimately decided against it. This has been enough excitement for one day. But curiosity does get the better of me, finally, and I bend over to spot a hole in the end. It looks like a trapdoor. I've never seen anything like it, but it explains precisely how the little raccoon got inside.

A memory comes to me.

I have heard of caskets used as rentals for bodies that are going to be cremated. Usually in cases where the family wants a real funeral with the body present.

I sigh, trying to get my heartbeat to regulate itself again. I wonder how many bodies have laid in this casket before they were cremated?

And now this little raccoon makes himself at home here.

Beside the casket is one of those easels used at funerals. The kind that a portrait of the deceased usually sits upon. This one is covered with a sheet like almost all the furniture down here.

I reached for the corner and pull it back, revealing

a full-length portrait of a subject I couldn't have guessed if I tried for a million years.

Staring back at me is a dog, but not just a dog. It's a dog posed like a human, wearing what looks like a general's coat. It's strange, macabre, even. There's something weird about it. It's like a human's body with a dog's head.

I let the sheet crumple to the floor beside me and it falls onto a small trunk with a lock that might fit a skeleton key. I make a mental note to check it out later.

The painting has to be at least two feet wide by three feet tall. The frame is gilded and flaking in places. It's old, possibly as old as the house.

Who in the hell has such a thing?

Even though it's weird and, I'll admit, a little creepy, there's something magnetizing about it.

The dog almost looks sinister.

Like he's looking at someone he doesn't trust.

The weirdness is charming. A bit like this house.

A bit like the circumstances that led me to buy it without giving it too much more thought.

I grab the painting and return upstairs. I shut the basement behind me and stare at the door handle for a moment.

Something makes me lock it. And then, painting in hand, I go up to my bedroom.

TEN

UPSTAIRS, I try to push my little raccoon friend out of my mind. The idea that he might come up here in the night is a little disconcerting, but nothing I can't handle, I remind myself.

I'm not sure I ever had a furry little visitor quite like him at the old house. But I'm trying to open myself to new experiences, right? Still, I make another mental note: aside from light bulbs, I need to call that exterminator. A brief thought dances through my head. I want to make sure that they're not going to hurt him.

I make another mental note: humane raccoon trapping instead of an exterminator might be a better search engine term. The last thing I want is a dead raccoon on my hands. There's already a coyote in the bottom of the pool out back.

I sit on my bed, having placed the portrait of the Frankenstein dog against the balcony doors.

It sits there staring at me, and I sit in bed staring back at it.

I wonder who commissioned the painting and why?

It seems like such an odd thing to have, or even to ask for an artist to paint. I don't have any nails, but I'll get some and tell myself to remember to add those to my list, too.

The painting is compelling.

There's something about it that almost seems alive. Like the paint strokes undulate and move when they're just in my peripheral vision. Like the dog in the picture wearing the general's coat might come to life at any moment and step out of the painting.

I wonder if he was a real dog that someone had or if it was just some strange vision of an artist. Either way, there's something eerie about it to me. Something other. Though I'm not the kind of person that believes in such things. There would be my dad's arena.

Still, I like having the painting up here. There's something about it that feels familiar. And maybe that has to do with my dad. Maybe it has to do with all the book covers and VHS tapes we had of information about alien abductions, Bigfoot, Loch Ness monsters, and other things that go bump in the night.

Maybe it feels familiar. Maybe it feels like home.

I think about Noelle telling me that I always liked weird stuff. That my dad always liked weird stuff, comparing the two of us.

Even sitting here, as much as I like the painting, I don't think we were the same. Not at all.

Still, he was my dad.

A smirk curves my lips. As I stare into the black canine eyes—eyes that seem to swallow up my stare and beckon me into some other world—painted on the medium-sized canvas, I think of my dad.

You'd be enjoying this, wouldn't you, Dad?

A little laugh escapes me. But it's followed quickly by sadness. I fought so hard for so many years against the things that my dad was interested in. I didn't want to be his weird daughter. I knew how people talked about him. When I was in high school, kids would ask me if I needed any aluminum foil to make into hats. I did my best to distance myself from whatever legacy he was creating.

It was particularly brutal, junior and senior year.

That's when Dad's career really started to take off. And he started appearing on talk shows. He started becoming more of a household name. Not for any good reason. No. Many of the people that knew his name only knew it in mockery.

There were hundreds of thousands—maybe millions—that took him seriously though every night.

Now I sit here in a rundown, old mansion staring into the eyes of a weird-ass human-dog portrait, wishing my dad were here to gush over how fucking cool he'd think it was.

My throat gets tight. It constricts inward on itself.

And when I try to swallow, it's almost impossible. I can feel gathering moisture threatening to sting my eyes. I fight back against it. He doesn't deserve my tears after all the pain he sent marching across my heart. I won't be soft on him.

I clear my throat and grab my laptop, determined not to think about that—about him—anymore.

At least for tonight.

I do a few searches and order some of the things I need. The light bulbs, the nails, a hammer, and, finally, I find a mattress and box springs and order those to fit the king-size bed frame that sits against the opposite wall.

I look at the ornate spires and the headboard with Medusa's face so intricately carved.

The gilding has flaked, but she's still beautiful.

I always thought the myth might have gotten it wrong. That she might have been misunderstood. And instead maybe it should have been her carrying Perseus's head with her out of battle.

I wonder who slept in the bed and if it belonged to the Solomons, and I wonder what memories were made in this room.

I glance around. The wallpaper is old, probably a remnant of the time when the Solomon family lived here. Or maybe the Horns. It looks like it's been restored once but might need a little boost.

I've got my work cut out for me. That's for certain. I go back downstairs and turn off the lights in each room, one by one. The house is so large. So empty, so much space for a single woman by herself.

And I wonder again briefly if I've made a huge mistake in coming here.

I try not to let fantasies involving regret plague me for too long. I tell myself that I'm just getting started. This is all brand new. My first night in the house. My first night away from my father's house since I was a teenager.

I retreat upstairs and close my bedroom door. I think about the raccoon once more and wonder what he's doing right now. Where he might be in the walls. I change for bed, grab my phone, and settle in under the covers.

I groan when I see the notification that's been waiting for me. The one I got earlier and rolled my eyes at. Stupid fucking Cash Kelly, wanting to talk to me.

I clear it. I just want to sleep and I pray that it's dreamless.

———

THE SOUND of chuffing wakes me. A heavy breathing animal, not a human.

My eyes shoot open and I'm immediately and violently jarred from sleep. Confusion settles over me. The raccoon? No.

Bigger.

My heart pounds in my chest, and blood rushes to

my head, thundering just beyond my eardrums. My skin is slick with a sheen of cold sweat. The sheets are damp and tangled in my legs. I frantically kick to get free in the moonlight, having the feeling that in a moment I'm going to need to run.

I look around the room, trying like hell to will my eyes to adjust to the low light.

I spot the painting standing exactly where I left it when I went to bed. Nothing is out of place.

But I swear that the dog's eyes are glowing in the portrait. Just subtly. Two little tiny pinpricks of light.

I grab my phone and switch on the flashlight feature.

I lean over close to the painting, shining it into the dog's eyes. It's as I thought.

There's no white in its eyes. No reflection painted into the portrait.

Its eyes are pure black.

I wonder if the painting could still reflect light somehow. I glance over to my left shoulder, looking at the bathroom. I left the door open. It could be moonlight from the mirror reflected on the painting.

I hold my breath, still for a moment.

There are no sounds of movement on the floor below me.

I'm alone. I tell myself. I'm safe.

What kind of nightmare must I have had?

I try to draw up my dream from the sticky spider webs of unconscious thought.

I'm too late. The nightmare has already retreated far into its cave, dwelling deep inside the lizard part of my brain. The part that reacts only with fight, flight, or freeze, and something about that is deeply unsettling. The idea that whatever terror I was facing, whatever thing that was chuffing right at my neck, is tucked neatly down inside my unconscious mind, my own creation. My own monster that has nothing to do with this house or its history.

I take a deep breath.

I look around the room once more. Just to make sure. Moonlight pours through the semi-sheer curtains. Curtains aged and in need of replacement. The light casts a dim illumination across the floor.

I reach for my phone.

I take my phone in my hand and check the notifications. A few articles have popped up. No messages, nothing from Facebook or Instagram. I go to my texts, just to make sure I haven't missed something. When I find nothing there, I go to my email, and waiting for me is the message I disregarded earlier. The one from Cash Kelly.

In the darkness after my encounter with whatever that thing was, I'm not quite as quick to dismiss the potential of connecting, albeit electronically, with another human being. Even if it's him.

I read the email.

Blair,

Oh, wow. He used my first name. This oughta be good.

I would really like to talk to you.
Cash

The first name basis rings false and irritates me.

What the hell could he have to say that's so important?

It reads like a line meant to sucker me in, so I'll contact him and somehow end up on his YouTube channel. What better thing for his slew of viewers than a one-on-one with their guru's daughter? Suddenly I'm filled with disgust and wish I hadn't opened the email.

I lock my phone and put it back on the nightstand. I lie there in the darkness for quite some time. My mind is no longer on whatever was terrorizing me in the nightmare.

I tell myself that's normal. I'm in a new place. There's new, old stress. All of that could contribute to me having some other worldly vision in the middle of the night.

My pulse has returned to normal, and my body's cooling off. I strip back all the covers, leaving only the sheet over me and I lie there, letting the cool air of the room kiss my damp skin. It's soothing. My mind drifts then back to its favorite scab to pick at. My dad.

I think briefly of a post I once came across on LinkedIn or Medium.

It was about daddy issues and how they shouldn't be a punchline, or a thing used to vilify women. Instead, it's a failing on a man's part. Somehow, though, a woman gets to bear the brunt of the humiliation from it.

I wonder briefly if I might have such issues. It's ludicrous to even ask the question.

I comb back through my relationships. There haven't been many after Colson.

I lay there staring at the ceiling in the semi-dark of my bedroom.

My bedroom in this house that I bought with Dad's money.

Damn, I miss him.

ELEVEN

THROUGHOUT THE NEXT week or two, I focus on the house. The interior, the exterior, just generally cleaning the place up and having the appropriate specialists out to give me quotes on work. Within that time frame, some of them actually start on it. I get a new light bulb down in the basement and the humane exterminator that I found on Yelp shows up that Friday wearing leather pants, a Pantera shirt, and sporting a bleached mullet.

The guy pulls his wraparound sunglasses down dramatically as I open the front door for him. A sucker sticks out of his mouth as he speaks.

"You called?" he asks, sounding almost like some sort of cartoon character. I stifle the urge to laugh because it reminds me of Lurch. A skinny, hair-metal version of Lurch. *You rang?*

"Indeed," I say.

"What's the issue?" he asks. I'm more than certain that the girl who took my information when I made the appointment informed him that there's a raccoon living inside the walls of my house. I'm not sure, but I think he likes the cinematic vibes he's putting off. It seems performative. Like he's too cool for school. I glance around out front just to make sure there's not a hidden camera crew capturing all of this for the viewers at home.

I see nothing, fortunately, and step back in letting him follow me.

"So, there's a raccoon in the walls," I tell him.

"Have you actually seen it?" he asks, glancing around the entry hall of the house.

I can see from the look on his face that he's judging every single thing that's wrong with this place right now. I want him to tell him to cool it until he gets rid of his mullet. I won't take home decor advice from a scrawnier version of Dog the Bounty Hunter. He's giving me the vibe that he thinks I'm some poor little woman who doesn't know a mouse from a raccoon.

"Yeah," I say. "I've seen him," I add, with an edge in my voice.

He glances around the house again as though he's weighing whether a raccoon could actually be living here. This time, he walks up to the wall next to the staircase. He wraps on it five times, then waits, like the raccoon is going to give him an answer. He presses his ear to the wall.

I wonder if the raccoon is knocking back at him or something? Is that how raccoons communicate with humans? I wasn't aware that they could. He turns to face me and dramatically pulls the sucker from his mouth.

"I think I'll be able to get him," he says, like he's talking about a crocodile or something. He acts like I've called him to tell him that there's an alligator in my pool.

"Without hurting him?" I ask.

"Without hurting him," he confirms. The whole interaction feels like it's out of a movie. Like this guy lives for the experience of being some weird action hero in an exterminator movie. Only he's the only one that doesn't know it's a comedy.

I nod and let him get to it.

A FEW HOURS pass and I wander around the house trying to stay out of this guy's way. Mostly just to avoid any unnecessary roles I might have to play in the weird little drama he's created for himself.

I don't want to hold the bag when it's time to catch the raccoon.

I walk into the second living room—the parlor that was used as a visitation suite when the Horn family owned the house. It's still empty with me not having let the furniture movers put anything in this room. It was just too creepy.

I look out the windows. It's a dreary winter day. No snow. The yellow grass looks sharp to the touch, even from here. The sky is cloudy, and the sun is buried somewhere behind it, casting the landscape in cool hues.

I remember this.

I remember these sensations. The way that this time of year feels on my skin. The temperature, the barometric pressure, the cloudy sky with no direct sunlight.

It all feels like the day my dad became a missing person.

I remember going outside the night after I talked to the police. After I realized that he wasn't just heading out on some sort of business trip.

I lit the fire pit on the patio and I stayed out there by myself.

I tried to call Blake, but he didn't answer. At that point, he was gone, and I didn't really have any friends other than Noelle, and she was out on a date that night.

I wanted to talk to someone. The house felt big and lonely. And terror was beginning to creep in at the edge of things.

I was on my own for good, even though I didn't realize it at that point.

I remember looking up at the stars.

The overcast day had turned clear in the night and

the moon was full. It seemed appropriate for him to go missing on a full moon. It wasn't something I realized until after the fact when theories started popping up online about what really happened to him.

Looking out at the property, I realize how different this place is from the one I came from.

The road that leads to the house is longer.

There are bigger bushes out by the road that mask the entrance to the place. Dad would like that. He always said the bushes needed to be bigger outside our place.

Just then, as I'm staring out into the gated entrance, I hear the tires of a large vehicle coming down the road and then a moving van emerges out of the trees surrounding the driveway. I stare for a second, puzzled, then I spot the logo and realize it's the box springs and mattress for the bed.

I rush to the front door and then outside. I quickly sign the papers offered to me by the delivery guy. He and another dude wrangle the box springs upstairs while two other guys follow with the mattress.

I follow them up.

"You want us to set it up for you?" the first guy asks.

"If you don't care," I say, not wanting to tell him if he leaves it leaning against the wall, I'm not sure I can manhandle the thing onto the bed frame by myself. I could call Noelle.

I don't tell him that.

Instead, I smile solicitously and he accepts. The guys place the king mattress atop the box springs and the bed looks vast. So huge compared to the one I'm getting rid of. I thank them and tip them when they take my old mattress and box springs downstairs and load them into the van.

After they leave, I go back up to the bedroom, still intent on avoiding my hair metal raccoon extractor, and I admire the bed. It looks even better with a box spring and mattress on it.

I slide on to it. It's huge, cushy and luxurious. I went all out on the purchase and I'm glad that I did. I lay there, my legs dangling off the edge for a few moments, and I close my eyes.

My nightmare from last night comes to me.

I think about the chuffing of hot breath on my neck.

It reminds me of an alien movie. Where the monster is breathing, salivating, and so very close to Sigourney Weaver's face.

The thought is chilling. My eyes shoot open, and I get up, pushing myself up on my elbows. I look over at the portrait of the dog again. Except something's wrong. I can't put my finger on it. Is he looking in the opposite direction? Is his nose pointed to the right now instead of the left? Is there something about his eyes?

I stare for a long while.

My pulse picks up. It's like my body is responding to an unseen threat.

"Got him!"

"Jesus fucking Christ!" I shout, jumping from the bed.

I turn around and see my very own bargain bin Axl Rose, holding a big fat raccoon by the scruff of its neck. The thing hisses and snaps like a possum. It's angry, trying its damnedest to bite the fucker holding it.

I can relate.

The guy just stares at me, clutching the snarling raccoon and holding him up like a prize. Like I'm supposed to give him a gold star.

It reminds me of Tinder images of guys holding up fish that they caught.

This is better, though.

Why can't more guys hold up raccoons that they humanely extracted from a house to re-home somewhere else? It would be more attractive. Although this particular guy that's holding the raccoon doesn't really have the market cornered on attractiveness.

"What do you want me to do with him?" he asks.

"What?" I snap. "What do *I* want you to do with him?"

"Yeah," he says with a nonchalant shrug.

I rub my face, trying to snap back to reality after worrying about the weird dog portrait.

"I guess just take him to the woods out back," I say, pointing in the general direction of the back of the house.

"Sounds legit," he says with a nod.

He turns and leaves the bedroom. I watch the pair of them descend the stairs.

New best friends.

I CALL NOELLE THAT EVENING.

"Come over," I say. It's not a question or an invitation. It's a statement. And I'm not planning on giving her an out. She hesitates. "Bring Hooper," I say with an exasperated sigh.

"How did you know I was with Hooper?" she blurts.

"I always know," I tell her with a smile in my voice.

Even when we were younger, I could tell when Noelle was doing something she thought she shouldn't. And context clues told me that right now that thing is hanging out with Hooper. Despite that, I'm pretty certain that Hooper might be incredibly good for her, even if she doesn't realize that yet.

He's not that bad. I wouldn't mind for both of them to come over.

"Okay, I'll ask him," she says.

"You *tell* him." I reiterate the fact that her presence tonight is non-negotiable. I wonder if she hears the desperation in my voice.

Part of me wishes I was still staying with her. An ache in my chest betrays just how lonely I am.

"Okay, pushy," she says, there's an inflection in her

tone. She's teasing. I smile as we hang up and grab a bottle of wine and throw it in the fridge, ready for when they arrive.

NOELLE AND HOOPER are there less than an hour later. I smirk as I see their headlights in the driveway. Eager for an evening not spent in my own company.

She parks, and in a few moments I hear them on the porch. I go to open the door.

"Jeez," Noelle says, looking around as I lead them into the entry hall.

"I hope that's a good jeez," I quip. Hooper follows her in. "Hey Hooper," I say as he gives me a sheepish grin.

"Hey, Blair," he says. The three of us haven't been together in quite some time. I think the last time I remember being around him, we were at a bar. He was hanging on every stupid thing that Noelle said.

And believe me, she was saying a lot of stupid things. She'd had quite a bit to drink that night.

What I wouldn't give to have someone do that for me.

But that would require letting a man close enough that he could well and truly destroy me. It reminds me of my dad. And we weren't even that close, only bonded by blood and proximity to one another.

I lived with him for years, existing inside his shadow.

Now that's gone and I'm not sure what my life is supposed to be.

"You okay?" Noelle asks, glancing away from the trappings of the house and back to me.

"Fine," I fake a smile. "So, what do you think?" I wave my arms around. Some of the furniture has been re-upholstered and other pieces have been restored. I've gotten rid of some of the more modern pieces of my dad's that didn't fit. That was the hardest part.

But our green velvet couch and matching chairs still sit in the living room. Beautiful Tiffany lamps that came with the house stand on either side of the couch, a little elbow grease and some love and they're glowing once more.

Noelle looks around again.

"It doesn't even look like the same place," she says. "It's amazing. It's shaping up so nicely." She squeezes my arm and gives me a smile.

I smile back at her, filled with warmth in her presence, and glad to have company on such a lonely night.

"Wine?" I ask the pair of them and lead them to the kitchen.

TWELVE

BACK IN THE LIVING ROOM, we settle in for a night of laughter, booze, and avoiding the frigid cold that awaits outside.

Hooper gets a blaze started in the fireplace and the room fills with warmth. He and Noelle go back and forth. The two of them are trying to tell me a story.

"No, that's not what happened," she tries to insert.

"I think you just don't remember it that well," he teases.

"I think you *wish* that's what happened," she teases back. I watch them banter. My heart is full for her and it aches for me. There's a part of me that's always dreaded the idea of Noelle finding someone. The same part of me has always thought that I'll be alone forever. I have to fight the urge to cling to her, to keep her from embracing this new part of her life. I have to tell myself it's wrong.

They keep talking. Apparently, they've gone out a few times in the past two weeks. Restaurants, bars. She's met some of the crowd he runs around with now. But apparently I'm the first of Noelle's friends that Hooper has gotten to meet, and he already knew me. It makes me wonder how serious she's taking this. He's already introduced her to the people he works with and some of his friends outside of work. Chances are that Hooper might have higher hopes for this relationship than Noelle does.

We keep on well into the night. Hooper adds another log to the fireplace and Noelle retreats to the kitchen for a moment to grab another bottle of wine.

Hooper stares at the fire and I do the same, tracing lazy circles around the mouth of my wineglass.

"She's something else," he finally says.

I start from my reverie, having to pull my drunken brain back to the moment at hand. Slightly tipsy, I'm not immediately certain about whom he's speaking.

Noelle, of course.

"Oh," I say. "Yeah, she is."

I smile to myself and see that he's doing the same.

"I think I'm in love with her," he blurts out. I sober up immediately.

"What?" I ask, processing his statement. I surreptitiously glance at the kitchen, trying to make sure that Noelle isn't coming out right now.

"I think I always have been, Blair," he says. "I just hope she feels the same."

It's something that we've all known for a long time.

Hooper has always been in love with her, but for him to say it is something else.

This is really the first time Noelle's ever given him a chance.

I stare at him for a moment, trying to find the right words and trying not to say the wrong thing. Ultimately, I decide silence is my best bet, especially in my current state. I don't want to give Hooper false hope.

I also feel like I should talk to Noelle about this and let her know that she needs to tread delicately and end it if she doesn't have any intention of this going anywhere. I dread that conversation.

Hooper fills the silence, though.

With a smile on his face and the orange glow of the fireplace illuminating it, he speaks.

"You know, I met your dad once after high school," Hooper says, changing the subject. Something we're both obviously grateful for.

"Really?" I ask.

It's rare for any of my friends to talk about my dad. It's not like he really made himself available for them when they were hanging out at my house.

"I was just starting college and there was this cryptid convention type thing at the Myriad Gardens downtown. It was sort of half art walk, half speakers getting up and presenting their research. I was heavy duty into that shit back then," he says as the ghost of a wistful smile dances across his face.

"You never told me you listened to my dad's radio show," I say with a smirk in my voice. I imagine there are a lot of people that listen to my dad's radio show that didn't tell the people in their lives.

I try to remember the event, but it bleeds into so many others. My dad did stuff like that all the time. Hooper knew my dad existed, but he never let on that he knew anything about what my dad did. Other than what I told him.

"Yeah," he says. "I guess I kept it a secret," he pauses.

"Because everyone wants to make fun of you," I say. He looks sheepish for a moment, then he swallows.

"Yeah," he says. "I guess so. But your dad was so great. You know, your dad really cared. I got to talk to him for a while," Hooper goes on.

I'm skeptical, imagining my dad really caring about these people that it seemed so obvious that he was exploiting.

"What was he like?" The question is out of my mouth before I even have a second to think how weird it must sound for me to ask Hooper about my father, the way I might ask him about the time he met Eddie Vedder at a coffee shop in Seattle.

"He was the coolest fucking dude I've ever met," he says. "Still to this day."

The way he says it makes me think it's the truth to him.

Hooper goes on.

"I caught him as he was packing stuff up. I'd seen him speak on a panel. I asked if he would sign a book of his that I'd had for a few years about aliens and UFOs and all that good stuff," he says.

I don't bother to ask which book it was. My dad had written several on UFOs and aliens.

I have all of them.

I wanted copies when I was little.

Up until the point when I became a teenager, I boxed them up and put them on the top shelf in my closet. I didn't want to look at them.

As a kid, I'd read a lot of what he'd written, mainly in an effort to get him to pay attention to me. To win his approval and to have something to talk with him about, but he just never seemed to have time.

"Do you still have the book?" I ask Hooper. He's still waxing poetic about my dad.

"What?" he asks, thrown off the track of his story.

"The book," I say.

"Yeah," he says, and then he goes on, unencumbered by my weird questions. "He was seriously so cool, Blair. So nice. And we talked for a really long time. He didn't have to do that. He was on his way out. He probably had places to be, probably wanted to get back to you guys."

I fight back a laugh at the statement.

"I actually ended up exchanging emails with him for a while after that," Hooper says. "We talked about all sorts of stuff. He talked about you and Blake a lot."

That last part catches me off guard, and I don't know what I feel.

"He did?" I ask. My voice is meek, soft, the kind of voice someone has when they're about to be choked by a strong emotion.

I hate that it excites me and devastates me at the same time.

"Oh, yeah," Hooper says. "He was so proud of you, Blair." He goes on. I feel the sting of tears in my eyes. "Your brother and him butted heads a lot. I could tell. Same with you," Hooper adds with a laugh. "But your dad loved you so much. You were definitely the favorite," he says with a smile.

A single tear escapes and slips down my cheek, like velvet over glass.

It's on the opposite side that's facing Hooper.

I swipe it quickly, making sure that he doesn't see. A smile comes to my face, thinking about all the times that Blake has told me I was my dad's favorite.

And all the times I told him that just wasn't true.

And then I have Hooper here confirming it.

I imagine a situation in which Blake might be here. A situation where talking about our dad would be fun, us reminiscing about the good times. And that maybe his idea that I was the favorite would be casual teasing.

Like brothers and sisters do. Him saying, *You know he let you get away with everything.*

The thought is heartbreaking. Wishing for a history that never existed.

And never will.

Hooper and I are silent. The fire crackles.

And my face falls at the sadness of it all.

"Jesus, who brought the party down?" Noelle asks when she emerges back into the living room.

"We were just talking about Graham," Hooper says.

"What? Hooper!" She punches him in the arm a little harder than necessary.

"Shit!" he gripes at her.

"It's fine," I reassure her. "Really, it's fine." And I smile.

Hooper looks nervously between us, realizing that it might be somewhat of a sore subject.

"I'm sorry. I wouldn't have brought it up–."

"No, Hooper," I tell him. "Really, it's fine. I'm glad you did."

And I'm telling the truth.

———

"IT WAS GOOD TO SEE YOU," Noelle whispers in my ear as she hugs me tight at the door.

I inhale the scent of her apple shampoo. I stroke her smooth strawberry blonde hair.

"It was good to see you, too," I tell her. As we pull apart, I look at Hooper. "It was good to see you, too, Hooper," I say.

He nods and smiles bashfully, probably still

wondering if he fucked up by talking about my dad. I want to tell him he didn't, but it's one of the few times that someone's brought him up.

I try to show him with a grin that it's okay.

They depart and I close the door, watching the route of Noelle's taillights disappear down the drive-way. Once more, I'm alone in this house. I lean back against the door and listen to the crackle of the fire in the fireplace. I'm not quite ready to put it out yet.

I want to sit there again, staring into the flames and think about what Hooper said. To try to imagine that my father would talk about me so warmly to a stranger. I want to think about all the ways I didn't know my dad, and imagine how things might have been different.

There are so many things I didn't know about him. I couldn't even tell you what his favorite TV show was.

I look around, wondering how to fill another hour before bed.

And my eyes land on the door that leads to the backyard. My favorite little furry friend.

Instead of sitting in front of the fireplace, I decide to grab my coat, scarf, and some mittens.

I go outside to spend a little time and see if I can spot the raccoon out back. I walk to the edge of the empty art déco pool. I glance at the bottom, now clean and free of other animal remains, and my eyes travel upward to the tree line at the back of the property. I narrow my eyes, trying to make out any shape in the darkness.

And that's when I hear it.

Chuff. Chuff.

Almost a snort.

A huge exhalation through a snout that must be massive. An animal much larger than a raccoon, and the same sound that woke me in the middle of the night.

A chill descends on me. My heart begins to race and an instinctive part of my brain suddenly shifts into prey mode. That's what I am. Prey, meat, sustenance. Whatever was making that sound views me that way.

Why would I have heard it in the house in my bedroom, so close to my ear that I could practically feel the hot air being forced from its lungs?

I stand frozen on the spot. My eyes still try to make out shapes in the darkness, but now through the lens of fear. I feel like I see them everywhere. A shadow here, one over there. My eyes dart around and the shapes move, my eyes trying to follow whatever it is that I'm seeing—or *think* that I'm seeing. They seem to get closer, bigger. I hear the sound again.

Fuck, I feel crazy.

Suddenly I'm wishing Noelle and Hooper were still here. That anyone was here. That I wasn't surrounded by empty fields for miles. I'm sure of one thing though, as I slip quickly back to the house.

I may feel lonely, but I'm not alone.

THIRTEEN

I SLAM the back door and turn the lock, jerking my hand away like there's a fire burning on the other side. The silence of the warm house envelops me and somehow feels too loud. I can't think straight. I have no idea what that was.

Or why it was the same sound that I heard when I woke up in the middle of the night?

That part is the most unsettling.

The raccoon got into the house, right? So maybe something else could be getting into the house?

Fully shaken out of my tipsy state, I get a glass of water and chug it. I think about the time that someone told me drinking water can stave off a panic attack. And I feel like I'm about to have another one like I did a week or two ago.

Except this time, it's far less related to existential

angst and far more related to a very real physical threat.

Or at least that's how it seems.

What the fuck was that?

I draw my mind back to the raccoon. Back to its home inside the weird casket with the trapdoor.

Ugh.

I realize that I need to go down into the basement. I need to finish checking to see if there's another entrance into the house down there. Or a hole dug by some ungodly creature.

Do mountain lions come into houses?

I don't even know if there are mountain lions out here. Authorities have long insisted that mountain lions aren't in the state, but I know from living with someone who specialized in the strange and unusual that a lot of people take issue with that assertion. A lot of people have seen them, photographed them, and documented their tracks.

There could be one here.

Jesus Christ, Blair.

What the fuck am I thinking?

There is not an apex predator stalking into my house at night.

I stare at the basement door.

Maybe I heard the chuffing sound once when I was outside. Maybe when I was with the lady showing me the property. Maybe with Noelle. Maybe I tucked it into my subconscious and left it there to ferment into a nightmare.

My heart rate slows at that thought.

It's the first one that has any basis in logic. It's the first one that makes sense in a way that doesn't terrify me.

Whatever it is, it isn't inside the house.

It's in the woods, where animals (and monsters) should be.

Finally calmed down, I go downstairs and turn on the light. With a new bulb, the place is a little less creepy. I look around, rummaging behind pieces of furniture, looking for any holes that might be in the walls. I find only one, which it looks like my hair metal exterminator has sealed up with a makeshift board and nail situation.

That gives me a bit more peace.

Nothing is out of place. Nothing is unusual down here.

Other than the fact that it used to be an embalming room and that I now own a weird casket a raccoon was squatting in.

Perfectly normal.

At least by the standards of the Graves family.

I TAKE a hot bath in the clawfoot tub. Steam wraps its tendrils around me and snakes up the tiled walls like ivy. It fogs the mirror and puts my mind at ease. I grab my phone from the table placed beside the tub and check to make sure that Noelle and Hooper made it home.

Sure enough, a text from her is waiting. Along with another apology for Hooper's dalliance into my dad's past.

I reassure her one more time that it's not a big deal. I'm really glad he brought it up. It's so weird to think that I never really knew him.

And that's the first time I've let the thought fully coalesce. I roll it over in my mind, the way you do when you have a sore in your mouth. Your tongue pokes and prods, trying to make it go away, or at the very least, understand it.

But I'm not sure I'll ever understand the question mark left by my father.

This leads me to think about Cash Kelly. And his stupid messages.

He wants an interview about my dad.

I'm so lonely. So, so lonely.

Lonely enough that I open his e-mail on my phone and begin to type out a response. I think about the way Hooper talked about my dad. He talked about him like a man I'd never even met, let alone been sired by.

I wonder if Cash ever knew my dad.

It's possible. Likely, even, if he's always been into this stuff and it's not just a stunt for views and ad clicks.

Responding wouldn't hurt, would it?

And so I do.

AFTER I TYPE out a message several times, backspace, completely delete, copy and paste and cut a few parts out, I'm satisfied and I send it. Basically, I ask him what he wants to know about my dad. And what was so urgent that he needed to talk to me about?

I lay the phone down on the little wooden table I've pulled up next to the tub and I sink in all the way to my nose.

I remember being a little girl at the pool with my dad. He would do this very thing, lower himself down into the water until it just covered the tip of his nose. He would hum the theme from Jaws and Blake and I would flee, swimming like mad in delighted terror.

Dad would chase us, always making one of us rescue the other one from him. And it always ended in laughter.

I close my eyes and a brief, but dark, thought enters my mind. I wonder what it's like to drown.

A thought with more salience occurs quickly thereafter.

What if dad drowned?

I have absolutely no idea what happened to him. Or where he could be. And he's likely dead.

There's a unique kind of pain in not knowing what

sort of death someone that you loved might have suffered. It's worse, I think, than witnessing it.

You might never erase a memory so vile, but you'll be plagued forever by dark possibilities the other way.

The way I am.

I slink up slightly out of the bathwater, not really intent on drowning myself. At least not tonight. Instead, I let my body relax fully and I close my eyes, listening to the sound of the water lapping at the edges of the tub.

———

I COME to and the water is cold.

Jesus.

I fell asleep.

I sit up straighter and realize my ass is asleep in the bottom of the ivory tub. I pull myself out, letting my posterior wake up to a flurry of pins and needles. I lean on the edge until I'm relatively certain that I won't maim myself when I step out.

I stand and wipe the glass before me with a towel. I look into the mirror.

I see his face sometimes when I do that.

His features.

I see his stubbornness.

His unwillingness to let anyone in.

And then I think about Noelle and Hooper tonight. The playful banter. Even the way that Hooper tried to appease her after he knew he'd pissed her off. The way he gave a shit about her. And me. I wonder for a moment if I'll ever know what that's like.

Or if I'll just be alone in this old house, one more family name to add to the roster of people that have lived here.

Will I be a spinster? Is that even a thing anymore?

I hear the house settling and groaning around me in the winter wind. It's warm in here, even though the bath water has gone cold.

Finally, I wrap up in a towel and go to the door. I open it and start to step out into the bedroom when my bare foot hits the wet carpet.

That's strange.

I've been in the bathroom. I glance behind me, checking to see if there's water on the tile floor that I just didn't notice. Did it leak out while I was running the bath?

I move my dry bare foot and see a large circular spot of wetness on the thin carpet.

My eyes travel forward, following more spots.

And then it occurs to me that they aren't spots.

They're paw prints.

And they don't belong to a raccoon.

FOURTEEN

I STAND THERE and my eyes follow the wet paw prints. They're large. I was right about it not being the raccoon. A weird thought occurs to me. Never in my life have I wished so badly for there to be a raccoon in my house, or any other vermin that might be small and reasonable to deal with. Because whatever this is, it's not a raccoon, or anywhere near the size of one. This thing is large.

Like a *mountain lion*, large.

What the actual fuck?

My eyes dart to the balcony windows. I look to see if the door is open. It isn't. The painting still leans against them. I stare at it for a moment.

It seems different again somehow, but maybe that's just my imagination. I think it's getting the better of me.

My eyes travel back across the room to the door

that leads on to the second story landing. It stands ajar and I try to remember if I closed it when I went to take a bath.

Why would I have? I'm here alone.

The only reason I closed the bathroom door was to keep the warmth in.

I reach for the pajamas that I laid out for myself on the bed. My skin is sticky and damp. I fight my way into them. The clothes cling to my body, but finally, I'm fully clothed and ready to explore the house. Somehow, the pajamas make me feel more vulnerable than being naked did.

I look around the room once more and see nothing out of place. Just the paw prints.

I look at the portrait again. Somehow, it seems spookier than it did the other night.

Maybe I shouldn't have brought it up here. I think it's giving me the creeps at a point in time where I really don't need any more help to freak myself out. There's a part of me that's chastising myself for that, thinking how silly that is, letting a stupid portrait get to me.

That's not like me.

It reminds me of the kind of ghost stories that my dad would tell from time to time on his radio show. The stories that I loved as a kid. I couldn't get enough of them. I would tune in on Friday nights, listening to my dad read emails of ghost stories that fans had sent in for him to read on the air. He'd tell them with such performance, and he got into them—*really* got into them. He would discuss what it could be. Sometimes he'd have experts on the show with him talking about poltergeists or demon possession.

As a kid, I believed in it all.

I thought those things were possible. And I thought it was so cool. That my dad thought those things were possible. After I grew up and really figured things out, I never felt the same way about it again.

I kick on my house shoes, grab my phone, and track to the door leading out onto the upstairs landing. I reach for the doorknob cautiously, like it might burn me once I take hold of it, but it doesn't.

The brass is cold. Alarmingly, so. Almost icy.

I pull the door on its creaking hinges and reveal the empty landing. Nothing here is out of place, either. I look down at the carpet. More paw prints. Wet little splotches that walk in a circle on the landing.

Like an animal looking for something. Like it caught the scent of some vermin and was chasing it right up to this point.

My eyes follow them to the staircase. They descend. Little globules of water are gathering in circular shapes on the wooden stairs. I follow them down to the bottom. They turn heading to the back of the house to the kitchen.

The carpet terminates at the end of the hallway that runs through the middle of the house and the tile picks up. So do the circles of water, and then something strange happens. They lead right up to the door that opens to the back patio. The door that I retreated to so hastily earlier.

The one that I slammed and locked.

I was so scared. I think about the sounds I heard out there earlier.

And now the paw prints of some giant animal are in my bedroom, in my house. I lick my lips and swallow. I reach out for the knob. I see my hand trembling as my fingers stretch as I try to make contact.

In that moment, my phone dings, and I jump out of my skin.

I shriek.

"Oh, my fucking God!"

I don't have neighbors, but if I did, they'd have heard me. My heart thunders and adrenaline races through my veins. I hold the phone now in both trembling hands and see a notification from my email. A response from Cash Kelly. *Jesus.*

My boozy longing for connection with my father has worn off. Now I'm overcome with a feeling that I'm not alone in this house and that there's some sort of animal stalking me.

I feel like I need to call someone, but I don't know who. It's the middle of the night. What could Noelle do if she came back over here? And besides, she's probably in bed, deep asleep right now.

I silence my phone and look back down at the tile.

The little globules seem to keep going past the door

onto the pavement by the pool. That's odd. I steel my nerves and reach for the knob again. This time my hand is steady.

When I open it, I'm greeted with a sight I was hoping I wouldn't see. There are two paw prints coming out of the doorway, onto the concrete, and just as my eyes find those, another appears in front of them and then another and another and another, moving slowly at first and then quickly.

They look like the paws of a large cat or a wolf. I'm hallucinating. I'm imagining something big and strong with jaws that I'm not sure I'd be able to outmatch in a fistfight. *That's* what made these prints—or *is* making them right *now*.

What the hell is happening? I'm losing my mind. That's what's happening.

I close my eyes tight, keeping them closed for a moment, then I open them and look back down at the sidewalk.

The prints are no longer moving all over and it looks as though they've walked back around me and into the kitchen, straight through the door like it had been opened.

I'm so confused.

These prints weren't there a moment ago.

Earlier, the door was locked.

Whatever it was, it couldn't have just walked through the door.

I go over the memory with a fine-tooth comb.

Hooper could have gone outside. Sometimes, he smokes when he drinks, and he did step out for a cigarette. It could have happened when he walked out. He could have left it open. Maybe he walked around to the garden. And got his feet wet.

Oh, and turned them into paws.

Jesus, Blair.

I locked the door after they left.

Somehow, this creature opened it.

These prints weren't there earlier, which doesn't make sense, either, because when I got down here, the door was still locked. So, what? The thing walked through a solid piece of wood?

I really don't like how much my pattern of thoughts is reminding me of my dad. I feel crazy right now. Coming to conclusions that certainly aren't anywhere near the truth. I look at the paw prints.

They lead to the edge of the swimming pool. I follow them and there they stop. As if whatever it was just sat down at the edge and looked out into the forest.

I glance at the bottom of the pool, but it's just as empty as it was earlier.

"I'm losing my fucking mind," I mutter to myself.

All of this has been too much. Blake needing the money, me selling the house, Dad being declared legally dead, buying this place, renovating it alone, living here alone, and being alone in the world.

He's been gone for seven years, but tonight is the first night I feel truly on my own.

There's some sort of animal wandering freely around my property and I don't have a number with which to call my father. I have no idea where he is. And the dark and unwanted, though entirely logical, thought—that it wouldn't matter if I did because he's likely dead—is right there, hanging like a specter in the background of my thoughts.

I feel panic swelling my chest, not so much about the animal, not so much about this house that I have no idea how to fill, but more about the knowledge that my dad is really gone.

I LEAN a chair against the doorknob, and I stack three pots on its cushion.

If anything so much as jiggles the handle, the pots will crash on the floor and I'll wake up, even upstairs.

My ears will be tuned for it, waiting for the distinct possibility that someone or something could be entering the house. The thought occurs to me that someone might know I bought the house. Some fan of my dad's thinking it would be a funny prank.

That thought chills me even more.

An animal doesn't have ulterior motivations, but people do.

I check all the doors once more just for good measure and I return upstairs. I debate on leaving my door closed, but I might not hear the pots and pans if I do that, so I leave it open. However, I do push a large chest in front of it, blocking an easy path into the room.

Someone would have to jump pretty high to get over that thing.

All that's left of the view into the hallway once I do that is the ceiling.

I bite back on the thought that whatever made those paw prints would make easy work of jumping over that chest.

That's all I've got. At least it does stretch pretty high.

Maybe whatever that was would be too big to struggle between the space between the top of the chest and the doorframe. That's what I'm counting on. I climb into bed and sit in the silence, or near silence. The old house groans and whines constantly with the wind. It makes strange noises that my dad's house didn't.

Finally, I nestle under the covers and grab my television remote. I turn on the TV and find something to wind down to in the background, and then I grab my phone once more.

It's then that I remember I have an email from Cash Kelly, and I decided to check on it.

Blair,

I'm glad to hear from you. I was thinking about just doing a little interview about what it was like growing up with your dad. Him being famous and doing what he did for a living. Also, if you have any spooky stories of your own that you'd like to share, I'd love that. Here's my number.

Cash

I stare at the number. It's a Friday night and there's probably little chance that he's not out and about or, who knows, maybe doing some ghost-hunting, hoping to skew pieces of questionable evidence into proof of the supernatural. At least, that's what my dad would have been doing.

I program his number into my phone, save his name, and pull up the new message screen. I start typing.

> It's Blair.

That's it. That's all I send.

And within a minute, I get a response. I'm shocked when the phone dings.

> Hey, glad to hear from you. Can you talk?

I look at the time on my phone. It's close to three in the morning.

I send back a quick *yes* and realize that I would do

anything right now to fill the void of silence in the house.

And then my phone begins to ring.

"Hello," I answer.

"The mysterious Blair Graves, in the flesh," he says, his voice deep, exactly the way he sounds on his YouTube channel.

"Well, not in the flesh unless you're staring in my window," I tell him.

"I'm not," he says. "However, I do know that you bought the Solomon house," he adds.

"How?" I blurt out and I sit up straight.

It feels like an invasion of privacy of the first order.

What the fuck is he doing digging around enough to know that I bought a new house, let alone where it is? It reminds me of the thought that a crazy fan might find out the same information. Maybe Cash *is* the crazy fan.

"Word travels fast in these channels," he says.

"Who the fuck told you that?" I demand. "And why?"

"It's not hard to find out anything these days, Blair," he says nonchalantly. "When can I interview you?"

I'm shocked at his directness. I barely know this guy. I *don't* know this guy.

"Tomorrow?" I propose. The word comes out a little too quickly. Partially because I'm eager to hear what Cash has to say about my dad and partially because it would give me another day where I'm not entirely alone in this place. Even if I'm in the company of someone like him.

Someone who's greatest value to me would be as a temporary distraction.

"I can make that work," he says. I hear a pencil scratching on paper.

"Do you use a paper planner?" I ask. It surprises me a little bit. A content creator going old-fashioned. But he does sort of look like a world traveler that might be something of an anachronism. My dad had a day planner. In fact, one for every year since I was born up until the year he vanished, and they're all in boxes here.

"Indeed, I do," he says.

"Is there anything I need to do to prepare?" I ask him.

"Not at all," he says. "I'll bring the video and lighting setup. You just find a good place to sit. I know that house has all sorts of cool places to sit."

The way he says it makes irritation flare inside me. Him being aware of what the interior of my house looks like feels like another invasion of privacy. And why would he know that, anyway?

"I'll see you then," he says, and before I can tell him he's quite rude and strange, he hangs up, leaving me staring at my phone.

Feeling just as alone as I was before he called.

FIFTEEN

CHUFF. *Chuff. Chuff.*

The level of insistency wakes me. Heavy animal breaths shoot out of the creature's lungs, and fan across my neck.

My eyes open, but I'm paralyzed. I stare at the ceiling above me and I feel like I'm sinking into my mattress. Like it's swallowing me up. Everything goes black and I hear the chuffing again and again. It sounds agitated. Like the animal is nervous, fearful, maybe trying to solve a problem. Perhaps it's cornered. I'm dreaming and I'm aware.

I let the mattress swallow me up.

The plush surface opens and lets me sink down through the floor.

The wooden floorboards open up, allowing me to go lower.

And suddenly, I'm standing at the entryway to the

house. The walls shimmer and undulate like I'm under-water. But something is off. Something is different.

I glance around and see that the pieces of furniture that belong to me have been replaced. The pieces that I found in the attic and the basement stand in all their splendor. The house is new. The furniture is new.

A laugh as clear and crisp as a bell rings from deep within the house. The conservatory glass traps the sound, forcing the echo towards me. I begin to walk that way.

Step by step, I travel carefully. Suddenly, I feel like I may be intruding on a scene too intimate for my eyes. That whoever is here has no knowledge of me.

I know on some deep level that this isn't my house right now.

Something is off.

Something is different.

I walk through the old funeral parlor visitation room and back to the conservatory, tucked away below the stairs.

The laugh rings again. It's a pretty thing, musical and high, full of confidence and definitely belonging to a woman who, if I were to judge her just by that, has all the magnetism of a cult leader and all the beauty of a star from Hollywood's Golden Age.

I peer around the doorframe, trying to keep myself hidden. And then I see her. She holds a glass with amber liquid inside—maybe iced tea—and leans her head back to laugh again, and on her pretty neck rests a beautiful necklace. The object of her amusement is a child—a boy—of maybe two or three. He's atop a rocking horse, pushing it back and forth so hard that it begins to travel across the carpeted floor. She seems to find endless amusement in this.

I wonder if the boy is her son, or perhaps a younger brother.

She could be the eldest sister in the family.

Something tells me that the little boy belongs to her.

He has the same beautiful blonde—almost white— hair and his eyes are the same color of blue.

The two of them in this moment seem like they're in their own little world. Like nothing can interrupt them.

My heart aches for that.

Suddenly the laugh fades and a sharp voice cuts in. A man's voice. He's just out of sight.

I can't make out exactly what he says to her. But there's a bite in his words. I spin, trying to find him. Sounds like it's coming from behind me, but I see nothing. His voice echoes around us like an all-consuming presence. The room seems to dim like clouds have passed overhead and the air suddenly feels heavy with a storm.

Her laugh stops short. The little boy looks back in the man's direction.

The beautiful blonde woman looks at the little boy. She leans forward and takes his hand, still clutching the handle of a rocking horse. He looks up at her, wondering if he's done something wrong to anger the man. She whispers something quietly in his ear and his smile instantly returns with a giggle.

She looks up and then she sees me in the doorway.

I know for certain she sees me.

My blood goes cold under her gaze.

Her smile falters and my heart races. I felt like I was invisible up until this moment, but right then, she is looking directly at me.

Something happens then to her beautiful face. It melts away in front of my eyes and is replaced with lines of worry and her eyes fill with pain. Something not quite solid passes through me.

I'm filled with a chill that goes bone deep, as the figure of the man materializes before me, walking with purpose across the conservatory floor.

That's who the blonde woman locked eyes with that brought forth that look of pain on her face. It wasn't me. She was looking directly at someone else. The man.

He reaches for her hand and she flinches, but offers him a demure smile.

He says something to her and raises his finger to point at the little boy. The woman flinches at his words and gestures. Before long, he's yelling. The little boy is crying. And the woman is trying to keep the peace.

Then, in a flash, the undulating walls collapse in a crashing wave.

I run for the stairs as the water chases me up, nipping at my heels, getting my ankles wet.

Pictures hanging on the wall begin to float on the first floor as I take the stairs. Like this is a ship, and it's sinking down into the ocean, heavy with sorrow. I struggle in the rising water, now at my waist, now at my chest. The water swallows me up and I go to scream and I feel my lungs burn as I begin to drown.

———

I REACH FOR MY THROAT, waking with a gasp. My body lurches upright, resisting the pull of the water. Like I'm fighting my way to the surface even now.

My hands find the sheet beneath me and I clutch it desperately, like it's a life preserver.

My eyes adjust to the darkness and my heart flutters in my chest. My whole body is electrified.

It was a dream, I realize, but it felt more real than any other I've ever had.

I gasp again, my breath coming in ragged waves as though I really did almost drown.

I place a hand over my heart, feeling the beat of it. My lungs burn.

Like I've just coughed up a ton of water.

I clear my throat until it hurts.

What the hell was that?

A sheen of sweat coats my body just like it did the

first time I woke in the middle of the night here in the house.

The dream was intense. It felt real.

It *was* real.

I have trouble for a moment as I try to readjust my eyes to the darkness that surrounds me. I'm in the bedroom, *my* bedroom, and I'm perfectly safe. Everything is fine. Right?

I used to have vivid dreams when I was a child, up until I was in my early twenties. The last time I had a dream like that, one that felt so real, was right after my dad disappeared.

In the dream, I was on vacation with my brother and my dad. We were late to catch a train. He kept getting on the wrong one, leaving us behind on accident and going the wrong way. Blake and I screamed, trying to get his attention, but as soon as the train door closed, it was like they were soundproof. And it was like he assumed that we had just come with him like we should have.

We were attempting to tell him he was about to get lost.

That he was going the wrong way, and that we weren't with him.

In the dreams, I would watch as the train doors closed behind him, none the wiser that Blake and I were still at the station. He didn't realize he was leaving us behind.

I couldn't shake it for weeks. It was recurring. A

nightmare, really, even though there were no boogeymen or monsters. It was something worse than that.

The boogeyman in those dreams was the sense of being abandoned by someone you love deeply. But as vivid as those dreams were, the one I just had was more vivid still.

I rub my upper arms as goosebumps break out across them in a wave. My scalp tingles. Hopefully, with cold, I tell myself.

Jesus, I sound like my dad. Even contemplating the possibility is ridiculous.

Being in this house alone has me losing my damn mind. Suddenly, I'm once more wishing that I was still staying with Noelle somehow, buying earplugs to avoid hearing her and Hooper going at it every night seems like a way better option than what I'm currently experiencing.

I'd rather be annoyed than scared.

I sit there in the bed, the cool air putting a chill on my skin.

I grab my phone to check the time. 3:33am

Isn't that significant?

I remember being with my dad in his studio once as a kid. He was doing a show about witches and he was talking about the devil's hour. Sometimes called the witching hour. 3:33 in the morning holds a lot of significance for a lot of people, apparently. People like my dad and people who listen to his show.

Supposedly, it's the moment during the night, when the veil between the living and the dead is at its thinnest. It's a spookier train of thought than I want to entertain. It's also something that I've never given a second thought to until right this second.

I rub my face and fall back into bed. I pull the covers up to my chin. Tomorrow will be better. This is all just about adjusting to my new surroundings. This is all about adjusting to the idea that he's really gone. The case is closed, and no one's still searching for him.

I feel an aching hollowness. A single tear escapes one eye. I swipe at it, much like I did when Hooper unintentionally made me cry.

I force myself to get some rest before my meeting tomorrow.

SIXTEEN

THOUGH I DO my best to sleep, I don't.

I pull myself out of bed early in the morning, way earlier than Cash and I agreed to meet, and the idea of taking a nap is appealing. It seems like sleeping in the house during the daylight hours might be safer, or at least it wouldn't be as disconcerting as waking in the night from another nightmare if the sun was shining through the window.

My head pounds, and my chest feels heavy as I make coffee. It's almost like I have a cold. I inhale sharply, feeling a burning sensation in my lungs. That same burning that was there earlier. A remnant of my dream. Like I coughed up a bunch of water, even though that's absurd. I was inside the house, on the second story, in my bed.

It was like I really did drown. I can't really explain it, and I don't like it.

Even when I had super realistic dreams about my dad, or tried to scream and scream but made no sound, I never woke up with any kind of physical symptoms reflecting what had happened while I was asleep.

I realize I've been standing in the kitchen longer than I thought, waiting for the coffee to finish brewing. It's already done and waiting for me to add sweetener and creamer to it. I just need to pour myself a cup. I do so, going through the motions. I take the hot mug in my hands, appreciating the grounding effect of the heat against my palms. It reminds me that I'm in the here and now. That what happened last night was a dream. This is real.

I clutch it tightly as I begin to drink the coffee. The hot brew feels good against my raw throat.

That still leaves me talking to myself. I wonder what the hell that's about.

I drink the cup gratefully, even though I know I'll definitely need another one before the day is overdue. Hopefully, I'll be so tired tonight that I can crash like a rock, which is to say, experience a dreamless sleep.

I GET everything as ready as I can. I'm not sure what more to do other than tidy up and set up a couple of chairs. I find the coolest ones I can and sit in each of them, making sure that they're not going to collapse under either one of us. I check his YouTube channel to look at other interviews he's done. It seems like a pretty standard setup and this will do.

I have two chairs set up on either side of the fireplace. I grab some logs from the rack on the back patio, but when I step out there, I glance toward the pool and something strange happens. Like a veil is pulled back for a split second. I get a glimpse of something else. Something that isn't my present reality.

Something from years ago, decades ago.

Sunlight glints off the dancing surface of the water that fills the pool. A woman, nude, steps into it at the shallow end. It's nighttime. The moonlight makes her skin shimmer when she stands up out of the water. After a moment, she looks up at it, like maybe she's making a wish.

And just like that, it's gone.

I stand there for a second, trying to reckon with what I just saw. That was a full-blown hallucination, I realize.

I've never been diagnosed with any severe mental illness, but right now, I'm feeling precariously close to one. What if I do have something going on?

Maybe I finally reached my breaking point.

The hallucination wasn't long enough for me to be sure that it was the woman I saw in my dream, but I feel like it had to be. The same blonde hair. Slender. And in the pool here at the house.

I shake my head and grab the logs. I grab extra so I won't have to come back out here, more than necessary, and I lock the door behind me when I reenter the kitchen.

MY TIREDNESS DRAGS ME DOWN, making me feel like I'm moving slower, both mentally and physically. When I hear a knock at the door, it wakes me up. I feel my heart begin to beat faster. Meeting Cash Kelly wasn't something I thought I'd agree to do only a week or two ago.

Now he's banging on my door to come inside my house because I invited him here.

Everything has happened way too fast.

Too much change in too little time.

I step out into the little room between the house and the front porch. When I swing the front door wide, he fills it. Well over 6'6", he's way bigger than I thought he was just from watching his YouTube videos. His massive frame darkens my doorway quite literally. And his shoulders are just as broad as I thought they were.

He fills the entire frame around him.

It'd be impossible for someone else to come through while he's standing there.

Sunlight casts a halo around his messy blond hair. He runs a hand through it and meets my eyes.

"Hi," he says. He offers the other hand quickly.

I shake it.

"Come in," I say, unsure of what else is appropriate in this context.

I don't want to come right out and tell him the whole reason I agreed to let him in my house is that I think there's a possibility that he might have information about my dad that would be of value to me. Not necessarily where he might be, but that he might have met him and have a different perspective to offer on who he was because I feel like I never knew him at all.

And the experience the other night with Hooper made me realize with crystal clarity that I really didn't know him. It also made me realize just how badly I want to fix that. And how wildly impossible that is at this point.

But nothing that rational is going to keep me from swimming upstream on this.

I don't say anything, though. It's too soon.

Cash ducks his head slightly, having to make the adjustment for his height to accommodate his huge stature in the antique door frames. He picks up two insanely bulky suitcases on the porch and carries them inside.

"Where would you like me to set up?" he asks. "Also, Blair, I really appreciate this."

"In there." I point to the living room and lead the way. I'm tiny in comparison to him, standing only 5'3". It occurs to me at that moment that I've let a very large man into my house and I don't really know him at all.

Everything that I do know about him is from what

he made available on social media. What I've watched on YouTube. A curated image that he's put forth for the world.

"Oh, this is perfect," he says, his voice is deep just like in the videos. At least that part's genuine, it seems. He wears a bomber jacket and jeans, a gray t-shirt beneath the jacket.

I watch him as he unpacks and sets everything up.

I feel anxiety rising in my chest. Why the hell did I agree to this? I have no idea what he's going to ask or how deeply he's going to probe. This was a stupid, stupid fucking idea.

As he sets up lights and turns the old living room into a regular movie studio, my dread mounts.

He sheds his jacket, and his biceps are huge, muscular indentations coming alive with each move he makes. I catch myself staring but don't look away quite in time. His eyes meet mine briefly and I do look away. I cross my arms over my chest.

"You'll need this," he says and hands me a wireless microphone. His fingers brush my palm and he drops the device there. I fiddle with it, looking at the device and the little clip on the back.

"Oh, sorry," he says. "I didn't turn that on."

He takes it from me for a moment and presses a button on the top and then he reaches out, towering over me, and clips it to the collar of my shirt.

I inhale sharply, and the dread returns like a pit in my stomach. Like there's something inside of me, wriggling and writhing to get out. I feel it snaking its way up my ribcage, climbing it like a ladder and seizing my heart, twisting and winding around it until it's constricting, like a fist squeezing the muscle at its own rhythm.

I realize we've reached the point where I'm going to have to tell him we can't do this. I can't talk about my dad like this. It feels exploitative. My heart says as much, painful in my chest.

I watch Cash as he gets out his own wireless mic and clips it to his collar. He checks what seems to be a central module that he connects to a computer and places it on the coffee table. He logs into some software and I stand there, helplessly watching him. He brings up an audio recording studio.

Or at least that's what I think it is.

I feel the panic begin to rise in my chest again, swelling to a crescendo like a giant wave. It grows taller and taller, beyond my control. I feel my breathing pick up and I start to inhale faster and faster. I tell myself to calm down.

I force myself to breathe slower.

And I find comfort in the fact that he's here.

The presence of another human being. That closeness, even if it is someone I don't know.

My heart aches for a second, reminding me just how lonely I truly am.

I watch as he returns to the cameras, both set up

facing either chair so that each of us will have shots for him to edit.

Watching him engage in this mundane task settles me. It's a relief to have someone else here, even if it's someone I barely know. It has nothing to do with Cash himself. He could be anyone, except when he backs up and sits down across from me, he looks at me with a kindness that I didn't expect at all and that's all it takes for me to come undone. Suddenly, the panic returns, swelling huge in my chest and constricting on my heart.

My pulse picks up, thundering in my ears. I can hear the blood rushing by. I gasp, grabbing up at the collar of my shirt, feeling like the neckline of it is choking me. I feel like I can't breathe. My vision tunnels and I choke out a sob.

He rushes to my side. Cash is out of his chair before I can even realize I need help. I feel the warmth of his palms on my cheeks. I feel like I'm overheating and freezing at the same time. I feel like I'm disappearing inside myself. Like my own insides are about to swallow me up. I feel like I'm dying. The intensity of the panic attack is like none I've ever had before.

"Blair, take this." He pulls something out of his pocket and fumbles with the cellophane wrapper on a piece of candy. Before I can protest, he pops into my mouth. Overwhelming sour shocks my senses. I almost spit it out. "Don't spit it out," he says. "It's super sour and it'll ground you."

He places a hand on my back, rubbing in circles. I focus on the taste. The overwhelming and shocking sour candy that I remembered from childhood. I remember taking them after lunch on recess with my friends, trying to see who could eat one without making a face. None of us ever succeeded.

I scrunch up my face, feeling my heart rate begin to slow down. The blood in my veins is no longer fire traveling through me. The sensation that I'm sinking into myself abates, whispers, and I feel myself coming back to the present moment. Cash continues to rub circles on my back.

"Are you okay?" he asks. "You had a panic attack."

"I know," I breathe. The words come out with a hitching sob. "I can't do this," I say. I blurt it out and stand up, shrugging out from beneath his touch. He stays kneeling beside my chair and, when I turn around, the kindness in his eyes remains.

"Okay," he says as he stands.

"I'm sorry I let you come here. I'm so sorry. I let you set all this stuff up and I can't even do it. I'm—"

"Hey," he whispers, grabbing me by my upper arms. I look at him. At this complete stranger standing here in my living room. How is this the most comforting thing that's happened in weeks? And how embarrassing is that? How embarrassing is it that I'm having a panic attack after telling him he could come here for an interview? And now I'm shutting it all down.

"Look," I try to speak, but another sob chokes me.

"Blair," he says, holding up a finger, instructing me to be quiet. "I understand."

"You don't understand," I say, shaking my head violently with the candy still in my mouth.

"I understand more than you realize," he says. I look at him, puzzled. "We don't have to do this today. We don't *ever* have to do it."

I want to tell him I asked him to come here because I thought there might be a small chance that he could offer me insight into the man my own father was. How fucking pathetic is that? I want a complete stranger to tell me who my dad was.

Damn, dad. How the fuck did we get here?

SEVENTEEN

"I ALWAYS WONDERED what it would be like to have a twin," Cash says, handing me a glass of water from the kitchen. He went to retrieve it and instructed me to sit on the couch and chill the fuck out. He didn't use those words, but I think he wanted to.

I take the glass and drink happily, feeling thirstier than ever before in my life. He sits across from me on the opposite end of the couch. I curl my legs under myself and lean back into the corner behind me. For the last few minutes, he's been making ridiculous small talk, obviously not comfortable leaving me alone yet.

I'm also a little impressed that he knows a few tricks when it comes to panic attacks. It makes me think that he's dealt with it before. I wonder if he's ever had one and if he still does.

When I finish gulping down the water, I speak.

"It's overrated," I say. A note of bitterness creeps out that I wasn't anticipating.

He arches one eyebrow, indicating he realizes there's more of a story here than I'm immediately divulging. Having already had a panic attack in front of him, my adrenaline having dumped into my system, exhausting me and making me feel like it can't get much worse, I decide to talk.

It's not often that I talk about Blake, especially with strangers.

Noelle and I barely talk about the subject.

And she only gingerly brings it up on occasion, usually to see how I'm doing with the whole situation. It's never something that we talk about lightly. She never brings him up and says, *Oh, how is Blake?* Like it's no big deal.

Everything about my brother is tied up in everything about my father. They're inextricable from each other..

"Blake and I were really close as kids," I tell Cash. "We were sort of inseparable. But all that changed in high school. I guess right around the time that Blake sort of started realizing what kind of person our dad was. He always said I was the favorite," I think back on Hooper telling me that my dad just about said as much in his email correspondence. "That caused a lot of tension, even though I always told him it wasn't the truth. He's always said I couldn't see dad for who he was."

"And who does your brother think he was?" Cash asks.

"Probably the same person I think he was at this point in my life," I tell him. "When I was younger, I looked at him with rose-colored glasses. It wasn't until I was a late teen that I kind of realized how things really were." Cash arches his eyebrow, waiting for me to say more. What the hell? "I don't think my dad was in it for the right reasons," I say.

I'm not sure I want to get into it more than that. But it's more than I usually admit to anyone.

"Your mom died when you guys were young, right?" Cash asks casually. The way he says it makes me think he's already done his homework.

"Yeah, she died soon after we were born."

"Do you have any pictures?" he asks.

"I do." I think there are pictures in the boxes full of my dad's shit that I've done my damnedest to avoid going through. It was all I could do to get his journals and books out of his office. I couldn't bear to go through any photo albums or actually read anything. But I'm sure they're in there. I know they exist.

It pains me to realize that I haven't looked at a photograph of my mother in years. After dad disappeared, I put them away. They were a painful reminder of how much we had lost and how much we had grown apart.

"Not exactly on hand, though," I admit.

I feel sheepish about it. I feel like I should have a

picture of her. Maybe I should carry it in my wallet. Maybe a picture of her, dad, me, and Blake. Wouldn't most normal people do that?

I want to probe him further. I wonder how close Cash is to his family. It might be a good change of subject.

"What about you?" I ask. "You close with your family?"

"My dad and I—" He hesitates. "We aren't very close. My mom, on the other hand, is probably overly involved in my life."

A smirk curves my lip. There's a sadness to it, though. He looks at me.

"I know a lot of people would be glad for that," he adds.

I nod, silent and sad, agreeing entirely with him on that.

I would love to have a mother that was overly involved in my life at this point.

Or even a dad that called me from time to time. Or a dad that I had a bad relationship with, just to have a relationship at all.

I don't think people who have harmonious home relationships ever realize how hard the most basic things are for the rest of us. Birthdays, holidays, calls home, setting out pictures, keeping anything sentimental.

"How are you feeling?" Cash asks, interrupting my train of thought.

"Fine," I lie to him, but I'm grateful for the interruption.

He nods, looking around at his equipment. I feel a pang of embarrassment flush my cheeks. He glances at me and spots it.

"Blair, seriously," he says. "Don't feel guilty. I don't care," he pauses. "At all," he says emphatically. He waves his hands, indicating just how big his level of nonchalance is about getting the interview.

I nod, accepting it, but I don't really believe it.

"I should probably go," he says. "Let you have some time to rest, hanging out on your own without me in your personal space," he teases. I bite back the urge to ask him to stay. Why do I want him here? Am I really that lonely? Or am I afraid of this place?

He begins moving around, packing everything up too quickly for my liking. I want him to stay. I don't want to be left alone here. Not after the panic attack. Not after the dream of drowning. And not after the vision out by the pool.

I throw out a life preserver.

"Did you ever meet my dad?" I blurt out the question before I can censor myself.

Cash pauses as he winds up cables and looks at the wall. A smile breaks across his face.

"I knew him pretty well, actually," he says.

"What was he like?" I'm unable to keep myself from picking at the scab.

"Coolest guy I've ever met," he says. "Super nice. He helped me in so many ways."

"So you really knew him?" I ask. "How'd you meet him?"

"I was really into all this shit from the time I was a kid," he says. He pauses like he's debating on elaborating. "Anyway," he says, choosing not to. "I actually shadowed him at the radio station for a while when I was first in college and he ended up hiring me. I was kind of like his assistant for a while. Assistant Producer —something like that. I got to be there when he was making live broadcasts."

I do the mental math estimating how old Cash would have been and how old I would have been. What my home life would have been like at that exact moment in time.

How my father would have been towards me and Blake versus how he was towards Cash.

Cash goes on.

"I wanted to be just like him. Go into radio. Talk about spooky shit late at night. Get those confessions from strangers they feel easier about giving on a frequency that only true believers tune in to," he says, and a wistful smile crosses his face. "At any rate," he goes on. "He was a cool guy. He believed in this stuff, you know?" Cash looks at me, gingerly testing the waters after what I said earlier.

I stare into Cash's eyes, searching them for the memory of my father. Like I can draw it out of him.

Like I can possess it myself. I'm eager for any piece of information about the man that remains a question mark for me.

"He really did believe this stuff," Cash says again. "He was never shitty about the people he interviewed. And some of these guys that do this stuff are. They don't actually believe, they just want the shock value. You know, it's easy to make fun of someone who thinks they were abducted by aliens," he says. His voice drifts a little. "But that kind of experience and the aftermath can ruin a person's life. It's a serious thing." He says the last with heaviness I wasn't expecting, like he's seen people who've experienced this very thing.

I wonder how many of those people my dad met, how many of them were on the radio show.

Watching Cash's videos on YouTube, I would have pegged him for a nonbeliever. For someone who just exploited people. Kind of the way I had pegged my own dad.

"You really think he believed?" I ask. My voice comes out meek.

"I know he did," he says with a smile. "I'm sure of it."

"Do you think he's still alive?" I ask.

The intimate question comes out before I can stop myself. My cheeks flush at the realization of what I've just said. The only person that I've even talked about the subject with is Noelle. I haven't spoken this ques-

tion aloud to anyone other than her. And I'm not sure
it's something that I even really want the answer to.

Cash seems to weigh his words carefully as he
resumes winding the cables.

"I don't know," he says.

"You can tell me if you think he's dead," I say.

"No, I'm serious," Cash says. "I'm not sure."

"It wouldn't make much of a difference," I mutter.

He's been gone so long. I've operated as an orphan
for all that time. Why does it feel so different now?
Why do I feel so vulnerable?

Is it the fact that I've realized I've bitten off more
than I can chew with this house? That I have no one to
turn to, that there's no backup plan? No house for me
to return to when this all goes wrong?

For fuck's sake, why am I having this conversation
with a stranger?

"It would," Cash says, pausing his task again. He
looks me right in the eye. "I can't imagine what that's
like," he says. "Your parent being missing, and for that
long. It's not the same as death."

It's the first time that I've heard another person say
what I already feel.

I feel a tightness in my throat as I try to respond to
him. He's right.

"It's absolutely different from death."

"The wondering is worse," he says. "Death is defi-
nite. Death has closure."

By the way he says it, I'm not sure if he's

completely untouched by the thing that scarred me. The idea of a missing parent, a missing loved one. I want to ask him.

Maybe he's trod this path before.

"Anyway," he says, taking us down a different track before I can screw up the courage to ask him anything else. The moment in which I could have done that is gone. "Are you sure you're okay?" he asks me.

"I'm fine," I tell him again, though I'm very unsure of the veracity of my assertion.

Cash gathers everything up. When he finishes, I stand, and he grabs his equipment in the cases. We walked toward the door.

"You know," he says. "There are rumors about this place being haunted."

I stop statue-still.

"What?" I ask.

"Oh, they've gone around for a long time," he says. "A family owned this place after the old man. What was his name? Anthony something," he trails off.

"Andrew Solomon," I correct him.

"Yeah, that guy," he says. "And the family with the funeral home. What was their name?"

"The Horns," I tell him.

"Yeah," he nods, as if recalling it now. "Apparently, they had some experiences here."

"Like what?" I ask. The question comes out too fast.

"I'm not sure. I can't remember exactly. I came

across it a long time ago on a message board, I think," he says. "That's where all the pictures of the house were posted. It's why I knew the place had the right ambience for an interview. Why?" he asks with a chuckle. "Are you experiencing any strange phenomenon?" he asks the last question in his professional broadcaster voice.

"No," I tell him, shocked at how definitively I say it.

He glances around the house before walking out onto the porch. He looks back at me again.

"If you ever do," he says. "You know who to call." He offers me a smile. It's friendly and warm.

"I do," I say and smile back.

I watch Cash get into his truck and turn out of the circular drive, head down the gravel driveway, and disappear into the trees and out onto the road. I listen until I can no longer hear the sound of his vehicle.

I step back inside.

I stand there looking out the window a little longer than entirely necessary.

This place is not haunted. It's just not. That's not a thing.

Is it?

EIGHTEEN

AFTER CASH LEAVES, I find myself at loose ends trying to decide what to do. The largeness of the house seems to swallow the day up and make it seem infinite. It seems like so much more time spent here than inside a cozy home. The hours are lonelier.

I decide to get online and start shopping for some decor. I browse around on Pinterest and kind of settle on restoring the art déco designs. I think it would be charming, beautiful even.

There are some images that I find of modern houses with styles that harken back to that era.

I start shopping on Amazon, adding different things to my cart. Some of them are art, portraits, paintings, little items of decor, but other things are for bigger projects. I want to make this place more inviting.

I want to make it my own.

I lived with my father for so long that I don't really know how I would style a house.

But the Solomon house is beautiful, regardless of whatever's happening inside it. It deserves someone to show the love, care, and attention it needs to make it something of its former glory.

A warm thought fills me when I think about hosting a party here someday.

How full the place could be. How many people it could fit. Then a sadness swiftly follows that thought. I don't know that many people. I don't have that many friends or family.

I laugh, but the sound is hollow. There's no mirth in it.

I grab my phone and text Noelle, seeking some solace from the silence of the house. Even the dinging notification of my phone would be welcome. I shoot her a message asking how things are going with Hooper, and it's only a moment or two before she answers me.

Really good, actually.

I smirk down at my phone, resisting the urge to tell her that I knew she would have a good time with the guy if she would just give him a chance.

I type back a message.

I'm really happy for you.

I know Noelle well enough to know how stubborn she is. And if I say anything about this being a good idea in my eyes, I know it won't go over well.

She'll dig her heels in and dump him immediately.

She has a bit of the same issue when it comes to dating that I do. Not knowing what's good for her and sometimes seeking out the worst.

I browse for more decor.

I find some accessories to go in the bathroom that have to do with tarot and astrology. Things that would match with The Lovers painting above the tub.

My phone dings again, and I answer. Noelle. We talk back and forth for a bit and I'm laughing as we get into a conversation about Hooper.

And then something happens.

There's a clanging in the kitchen.

The sound of something solid hitting the floor and the slamming of the door.

A cupboard door.

I sit upright, and my blood runs cold.

I wasn't expecting that.

My heart beats faster in my chest. How the hell could something already be happening right after Cash left? And why didn't anything happen while he was here?

I grab my phone in case I need to call 911 and head down the hallway to the kitchen, dreading what I might find when I get there.

I peek in and I see a bowl sitting neatly on the hardwood floor. There's nothing in it and it's not cracked. The cabinets above are closed and I know that the bowl was in one of them. Everything was shut.

There were no dishes in the sink. There was no way that bowl just jumped out of the cabinet. And onto the floor.

Especially without breaking.

I stare at the scene for a moment, reminded of *Poltergeist*. The only thing that could make this worse is if all the cabinet doors and drawers were open. I thank whatever gods may be for the fact that they aren't.

But this bowl being on the floor really disturbs me.

I think about the fact that someone could have come in and put it there. Someone could be in the house right now.

It's chilling. But why would anyone do that?

I force myself to go through the house room by room, making sure that no one is here. I lock all the doors and make sure all the windows are locked, too.

I spend the rest of the day in a heightened state of anxiety.

By some miracle—perhaps my spent adrenaline—I don't dream.

I wake up the next day like a normal person, stretching my arms and back like a cat fresh from a nap. My eyes adjust to the daylight slowly. For December, it's an awfully crystal-clear day. The sun streams in through the curtains, painting the room in shades of gold. Threads of the carpet glisten and the natural light reminds me of a time gone by. The time in my dream the other night. Even without revisiting it last night, it's not far from my thoughts.

Neither is my encounter with Cash Kelly. He shocked me honestly. The kindness wasn't something I expected. I feel like that's fewer and further between these days.

And in his position, I really didn't expect it. Especially since he was here to get what was probably the prime interview of his career within the paranormal community.

My back pops as I stretch.

I get out of bed and head downstairs to make coffee.

The stairs creak beneath my weight. It's still taking some getting used to this old house.

It makes a number of noises that my dad's house didn't, just by virtue of how new it was. I glance at the walls, bare and seemingly naked, without anything hanging on them. The thought occurs to me that I could move that weird dog portrait out here into the hallway. Maybe that would help with the weird dreams. It's an awfully strange painting. Not something that I'd have ever chosen to have made myself and I can't really explain my attraction to it.

A tiny chill runs down my spine.

I make coffee and ruminate on that. A dog made into a portrait, let alone one that strange, probably cost a fortune, which I'm sure the Solomons had. Still, it's odd for some reason. It makes me wonder if Mr. Solomon preferred the dog to his wife.

Maybe it was a loveless marriage. I think about him yelling at her in my dream.

But that doesn't jive much with the story Diana gave me when I was touring the house for the first time.

According to her, Mrs. Solomon suffered a stroke that rendered her incapable of caring for herself. And then she drowned tragically, so tragically that Mr. Solomon went crazy afterwards.

I can't imagine how anyone could have stayed in the house if the love of their life and their only child perished here.

It makes me think about my dad's house. He didn't exactly disappear there. But it was the last place I ever saw him alive. The last place I ever saw him, period.

I go back to my conversation with Cash. Him telling me he's unsure if my dad's still alive. I think it's probably naïve to assume that he is. How could he manage not to be spotted or contact anyone that would have had an inclination to let his kids know that he wasn't dead after all?

He ran with a strange crowd, though. So there's no telling what sort of motivations his friends might have.

I debate on what to do with the day. Lingering guilt about not giving Cash the interview that he came here for clings to me like cellophane. I got what I wanted, or a little of it, from him, but he didn't get anything in return besides a side show of how bad my anxiety has gotten since I sold my dad's house.

As I sip my coffee, I scroll through my notifications on my phone. Nothing too exciting. I think about calling Noelle and making her and Hooper come back over. But I feel like I shouldn't. They probably have way better ways to spend their time together that don't involve entertaining a third wheel.

I stare across the kitchen at the opposite wall. It's blank, just like the stairway walls. Maybe decorating would be good for me.

I know it would. And I decide to purchase everything that I put in my Amazon cart this morning. Then I decide that I'm going to go down to the basement again and up to the attic to root around and find some more things to hang up.

Maybe things that aren't as creepy as the dog portrait. I decide that's how I'm going to fill the day.

I GET into a rhythm in the basement.

I unbox various items, all of them belonging to either the Horns or the Solomons, and go through them meticulously.

The Horns left behind bookkeeping records from years past.

Filing cabinets line the walls of what was once an

embalming room. I pull the sheets off the two embalming tables and run a finger down the ivory lip that runs the entire perimeter of it. A drain sits at the end, no longer attached to a hose, which I'm sure was meant for draining the blood during the process. The thought sends a little chill through me.

It's a bit strange to think about leaving a house behind in such a hurry that none of this mattered to them.

Maybe it went under. I make a little mental note to do some digging on the internet about the old funeral home.

I find one stray family photo album belonging to the Horns. Leather bound and cracked, time has taken its toll on the album. It looks like it might be a remnant that wasn't meant to be left behind. In the front of it, on yellowed paper, someone has written the names of the people featured inside the album.

Each one of them has a date of birth and a date of death except for one: Jean Horn.

Her date of birth reads February 13, 1945.

I wonder briefly if the handwriting is hers. I flip through the album, seeing the various family photos of predicaments around the house. Candid shots. The photos are black and white, an older album. Some feature a woman who I assume is Mrs. Horn, cooking in the kitchen with the kids running around her feet.

One of the photos features one of the boys peeking

on tiptoes into an empty casket in what must have been the showroom.

The image is odd and a little macabre, but I smile, nonetheless. There's something warm about it. The person behind the lens captured the child's curiosity. I rub my thumb over the cellophane covered images. It crackles beneath my finger and I wonder what sort of pictures are in the albums that my dad left behind.

I think about how I've never looked at them. I've distanced myself so much from the pain I might feel.

I look up, drawing my mind out of the images of another family, peeling myself from their happy memories, to confront the ones in my own mental filing cabinet that aren't quite as jolly. Memories of the holidays that Blake and I spent with Sheryl. Years when Dad didn't even come home at all for Christmas. Phone calls where I pleaded with him to do just that and he refused, telling me that he had to work.

I wonder how he feels about all that now, or how he would feel if he was around. If he'd regret it or be happy with his choice. That hollowness returns to my chest and I close the family album. I walk over and place it on the steps leading up to the kitchen.

I gather some other items from the basement. Things I think will look nice in the house and match some of the things I ordered today. I carry them upstairs. Returning finally for the photo album, I open it once more and trace the indentation of each hand scrawled letter of all their names. Finally, resting my hand when it comes to Jean.

I glance at the pieces I brought up, standing in disarray in the kitchen, waiting for their new homes.

They can wait.

I need to look her up right now.

NINETEEN

IT TAKES all of thirty seconds to find her on Facebook. One of the joys—and sorrows—of modern society. I wonder what it must have been like to be an adult prior to the age of the internet and social media. What it must have been like to be able to slink away for a time and get your life together without anyone being the wiser.

It's an impossibility now.

My mind drifts to my dad. What might he be doing right now if he really is alive?

The reality and the alternatives—visions in which he's being held captive as some sort of prisoner—are too gruesome to think about. I tuck it away and save it for another day when I need something sad to think about. I seem to be in no short supply of those types of thoughts.

But not today. Not right now.

Right now, I'm fixated on Jean Horn, though I can't really explain why.

I click on the first profile. It lists her as living in Oklahoma City, which tracks with everything I do know about the Horn family. I browse around, looking at Minion memes that she's shared alongside political posts. It seems that Jean also has an interest in Tom Selleck, though she laments his involvement with the NRA in one post, describing it as the only imperfection in an otherwise splendid man.

That makes me chuckle.

It seems that Jean isn't married. Or is perhaps widowed. There are some posts about a man that seems to have been important to her. I wonder about the fact that she never took his name. Maybe she doesn't believe in that.

Whatever the reason, I'm glad that her maiden name was retained when she signed up for Facebook. It made this a hell of a lot easier for me.

My mouse cursor hovers over the button that reads MESSAGE. I debate on clicking on it. What would I think if someone suddenly wanted to talk to me based on something they found in my old house?

I'd be excited, I realize.

I'd want to hear from them.

I long for any sort of contact that brings me closer to my father. Jean Horn might be in the same boat.

Doubtful, but it's a possibility.

And it gives me the courage to pen a message, so there's that.

Jean,

My name is Blair Graves and I recently bought the house that used to belonged to your family. I found a photo album that I thought you might want to have.

Take care,

Blair

> I hit send.
> And hope for the best.

I PASS the afternoon moving things around, getting the decor just right. I hang the dog portrait on the wall at the second story landing and stare up at it for a moment. It seems bigger now that it's up on the wall. It seems more intimidating, like a presence all its own.

I look into its eyes, still pitch with their own gravity.

It's an alarming feature of the portrait.

My mind drifts back to the vision—the nightmare— about the woman in this house.

I don't know how much ownership a woman could

have really exerted at that time in the state of Okla-homa. That's assuming that the person I saw in my dream ever existed at all. She likely did not because she was probably a hallucination.

It's just part of the price I'm paying for living in a house this old with that many unhappy memories. When you're dealing with unhappy memories of your own and a little stress, I think it makes it easier to start seeing things. Suggestibility is real and I wonder if that's what I'm experiencing right now. I'm vulnerable in the wake of everything that's happened.

I take one last long look at the dog in the portrait. It's so strange.

I find it enchanting in a weird way. It's something that, should I leave the Solomon house, I'll most likely take with me.

I go downstairs and do some more rearranging, getting things just to my liking. And with a bit of a change of scenery throughout the house, it begins to feel more like a home. More like my mark is here on it. Like I've legitimately become the next owner of the Solomon house and that's a strange feeling.

When I get done, I log back onto Facebook, pulling my laptop up onto my cross legs on the couch. Having lit a fire in the background, it crackles now, giving me some white noise to the mostly silent house.

And I have a message waiting for me, though I didn't expect it. I realize that when my heart leaps. That it was what I was hoping for. It's from Jean.

I open it.

Mrs. Graves,

I'd love to have the album. Would you mind for me to drop by this evening and pick it up? Thank you so much.

Jean

I quickly type out a reply and attach my phone number.

I almost give her the address when it occurs to me the woman knows exactly where the house is. I tell her that I'd be delighted for her to swing by this evening.

AS THE SUN begins to set, I brew some coffee to have on hand when Jean arrives. I'm interested and a bit nervous to hear her thoughts on how the house is shaping up under my care. It's definitely not done and I can imagine that she might have strong opinions about it, something that I try to prepare myself for.

I know that I would have strong opinions if I was visiting my old house and that surgeon and his wife had done something completely unthinkable with it.

It's after dark, which falls fast here in the winter, when I see her headlights begin to peek through the brush surrounding the drive. I see her car emerge and watch as she parks it in the circle drive. I go to the door and greet her, swinging it wide just as she's reaching up a hand to knock.

"Well, hello!" she says brightly.

"Hi," I say with a smile. I rush her quickly inside into the warmth of the house and out of the cold.

Jean is a plump woman with short yet voluminously curly gray hair. Her face doesn't betray her age. She seems youthful and moves with a lightness in her step that makes me think she must take good care of herself.

"Oh, my," she mutters as we enter the hallway. She glances around. "It looks wonderful." She turns back to smile at me almost conspiratorially. I grin back, a little embarrassed at how much I wanted her approval and didn't even realize it.

She brings her hands out of her pockets and cups them before her face, breathing a little heat into her palms.

"Would you like some coffee?" I gesture to the kitchen. "I just made some."

"That would be lovely, dear," she says and I lead the way. She follows, and once there I pour us both a cup. Jean takes hers black and I mix cream and sweetener into mine. She gratefully wraps her hands around the hot mug. "Arthritis is a bitch," she says with somewhat of a sad smile. "Getting old ain't for sissies," she adds with a wink.

We walk back into the living room, and she takes a seat at one end of the couch. Right where Cash was sitting. I think of him for a moment, wondering what he's doing right now.

I push the photo album with one hand across the coffee table toward her.

She places her cup next to it and picks up the album. She opens it and begins to lose herself in memories.

"Oh, my land," she says. "This was Christmas." She scoots to the middle of the couch and turns so that I can see the photos. She's pointing at the one where her mother is in the kitchen with a bunch of kids running around her. "That's me," she says and smiles. She points out a little girl sitting on a barstool near the island in the kitchen, munching on cookies. "I got in trouble every year for eating them before I was supposed to," she recounts the memory warmly.

She tells me about her brothers and sisters. There were five children in all, and Jean is the only surviving sibling, though she wasn't the youngest.

Her parents have been gone for some time. Finally, we arrive on the subject of the house.

"What made your parents sell it?" I ask.

"Oh, Dad had died before it ever came to that. I think it might have killed him if he'd been alive. Mom was still living here. I'd moved out. So had my sisters and one brother. The oldest brother was supposed to take up the family business, but he never had a heart for it."

"I understand," I say without thinking. I know a bit about that, I suppose.

I wonder if my dad ever wished for me to carry on in his footsteps. Somehow, I imagined the mantle was something he decided was all his own. Which is just fine with me. I don't think I could have, just like Jean's brother. I don't have the heart for it.

"At any rate, Mom got sick. She needed to go into the nursing home. My brother didn't want the house. None of us did," she trails off then, her voice becoming slightly distant and haunted. "Not all the memories here were happy ones."

I'm silent, letting her finish her train of thought.

"This house has a lot of sad memories," she says. "And not just from my family." She glances at me. "How much do you know about the Solomons?" she asks.

"The basics," I tell her. "She had a stroke. She and the boy died. The husband was wracked with guilt. And he sold the place and left."

She nods solemnly.

"It's a lot of death in one place," she remarks. "Even coming from a girl that grew up in a funeral home," she adds with a smirk.

I feel like she's holding something back.

Finally, she turns the conversation on me.

"Are you living here with your husband?" she asks.

She glances around as though she expects a man to materialize.

"I'm single, actually," I say. "Oh," she says. "I'm sorry. I guess I assumed since it's such a big house."

"I understand," I say. I feel like I owe her a tiny bit of explanation. "My dad had some money that he left me," I elaborate. "He's not here anymore," I say. "And I guess I needed a project."

She nods, silently understanding that I've gingerly phrased it in that way because I don't want to say more. She reads me correctly and respects it. She looks like she knows a thing or two about grief.

"I guess I should go," she says, clutching the album to her chest as though it might run away.

"You're welcome back anytime," I tell her as we make our way to the door. She glances back at the house and the room around us once more. She seems like she's taking stock of every memory that she has of this place. She looks at the hallway, glancing up stairs.

"I don't think I'll be back," she says softly.

I nod, a little disturbed by her response.

But on some level, I also understand it.

As I let her out onto the porch and she starts to make her way to her car. She turns and looks at me in the eye. I stare at her, waiting for her to speak.

Finally, she does.

"Have you seen her yet?" she asks.

A chill descends over me.

"Seen who?" I ask, my voice coming out sharp as a knife.

"You have, then," Jean Horn says with an arched eyebrow.

I try to formulate a coherent thought, but before I can, she slips into her car and she's gone.

And here I am, once more alone but not really, with a deep fear that I wasn't ready to confront all but confirmed.

TWENTY

JEAN'S PARTING words haunt me as much as any potential specter might.

My mind drifts back to Cash, asking me a similar question. And that leads me into thinking about the dreams—the nightmares—I keep having that seem so goddamn real that I can barely get myself to crawl in bed tonight.

I try to recall a time in my life when I might have suffered from night terrors. Even as a kid, even with all the stuff my dad put us through, and the spooky things he talked about on the radio, I never had this much trouble sleeping. Blake, on the other hand, was a certified insomniac from the day we were born.

I should probably call him.

I roll my phone over in my palm, thinking about giving my brother a ring. Then it dawns on me that the only time we've talked in the last several years was a few weeks ago when he asked me to sell the house and wanted to make sure his check was on the way.

It makes it hard to think about reaching out to him for nothing. Just some company before bed so that I don't feel so alone and so scared of turning off the lights.

It would be absurd.

I lay the phone facedown on the end of the table beside the couch and sigh deeply.

I rest my chin on my palm, my elbow on the arm of the couch, and I stare into the crackling fire.

It's beautiful, hypnotic, even. Jane's words return once more. It's the last thing I want to think about: the possibility that this place is haunted.

Because it isn't.

It can't be because no place is haunted.

That's absurd. And it's just the kind of shit that my dad would have eaten up. I remember Cash saying that he felt like my dad really believed in this stuff. Suddenly, I'm going through the Rolodex of my memory, trying to pinpoint anything I can that might shed some more light on whether my dad actually *did* believe.

It deepens the wound I feel about not really knowing him. It carves it out into a cavern in my chest. I can't even tell you if he legitimately pursued the things he did because he believed or because he got paid to do it.

The thought makes me feel slightly ill. Why does it bother me so much?

That thought, combined with the fact that both Hooper and Cash seem to have memories of my dad that don't jibe with my own, makes me want to throw up. Like my dad was an entirely different person with the rest of the world than he was with me. With us. I think of Blake again.

I roll my phone over, instinctively checking it for notifications, and briefly wondering how addicted the entire world is to their smart devices.

Sometimes, I'll open my phone and check one app and then check another and another, and then repeat the same pattern over and over again. Then I'll lock my phone. Leave it sitting beside me for a few seconds and pick it right back up to check the same three apps.

I think we're all addicted.

And I don't know that smart devices have done anything to better the world other than connecting us.

Seems like a lot of that is used for more harm than good.

And it seems like it might have made us even lonelier.

I unlock my phone and scroll through my contacts, finally arriving at my brother's name.

I decided to call him. What the hell could it hurt? I hit dial and press the cold glass of the screen to my face. I inhale and hold my breath. It rings once, twice, three and four times. And then it goes to voicemail.

"This is Blake. You know what to do."

And it beeps.

I'm silent as I hold the phone to my face.

As if he might suddenly pick up, but he doesn't. So, I hang it up.

IT'S WELL past midnight when I realize that I've been pacing the house. Looking at each piece I've placed in an attempt to make the house feel more like mine.

It's around this time that I realize just how tired I am and how much I'm avoiding going to bed. It's ridiculous. I'm a grown woman.

Absolutely fucking ridiculous.

I steel my resolve.

"You're being an idiot," I mutter to myself as I stomp upstairs.

I hate the fact that I even have to say it out loud. That makes what's happening feel real.

And that's the last thing I want.

Part of me thinks the stomping might be an attempt to get whoever or whatever to stop waiting, invisible, next to my bed each night.

Upstairs, standing in the doorway to the bedroom, I decide to change into pajamas. Afterwards, I crawl into bed. I flip my television on in another attempt to keep anything weird at bay. I put it on the classic movie channel. A black and white film that I halfway recognized plays softly in the background as I drift off to sleep.

I don't expect the Sandman to take me quickly, but he does. It happens sooner than I thought it would. I'm so exhausted.

THE TINKLING SOUND of silverware meeting glass pierces my eardrum so sharply that when I sit bolt upright, I'm shocked to discover there's not a dinner party happening next to my bed.

It takes a moment to orient myself.

I think of the noise I just heard. It must have been a dream of a dinner party happening downstairs. I strain my ear to hear that tinkling sound once more. I don't. There's only silence. It's a relief, thinking that sound was in a dream.

A dream that I don't remember.

That feels like peace.

I lay back down, pulling the covers up to my chin protectively in the darkness. I strain my ears until I'm so hyperaware of the sound of my own pulse that I can't hear anything else.

Then, just as my heart rate begins to slow, I hear something. The tinkle of silverware on glass.

I lean up onto my elbow and strain to listen once more. But this time I hear everything.

Music notes, high and melodic voices carrying on,

and sounds of general merriment fill the stairway leading up to the landing. The sounds of a party fill the house downstairs. It overflows up toward me. The conversations and laughter get louder, no longer potentially part of a dream.

My heart beats faster once again. Terror makes my blood run icy in my veins.

I feel trapped.

Someone's in the house.

What's going on?

The last time I checked, raccoons don't break into people's homes and host dinner parties.

I sit up straight and scoot off the bed quietly. I slip on my sneakers and glance around the room for a weighty object. If someone is going to die tonight, it's not going to be me. That's for damn certain. I spot a fire poker brought up one night to help get the fire going in the fireplace up here. That'll do. That'll do just fine.

I wield it like a baseball bat, resting it just over my shoulders, readying myself to swing when necessary.

My heart keeps racing, pumping blood just beneath the surface of my skin. Making me so conscious of my body that I feel like I might leave it.

As I descend the stairs, it strikes me how strange it would be to break into another person's house and be so loud. But I've heard horror stories in the news before about squatters and weird break-ins. Stranger things have probably happened.

Very probably in this damned house.

I know that I'm telling myself that for my own comfort. It's unlikely given the circumstances.

As I go further down the staircase and get a view of the entry hall, I stop dead in my tracks. My heart threatens to quit beating when my eyes start to send the visual input they're getting to my brain. This is impossible.

I'm still dreaming.

Shadows, half-transparent, in the shapes of humans gather in the entry hall. A figure opens the door for another couple to come in. He takes their coats. The shadows become more than that. They flesh out into people slowly. Glamorous women and men with expensive taste. I feel like an interloper on a period movie set. Like at any moment someone might yell cut and my life will go back to normal. I'll wake up because this is absolutely a dream.

I perch on the edge of the lowest stair, watching people enter the house. They're obviously here for a party of some sort.

Their voices become clear conversations. They are audible and it's no longer just a den of chaos, noise coming from every direction and filling the house.

I drop into another reality, and when I tried to dodge a woman making for the staircase, she walks right through me with a cold breeze that reaches my bones.

I feel an inexplicable chill throughout my limbs. My heart feels like it might have stopped and restarted in the time it took her to pass through me. I turn and watch her climb the staircase. Solid as anything I've ever seen in my life.

I return my focus to the people in front of me.

My heart feels like it might have stopped.

The dress is from quite a long time ago. A century ago, perhaps? Maybe not quite that long.

I watch as they socialize, greeting each other on friendly terms and exchanging pleasantries. There's an excitement in the air that makes me feel like tonight is significant. That this is an important event, not just a regular party.

Finally, the doorman is left unoccupied as everyone streams past the staircase and makes their way into the sitting room. The room that I've designated as a living room, I follow them, chasing the sounds that woke me in the first place.

The room is full of people and strangers to me, but not to each other. They smile and whisper to each other in their excitement. I pass through them, taking in the glamorous way the women are dressed, feeling a tinge of envy for a simpler time and for this kind of luxury.

When I emerge into the dining room, I see her once again. The blonde woman from my vision the other night. She raises her glass, clinking her spoon against it, gathering everyone's attention right there at her feet, and they fall in line quickly. She commands the room effortlessly. The man that sits at the head of the table casts his eyes to her just like everyone else. And then she begins to speak.

"So glad you could all be here once again for the annual Fourth of July party," she says. "I know this is the only time some of you get out," she adds with an incredulousness that makes it clear that everyone here is part of a party crowd. Her tone hints at decadent celebrations that aren't spoken of outside these walls. Glassy eyes, fuzzy with alcohol, follow her every movement. "I guess we should get on with drinking so we can get to the more memorable signature parts of the evening," she says with a laugh that invites the men in the room to speculate just what she's capable of behind closed doors.

I glance back at the man at the head of the table. Unlike the other men in the room, he's unfazed by her presence. A sneer curls his lip as she entertains their guests. Her husband, I think.

"Hattie," the man speaks, breaking his silence. "Why don't we let our guests seek their own bawdy forms of entertainment tonight?"

He quirks an eyebrow that indicates the question is less a suggestion and more of a demand. But it's a feeble attempt on his part to put reins on a woman who is clearly a wild horse never meant to be bridled.

I wonder if she's even happy within the constraints of marriage. The expression on her face and the way the guests nervously distract themselves from the couple's interaction tells me that she has little to no intention of doing what her husband wants her to do tonight, or any night, for that matter.

Her eyes roam from his to a figure that approaches him from behind. The maid. She whispers something to the man, and he excuses himself.

Hattie seems irritated for just a moment. But then she regains her composure quickly.

There's hurt in her eyes that her husband doesn't want to participate in their party. That he doesn't want the things that she wants. To be the way that she wants to be.

When I look at her eyes, there's a fire there. A desire for freedom.

And I think she has the resolve to get it.

TWENTY-ONE

I WAKE IN SHOCK, like my body has just been involved in a high-speed crash. Like I've been ejected straight out of the driver's seat onto hard pavement. My head pounds and I gasp, desperate for air, desperate to reconfirm reality.

"What the hell was that?" I mutter.

I look around in the darkness. Everything is just as I left it when I went to bed. Nothing is out of place, and the house is quiet.

The sounds of a dinner party are long gone, the house almost aching with the heaviness of the present silence.

I feel something in the bed beside me, something hard, cold.

I scoot over and reach beneath myself. I pull out the object, an ornate spoon.

The same spoon that was in that woman's hand as she commanded the room with a toast.

I stare at it, incredulous. That's impossible. I haven't had a spoon up here. How the hell did this get here?

An eerie feeling settles over me. Like I'm holding something I shouldn't be. Like maybe something bad has happened. An invitation has been made and picking up the spoon feels like I've accepted it without knowing a thing about what lies on the other side.

Every fiber of my being is telling me that this is bad. Turn back now. This is the point of no return. But I've already committed to this house and I think, because of that, I've already committed to this little ride I'm on.

Surely I did bring a spoon up here.

Maybe I was sleepwalking. Maybe that's what all this is. Night terrors, sleepwalking, and a little suggestibility. Jean's words still echo in my mind. I think about what Cash said, too. It's creepy. I don't want to entertain that idea, but it's right here in front of me.

I stare at the spoon, running my finger along the handle. I'm trying to tell myself that it's not real, but I know it is. It's right here, solid in my hand.

I place the spoon gingerly on the nightstand and grab my laptop. I pull it into bed with me, placing it atop a pillow, and switch on the bedside lamp. I crack open the laptop, log in and immediately go to my search engine. I hammer out a search.

I type in the name *Hattie Solomon*. In a fraction of a second, search results return. Pictures of women, both recent and from a bygone era, populate the screen. Line after line after line of them.

I keep scrolling down, down, down, unsure of what I think I'm going to find, feeling slightly better with each page that loads full of faces I don't recognize.

Until I see one that I do.

My blood runs cold. In a black-and-white photograph, there she is. Hattie Solomon halfway through a laugh, a champagne flute in hand.

She's unmistakable. It's the same woman that I've been seeing night after night.

And in the background, I see him. The man that seemed to be her husband.

The one that left the room disenchanted with her.

The caption confirms my worst fear. The people I just saw weren't figments of my imagination. People that maybe I'd seen in old photographs somewhere else, maybe in a magazine or in a movie.

I had never seen these two faces before.

The people I just saw were Andrew and Hattie Solomon, the first owners of the Solomon house.

I'm not sure that I'll ever sleep again. At least that's how I feel, sitting here on the bed, staring at images of the people that I saw in living color, full of life, moving, talking, emoting, and just existing inside the walls of this house not thirty minutes ago.

It had to be a dream, though.

I wonder about the implications of that to what I'm saying? That I'm psychic? That can't be it. I don't believe in that either.

I remember something someone once told me about how all the images in our dreams are faces of people that we've seen before, even if we have no recollection of them. We store away those faces we see every day deep inside our subconscious, only to bring them out at night when we need to put a face on a stranger in our dreams.

I'd never seen Andrew and Hattie Solomon before.

How could I have conjured their faces from nothing?

I keep looking at the constellation of pixels, arranged like human forms, wondering if there's some way that I'm misinterpreting what I'm seeing. Could I have seen pictures of the two of them? Could I have done that without realizing it?

That could be it, right?

Right.

The whole thing is enough to make me nauseated. I crawl out of bed, propelled by my need for a toilet and no longer stuck there by the level of shock I feel.

Funny how biological processes don't really care about whether you might have just seen a ghost.

In fact, they seem to be encouraged by such a shock to the system.

I rush to the porcelain god nestled in the old master bathroom.

Clutching the cold edges of the toilet bowl, I vomit promptly and with great accuracy. I flush the toilet feeling like I've thrown up my toenails and there's nothing left in there to expel except the experience itself.

I don't think I'm going to be rid of that for some time now.

I wash my hands and rinse my mouth, reaching for the toothbrush and toothpaste to finish up.

I spit, tasting the minty freshness of the paste, a welcome relief from the sour bile, but it's still clinging there in the back of my throat just like the memory of what I just saw.

Andrew and Hattie Solomon celebrating in their house, in living color, right in front of me.

I dry my face and wipe my mouth on a hand towel and head back to bed.

I crawl in, unsure of what I'm really doing, but knowing that I'm not going right back to sleep.

I sit there for a moment, laptop still on my bed. Finally, I reach for it. I browse a little more and see that there are more photographs. I come to another one of the couple and then another. I find myself on the Historical Society website for Oklahoma.

I look at the pictures, combing through them, trying to identify other faces that I saw in the scene.

This stirs me up more. I'm in shock. How could this be?

There's no way I'm going to be able to sleep.

And I think there's only one person that I can contact right now.

Not Noelle. Not Blake.

Cash.

I grab my phone and look at the time. It's past 3:30 in the morning. I have no idea what Cash is doing right now. What his life looks like and whether he might be awake, alone, or annoyed to get a text from a loose acquaintance in the middle of the night. But I think about the other night when I did text him and he called immediately. Maybe he's up, too. I feel like this is the only solid lead I've got and I need to know what's going on in this house. So I type it out. And then I hit send.

A MESSAGE COMES BACK ALMOST IMMEDIATELY.

I stare at it.

Can I call you?

That's all it says in response to everything I just typed out in the initial text.

I quickly tell him *yes*. Partially because I'm eager to hear what he says and partially because it will mean that I don't have to fill the time completely alone. The phone rings in my hand. The sound is unwelcome, loud, and startles me. I didn't remember that I had my ringer on.

Usually I keep it on vibrate, dreading when any notification makes a noise.

My hand trembles as I hit the button that begins the call.

"Hello," I say tentatively.

"What did you see? Tell me again," he cuts right to the chase. He's so serious. On the one hand, I want to laugh, but on the other it's a little alarming. Reminds me of a time when I was attempting online dating and I let a guy call me in the middle of the night.

He had the same insistency but for other reasons. The thought makes me chuckle. Cash is asking for a description of my paranormal experience with the same excitement that most guys ask for a description of what you're wearing.

"It's exactly what I described," I say.

"Well, describe it again."

I tell him about the vision of the party. The crystal-clear way that initial sound rang in my ears, waking me.

"I could see them all in perfect focus. First they were shadows, then they became smoke, and then something solid. I saw them. I saw the party they were having."

"Is this the first time you've seen something like this?" Cash asks.

"I've never been someone who sees things, Cash," I tell him, suddenly feeling defensive.

"That's not what I asked," he sounds irritated.

I hedge around it, unwilling to commit to what I know the truth will be.

"Blair," he cuts me off as I begin to hem and haw.

"What?" I ask him.

I hear on the other end the taking of a deep breath. He sighs.

"Have you seen other stuff inside that house?" he asks.

I hesitate.

I can hear myself swallow.

"I have," I admit finally. I cringe outwardly and pinch the bridge of my nose, not fully believing that I'm actually having this conversation right now. Let alone with a complete fucking stranger.

"Tell me," he says. He waits.

The silence between us grows thick, anticipation builds.

I wonder how many of these stories he hears every week. How does he determine what's bullshit and what's real?

None of it is real, I tell myself, even though I've

experienced everything firsthand that I'm about to lay on him.

"So," I begin. I feel like I'm about to say something I shouldn't. Like it's dirty, untruthful. "I keep hearing this sound."

He makes a noise, indicating I should elaborate.

"Like an animal," I say. "Breathing hard, like it's annoyed or threatened. Not a growl, but a noise that a dog or a bear makes when it's frustrated."

"I know what you're talking about," he says.

"So, I keep getting woken up by that noise," I say and take a deep breath. "And I saw paw prints in the house one night," I go on. "But they led to the back door, and they didn't stop. It was like—"

"They walked right through it." He finishes my sentence.

"Yes!" I exclaim, the excitement of being understood shining through my voice.

"Did you go outside?" he asks.

"Yes, because I thought that maybe it was the raccoon."

"Did you see it?"

"Not a trace of him," I admit.

It feels like I'm giving out a death sentence for any reason I have left in my body.

Like I've given into something primal that I shouldn't. Something that we've left behind as a society. The idea that ghosts and goblins and monsters rule the night.

It's absurd.

And the thought of how much my dad would enjoy this makes me laugh hysterically for a moment.

"Are you okay?" Cash asks.

I calm myself down.

"I'm fine," I tell him.

"What else, Blair?" he asks.

"I had another vision. A dream, I mean," I correct myself. "In it, I saw the same people. The Solomons, I guess. It was so real. And then at the end, it felt like the entire house sank underwater and I was drowning."

Cash makes a noise indicating that he's thinking.

"What does it mean?" I ask.

I want him to say that it means I'm stressed out and going through a lot.

"I think you know what it means," he says.

I sit there listening to the sound of my own breathing. I say nothing for a moment. I inhale, bracing myself. I think about repeating the question, but I'm too scared. Too afraid of what he'll tell me he thinks it is.

But he breaks the silence. He inhales deeply. I hear him chuckle, but the sound is mirthless, like he's the bearer of bad news, and it's the last thing he wants to tell me.

Finally, he speaks.

"That house is haunted, Blair."

TWENTY-TWO

WE GET off the phone just after five in the morning. Cash tells me he's coming straight over after finishing up some things he needs to take care of.

I forget to even ask him why he was awake in the middle of the night to begin with, not that it's any of my business. Lots of people have their own reasons for being awake in the wee hours of the morning. I should know.

When dawn breaks, I'm finally able to sneak in a nap.

With daylight pouring in, the house seems less oppressive. Like whatever's in here might have a harder time getting me with the sun out.

That's a thing that happens with certain traumas. Feeling safer sleeping when the sun is out.

It's something that I did after my dad disappeared. I associated him leaving with nighttime, so I would sleep during the day and stay up all night. Just in case something was going to happen.

Or maybe I was waiting for him to return.

When I wake from my nap around 11:00 in the morning, I ruminate on everything that happened to bring me to this point.

I feel this urge to connect with Blake, to call him and talk to him. Not about any business matters or money situations. But just because he's my brother, and I miss him.

I hadn't missed him for some time. I think the current circumstances have made me realize that I do want him in my life, even if he's difficult.

I think hard times do that to us. Make us realize what's really important.

Blake is the only remaining tie that I have to my dad.

The only other living person that shares his DNA that I know of. Our family, the extended parts of it, weren't very close. I barely ever saw my grandparents.

I think they didn't quite approve of what my dad did for a living.

They all thought it was silly and I can see why.

It is kind of silly.

I think better of calling Blake. It can wait.

I busy myself cleaning even though the house is already clean. I scrub the countertops and the stove like my life depends on it, hoping that doing something physical will keep my mind from picking too much at everything.

Like picking at a scab, knowing that it will bleed.

If I stay busy, I don't have to think about any of that. I don't have to think about Blake. I don't have to think about the fact that he's my only remaining connection to my dad, and I don't have to think about the fact that Cash is coming back over to my house to hunt ghosts.

I hate to bother Noelle right now.

I think things are going really well for her with Hooper.

And Cash isn't nearly as bad as I thought he'd be. He's pretty good company. He did help me through a panic attack, after all.

Around noon, the doorbell rings and I put my cleaning products away.

I run to the front hall and open the door for him.

"Come in," I say. He looks just as I remember, though a little tired. Dark circles ring his eyes and his hair is a little messed up. Clear signs that he really didn't sleep last night.

He's wearing the same clothes from yesterday, minus the bomber jacket. The gray shirt and jeans look a little worn. A little worse for wear, with wrinkles here and there.

He steps into the house and glances around like he's taking it all in again, but weighing it in new ways now. I follow the trail of his gaze, trying to see what he sees, but I can't. He reminds me so much of my dad that it hurts. That faraway gaze that I'm not sure I can relate to or penetrate.

Finally, his eyes find mine.

"Are you okay?" he asks.

"I'm fine." The way it comes out, I'm not even sure I believe it. He gives me a skeptical look. It tells me he's not sure about it, either. "I could use some decent sleep," I tell him. That's as much as I'm willing to admit.

"You and me both," he murmurs with a sad smile.

"You couldn't sleep either?" I ask, unable to keep myself from probing. I find myself wanting to know more about him. That's natural, isn't it? To want to know more about the person that you're spending time with.

"Okay, so I think what we need to do is set up cameras, first of all," he snowplows over my question, redirecting the conversation back to the problem at hand and making me feel like an idiot for trying to pry into his personal life. This is business clearly. And it's obvious that he doesn't want to talk about whatever he was doing last night.

It could be anything. He could be interpreting my interest as romantic interest. The thought makes my stomach turn. God, I don't want him to think that I'm into him like that.

I could just use a friend.

Maybe he was with someone last night. Maybe he

stayed at their house. Maybe that's why he's wearing the same clothes. And it's none of my business. I barely know him.

"Okay," I say.

"You alright with that?" he asks.

"Are you going to watch me shower?" I tease, but regret it immediately.

"Of course not," he says back, horrified by the thought. The contortions of his face are less than complimentary.

He steps around me and starts to survey the house some more. He walks around looking for places to plant cameras, I imagine.

"Have you ever actually caught a ghost on one of those?" I ask, a little irritated by his response to my joke.

"Do you know anything about platypuses?" Cash asks.

"Shouldn't it be platypi?"

Cash keeps talking, undeterred by my irritation.

"In 1798, a sketch of a platypus was sent back to England from New South Wales. The thing was totally foreign to them. It had a duck's bill and a beaver's body. Everyone thought it was a hoax, except for a zoologist named George Shaw. He examined the animal and said, 'On a subject so extraordinary as the present, a degree of skepticism is not only pardonable, but laudable; and I ought perhaps to acknowledge that I almost doubt the testimony of my own eyes.'"

"Why are you telling me this?" I ask, confused as to where he's going.

"At one point no one believed a platypus was a real thing," Cash says, looking around some more. "Even people who had seen it," he says pointedly.

He approaches one of the bookshelves and reaches up to the top, his extremely tall frame allowing him to do so. He swipes around feeling for the surface hidden by the lip.

"That'll do," he says.

"What the hell does the platypus have to do with this?" I ask, growing more irritated as I follow him around the house.

"One day," he turns on his heel, looking down at me with piercing blue eyes. "Someone is going to catch something on tape that's irrefutable."

"You mean a ghost?" I ask.

"Yes, Blair. A ghost." He turns and continues his assessment of the house.

I follow him upstairs and we reach my bedroom.

"This is your room?" he asks.

"Yeah," I say.

"May I?" He gestures at the doorway, asking for permission.

"Sure," I sound as annoyed as I am.

"Thanks," he says in a tone that indicates he has no desire to be in my personal space. I feel a flush hit my cheeks and chest.

We walk around the bedroom, and he investigates the bathroom.

"You think this is where the water came from?" he asks, referencing the paw prints.

"I think it has to be," I tell him. "You know?"

He seems to take that as another piece of data to be analyzed.

I follow him out of my bedroom, and we go back downstairs. He leads me out onto the patio. He looks around and asks a few more preliminary questions that I've already answered at least once, and sometimes twice. Finally, he goes for his equipment. He sets it up and, with my help, runs cables until the house looks like black spaghetti has been thrown up all over the floors. It's an eyesore, to say the least. And a bit of a hazard if I plan on making any late night trips to the kitchen. I'll break my neck and become the latest in a long line of people trapped forever in the Solomon house.

The thought makes me smirk.

The idea that someone just like me could be encountering my ghost a hundred years from now.

We finish up in the dining room, setting up something of a control center. Cash shows me where the video streams from every room can be monitored in real time as well as being recorded for further analysis later.

"You can sit here and watch if you think something's going on," he tells me.

"I have very little faith that we're going to capture anything on camera," I tell him.

"Honestly, you haven't been following in your father's footsteps." He hits me with a charming smirk that does something to my stomach that I don't like. But it's quickly followed by a chill.

Of course I haven't. I don't even know who the man really was.

And I've never been into any of the things that he was.

"I'm sorry," he says, reading the silence.

"It's okay," I assure him, shaking the moment off and trying to speak brightly.

He hands me a handheld recorder. He shows me on the on and off switch, the record button, the playback button, and he instructs me on how to use it.

"Basically, it's like you're having a conversation. You want to give the spirit time to answer. Pause after each question, then listen to it later." He says this like that's the most normal fucking thing in the world, which makes me laugh.

I roll the weighty recorder over in my hand and remember a night when my dad had Blake and I hunt for ghosts in our own house. We were kids. And it was so much fun.

This could be fun, I tell myself. For a moment, I feel a flicker of hope.

"What's wrong?" he asks.

"It's just all—" I search for the word.

"A lot?" he asks.

"To say the least," I tell him, trying to sound like I'm making a joke. Like the part about this that's heavy is the fact that there might be a ghost in my house.

"Blair," he says. "Let me tell you something."

I inhale and sigh, wondering what sort of pearl of wisdom he's going to impart to me.

Seems like whenever you don't need any advice, everyone's full of it.

"Sometimes people can have the most unexplainable, incredible, strange things happen to them and they still go to their deathbed uncertain that there's anything beyond reality as we currently understand it," he says.

"Oooh-kay," I draw the word with annoyance.

"Sometimes people think that if they can't understand something, then it can't exist."

"What are you getting at?" I ask him.

"Just keep an open mind," he says. There's a bit of pleading in his voice, like he really wants me to try. It triggers some emotion inside me. Some thought of my father.

"I'll try," I say and clear my throat.

"Okay, good," he says and begins gathering his things.

"You're leaving?" I ask.

The words come out before I can hide the desperation in my voice. I hate the way it sounds and I hate even more the implication of it. That I am *so* scared to be alone here that I'm begging a stranger to stay with me.

And it probably only serves to make Cash think I have other intentions.

"Do you want me to stay?" Cash asks. He looks up at me as he packs up his stuff.

I hesitate. I can't bring myself to say it. It seems so pathetic. And he's probably got way better things to do.

"No," I finally get out. "I just wasn't sure you trusted me to be able to use all of this," I say with a weak laugh.

"I think I have more faith in you than you have in yourself," he says with a smile. He stands and I do the same, then we head for the door.

"Thank you," I say, peeling away the armor I've been wearing for most of the day.

The entire set up takes all day, so by the time I'm walking him to the door, it's dark out.

"I'll be able to see everything from my laptop," he says. "And my phone," he waves the device before tucking it into his back pocket. "You won't be alone."

When he says it, it hits me like a ton of bricks.

"Cash," I say as he starts down the steps leading to the driveway.

He turns to look at me.

"Thank you, again."

"It's nothing," he says and clears his throat. "I do this sort of stuff all the time."

I nod.

"Right," I say, nodding more vigorously.

This isn't a special favor.

This isn't because he feels bad for me. Because of my dad. Because he knew him.

He pauses for a moment.

Looking down at the ground as if he's thinking about what he might say next.

He looks up at me and presses his lips together.

"Everything's gonna be okay," he says.

I didn't realize how badly I needed someone to say that and I feel emotion trapped in my throat.

I'm scared, I realize.

I say it out loud.

"I'm scared." He looks at me seriously.

"Don't be afraid," he says. "I'm here to help you."

He gets into his truck and I watch as he heads out, regretting letting him leave immediately.

He does this all the time. Nothing about this is out of the ordinary for him.

But it is for me, and that makes me feel alone all over again.

TWENTY-THREE

AFTER CASH LEAVES, I walk around the house, reexamining all the cameras that we set up. I step cautiously over the cables and make a note that I probably shouldn't drink too much tonight. Especially alone. I could trip over one of them and kill myself.

No one for miles. No one to hear me scream. That thought is entirely unhelpful.

"No one has ever been killed by a ghost," I say.

The words echo around me, and I realize how empty the house is again. It's a comfort to have all the cables running here and there. Evidence that another person has been here and that another person intends to return. The reality that I'm having to tell myself this is not just in my mind sends a shiver through me. I feel like I'm losing touch with reality. That sad thought brings me back to my dad in a heavy and unexpected way. I wonder what he was hoping to find all those years. The same thing I'm searching for now?

I wonder. He wanted answers, or at least, that's how he made it seem. Cash seems to be the same kind of person wanting answers.

I don't even know Cash that well. Now he has a bird's-eye view of every room in my house. A thought slips in. What if he uses this for his channel? Wouldn't he have to ask me first? Wouldn't he have to get me to sign some sort of release? I'm not sure exactly how all of that works. But I imagine he knows the ins and outs of it. If there's a way for him to do this surreptitiously, I'm sure he's aware of it.

Suddenly, allowing someone who is a virtual stranger to set up cameras inside my house seems like it might have been the dumbest thing I've ever done. Especially given the fact that said stranger profits off of visual media, such as videos about ghosts.

I can't believe I'm even entertaining the possibility that this house is haunted.

It's absurd. It makes me bark out a laugh. If anything, I think Dad would get a big kick out of this. I think it saddened him when I was a late teen and I'd kind of given up on believing in the things he did. When I was a kid, I was probably his biggest fan. I thought it was so cool that my dad chased down ghosts, demons, and monsters. That he shared the stories of people who were too afraid to speak up in their everyday lives. It wasn't until I was older that I realized why they were scared and the fact that my dad was probably exploiting them.

"Jesus fucking Christ," I mutter to myself, staring straight at one of the cameras in the living room. I wonder if Cash is watching it right now. It makes me mad that he left me here alone when it was probably apparent that I didn't want him to. I hope he's watching when I flip the camera off.

I SPEND the rest of the day trying to act like there aren't cameras everywhere. Going about my normal everyday business like I usually would. But it's hard knowing that there's a camera around every corner, watching my every move. It has me feeling ultra self-conscious. I don't know how people get used to that sort of thing. Performing on video, performing live, or being recorded. The kind of people that perform the way my dad did.

I feel like if I was put in front of a microphone, I would freeze up. Same with a camera, maybe worse. I watch television late into the night, my remote clutched in my hand. I think I keep it there because as soon as I lay it on the nightstand that's equivocal to giving up. That means I'm letting go and letting sleep take me, which puts me back in the position I've been in every night that I've seen things. I hate that it feels this way. That I'm afraid of sleeping in my own house.

Again, the thought that Cash could be watching me right now comes to me.

I look over at the camera pointed toward the bedroom. From the bed, I give him a little wave and a smile. Awkward.

I look over at the remote that I had sat down on the nightstand. I think about picking it up and finding something fresh to watch, making it clear that I'm not going to sleep right now. If I can just keep clutching it, even though I'm nodding off periodically, waking and seizing the remote before it can fall from my hand, maybe nothing will happen.

Finally, I wake up enough to think just how absurd this bit of magical thinking is. I'm quite literally a woman in her thirties trying to keep the boogeyman at bay by not falling asleep. This is beyond ridiculous. This is pitiful. In an act of pure defiance, I place the remote on the nightstand again and tuck my covers up around my chin.

I stare at the television, not really paying attention to anything that comes across it. Finally, sleep sneaks in and I slip under its warm embrace.

CHUFF. *Chuff. Chuff.*

My eyes shoot open. I feel the breath on the back of my neck. Hot. An animal's breath. I hear the sound once more and very clearly feel the burst of hot air that accompanies it.

It's real.

"What the fuck?" I shout as I spin beneath the covers, trying to face my non-human assailant in the darkness. When I turn, there's nothing there. My bedroom is empty aside from my own presence. Even the television is off.

My heart thuds in my chest at the realization that I felt it again. It was so real.

I rub my face hard with the palms of my hands, trying to wake myself up out of what might be another nightmare. But nothing happens. I feel it when I pinch myself on the leg. I'm not dreaming, this is reality.

There's nothing that's going to wake me from this and put me back in the real world because this is it.

And I heard that stupid goddamn sound again, the sound that very clearly belongs to an animal. Would it be worse if it were a person? I wonder. The answer comes almost instantly. *Yes.* Yes, it would. It would be much worse.

I am undoubtedly of the belief now that it has to be an animal because my sanity can't take the alternative, ghost or not.

I lay there in bed and I listen. I strain my ears wondering if I'm going to hear the peals of laughter that I heard the previous night. They all seem to be bleeding together now. I feel like I can't distinguish one experience from another. They've become numerous, which is alarming. It's becoming the new normal and I don't like that. Not at all. Just a few weeks ago, my normal was wandering through a house, my biggest worry being that if I played music on the patio too loud, I might disturb our neighbors half an acre over. Now my biggest worry is that this thing I keep hearing every night is a person.

Or worse, a ghost.

I look over at my nightstand, at the camera Cash set up to survey everything in the bedroom except for me. He set up another camera's angle so that it includes the foot of my bed and the door to the bathroom, but the one camera is pointing at me in the bed, which is disconcerting. The idea that he thinks he might catch some sort of evidence involving me scares me.

I grab my phone and realize with an eerie clarity that I've woken up again in the middle of the third hour past midnight.

Is that significant? Do I need to tell Cash about that, too? I feel like I'm out of my depth in a land of make believe. I feel like a crazy person. Maybe I'm losing my mind. Maybe that's all this is. I close my eyes, intent ongoing back to sleep, ready to reclaim my sanity in the morning. Just then, a vision of Jean Horn comes to me, standing on my porch, casting a glance back at me and asking a very simple question.

Have you seen her yet?

I can almost hear her. My eyes shoot open once

more. This isn't just in my head. Other people have seen what I'm seeing.

I don't sleep. I don't go looking for the source of the noise, either. I'm resigned to admit that this place might be haunted.

I lay there, staring at the moonlit ceiling until finally dawn breaks and I feel safe again.

I MAKE coffee in the morning. I drink three cups before eating breakfast and I feel the anxiousness that comes with too much caffeine begin to permeate my brain.

I regret my decision immediately, but I also know without it I'll be asleep most of the day, which will ultimately lead to an inability to sleep at night. Would it be the worst thing?

My dad always struggled with insomnia. The entire time I was around him. I remember him being up well into the wee hours of the night, working in his office. The sound of him puttering around at night always made me feel safe enough to fall back asleep. If I ever woke up before morning, the idea that someone was on guard—someone was watching out—always made me feel safer.

I've always chalked it up to being a kid with an overactive imagination, perceiving threats where there were none. But now I wonder if my child-size self knew something that my adult-size self isn't ready to recognize.

The thought is too much for seven in the morning. Especially after another sleepless night. I can't imagine it leading me anywhere good.

At least I was able to keep myself from calling Cash. That's a small victory. It seems like that's the only kind I get these days.

Finally, when I can't keep myself from it any longer, I pick up the phone and call him. At least it's close to noon, or at least closer than it was when I thought about it earlier.

"Hey, Blair," he answers. Something tugs at my chest when he says my name. A sense of familiarity lies in his voice that I wasn't expecting. He sounds as tired as I feel, though.

"You not get much sleep last night?" I ask.

"The more important question is whether you got much sleep last night," he points out. "Judging from the fact that you're calling me before noon, I'd say that you didn't." I'm silent for a moment. He's right. "I guess there's my answer," he says.

"Have you looked at the cameras?" I ask him.

"Have you?" he asks.

"I haven't." I didn't want to. I don't want to admit that to him now. "I'm not great with technology," I lie through my teeth.

"That sounds like a lie, but okay," he says with an edge. "What happened?" he asks.

"I heard that animal noise again." I tell him I was in bed as usual. I cringe at the last part. That shouldn't be an as usual type of situation. I hear him surfing around some more on whatever program he's using to monitor the cameras.

"Oh," he says softly. "Oh, wow."

"What?" I snap a little too eagerly.

"What time did it happen?" he asks.

"I'm assuming around 3:30am because that's what the clock said after I woke up."

"Okay, yeah," Cash's tone becomes serious. The irritation with me fades. He's zoned in to work mode now, impervious to personal assaults or annoyances.

This makes me feel sick. This makes me think he's got something.

"What is it?" I demand again. "Tell me!"

"I think I'd rather show you," he says. "That's not what I wanted to hear," I murmur.

TWENTY-FOUR

I PACE back and forth in the dining room. The mountain of monitors sprawls across the table and I'm tempted to begin looking through each camera feed. Something stops me. The same thing that made me tell Cash I'm technologically challenged. If I'm being honest with myself, I don't want to see whatever it was Cash saw on the footage, and I really don't want to see it alone.

If I'm going to see something that's going to change my entire paradigm of reality, I'd rather do it in the company of another person. Someone that can ground me back in the present moment and remind me that these things aren't real.

The thought makes me laugh. Cash isn't that person. Cash is going to tell me it is real.

The realization makes me feel weak. Not like the kind of girl my dad would be proud of. I think my dad would have been down here in the middle of the night analyzing this stuff, or at least he would have if he were a believer. Cash and Hooper seem to be under that impression.

Maybe he was. Maybe they're right.

I roll that idea over in my mind a little bit.

The late nights, the trips.

Why would he have gone to all that trouble if he wasn't a believer? If he was just in it for the money, why go to all those places and spend all that time away?

A grim thought occurs to me. Maybe he wanted to be away from me and Blake. Maybe he didn't want a family. Maybe he felt like he was better off on his own. Since he had the money to afford someone to take care of us, why not be on his own most of the time?

Maybe he really did believe in this stuff. Maybe he just didn't want to be a dad.

The idea is bleak and not one I thought I'd be having right now. Especially not as a result of anticipating seeing a ghost on film. Finally, I hear a knock at the door and I let go of the thoughts plaguing me. Cash is here.

I open it. He immediately makes for the dining table and sits down at the computer station we set up the day before. He doesn't say a word to me. It almost makes me laugh. This time nervously. I hover behind him, arms crossed over my chest. He barely says anything, which only serves to make me a million times more nervous. He's being serious.

Yeah, he thinks he saw something.

"Are you going to tell me anything or not?" I snipe behind him as I pace.

"I want you to see it for yourself," he mutters. Still fiddling with the footage, he rewinds and fast forwards, examining the timestamp. "Sit down. You're making me nervous," he adds.

"Me making *you* nervous?"

"Yeah, so be quiet and sit still," he says without looking up from the computer screen.

I sit down at the table. If anyone should be nervous right now. It's me.

Arms still crossed, I stare holes into him. He's so engrossed in what he's doing that he fails to notice. A wave of something I wasn't expecting hits me in the gut like a punch out of nowhere.

Gratitude.

That I'm not dealing with this alone. That I have a friend with me. Or, at least, someone who might be a friend. I'm grateful for him. I'm grateful for his presence. For him being here and doing this.

I glance at the monitors and all the cables strewn about the room leading to other parts of the house, all of it under constant surveillance. I think about how long it took us. The effort involved.

He sits there staring daggers at the screen, trying to get the information he wants. I'm not sure anyone aside from Noelle has ever put forth this kind of effort for me. It's a sad realization and thankfully, I don't have long enough to sit with it before Cash opens his mouth.

"Here, come here." He gestures for me to sit next to him. "I've got it."

I get up and take the seat next to him. He does something then that surprises me. He grabs the side of it and pulls it up close to him. Our bodies touch. I feel the warmth coming off of him. He reaches a large hand towards the screen and points.

"There," he says.

I'm staring at my bedroom and it's night. The time-stamp indicates it's around the time I was about to wake up. I see myself start to shift under the covers and my face is contorted with worry. My left arm hangs off the side of the bed, my hand dangling over the edge. Suddenly, I'm overcome with a feeling of dread. I want to tell myself to wake up. Anyone who's ever seen a horror movie knows that you don't let your appendages dangle. Ever.

My arm is limp in the picture. My muscles make no movement but suddenly my hand flops upward as if hit by something. It happens again. It's like something is tossing my hand up. Then it looks like something gets under my hand and raises it, gently moving it up and down.

And then, just as quickly, I see my hand jerk back. I see myself scooting up and my legs go out of the picture. I pull them up and cross them beneath me. I remember something was there, touching me.

My fear that I'm alone has been dispelled. Something is here for sure.

"IT DOESN'T MEAN ANYTHING," I keep telling Cash.

"Would you stop saying that?" Cash asks, irritated now that I'm going over all the reasons that this can't be real for the fortieth time.

"Couldn't it have been my hand moving involuntarily in my sleep?" I ask.

"Did you see your muscles or tendons contract? Because I didn't," he says. He stares back at me with a look that's very matter-of-fact.

I know he's right.

I didn't see any of that. Something moved my arm and I know it. I can remember feeling it. It came right before the chuffing, and that was very real.

"Okay," I say. I pace some more. I bring my hands up, animating the words that come rushing out of my mouth. "Let's say that this thing is real, okay?" I look up at him and he nods. "And it's here in this house, waking me up, night after night." I look once again for confirmation that he's following. "What's the point?" I ask. "Why? What does it want?"

Cash seems to think about this a little longer than I'd hoped he would.

"I think the important thing to figure out first isn't what it wants, but what it *is*." His eyes come up to meet mine on the last word.

"I don't like the way you said that," I spit out.

"What did you want me to say?" he asks.

"Oh, I don't know," I say. "I thought maybe you'd have answers since you're Mr. Ghost-man or whatever it is that you do."

He gives me an irritated smirk, telling me that he doesn't find me funny at all.

"Blair, if people knew what these things were, it wouldn't be in the realm of the paranormal. There's not a one size fits all answer. We don't have a blueprint that tells us what we're dealing with. In these cases, we have mythology, folklore, and anecdotal evidence."

"So what you're saying is that you have nothing," I snap.

"Not nothing," Cash says, his voice patient. I get the feeling that he's had to calm down a homeowner in a similar situation before and it makes me even more angry for some reason. He goes on. "We have a few things to go on here," he says.

"Do tell," I say.

"Well, the home has been owned by at least two other families prior to you buying it," he says. "From what I found on the internet, it seems that the Solomons were plagued by tragedy. The wife had a stroke. She drowned. The husband was driven mad and left. A lot of people thought it was because he just couldn't get over what happened in the house. Then the Horns owned the place. It was a funeral home. Lots of sadness there, too."

"I don't think it has to do with the Horns," I interject quietly.

"Why is that?" Cash says.

"I met Jean Horn," I say and meet his eyes. "She came over the other day. I wanted to return a photo album to her that I found in the basement. And when she left—" I trail off, debating on whether to finish my sentence. If I say it out loud, then we're officially talking about ghosts here.

"What did she say?" he proceeds.

"She asked me a question. She asked, 'Have you seen her yet?'" I look at Cash and let the question hang there between us. One of his eyebrows raises. This has definitely piqued his interest. I know he's going to tread lightly. "I tried to ask for more clarification, but she left before I could," I finish. He nods, slowly taking this in and digesting it. I want him to spit out whatever he's going to say.

"That indicates to me that whatever you're seeing, she must have seen, too," Cash says, thinking out loud. "And she said 'her?'"

"Yes," I say.

"Mrs. Solomon?" he asks.

"That's what I think," I admit out loud for the first time.

The idea that the person that I'm seeing is Hattie Solomon is chilling. A woman who died a tragic death in this house could be trying to communicate with me in some way. Is that how it works? Is that normal? The thought is crazy. There is no normal when it comes to these things.

"Go get your computer," he instructs. He grabs his laptop out of his messenger bag, opens it, and starts typing something into a search engine.

"Why?" I ask.

"We're going to dig up every single thing we can about the Solomon family."

"I've already searched them. I didn't find much."

He looks at me with mischief in his eyes. He's got something up his sleeve.

"Yeah, but you didn't have me on your team yet." He winks at me, and I can't help but smile back at him. "Go get it," he says.

So, I do.

TWENTY-FIVE

I BRING my laptop downstairs and plant myself back at the head of the table while Cash keeps working. He's right where I left him.

I open my laptop, navigating to my usual search engine and doing a general search.

I don't find much more than I did the first time, then Cash interrupts me.

"You're going to want to search through historical records. You're gonna need to go to the library website."

I don't bother arguing with him, and I do as he says.

Once there, he logs me in with his card and gets me to the Newspaper Archive.

"Now," he says. "You're going to search both of their names and you might want to narrow it down by dates, if that's necessary. You're just going to start looking through articles. See what you can find about them. About their lives. About the house," he says.

"It's like being back in college."

"It is," he says. "A lot of it is exactly like that. You'd be surprised how much ghost hunting goes on in the libraries and newspaper archives, trying to confirm stories, trying to identify people. All of that. I use it all the time just for research. It's great for that."

I'm wondering for a moment what life is like in Cash Kelly's bubble. Then the two of us get back to work in silence. We hammer out phrase after phrase and name after name into the archives search engines to see what we can find. He starts searching for anything he can find about Andrew Solomon and instructs me to do the same with Hattie.

So, I do.

The first searches seem fruitless and it takes me a bit to get the hang of exactly what's required when searching through newspaper articles. Finally, I find a few that center around the Solomons' annual Fourth of July party.

It's the party that I saw in my dream—vision—or whatever you want to call it.

Call it any of those, Blair, but it was real.

I hear the words in a familiar voice, my own father's.

I glance over at Cash, not entirely oblivious to the fact that my dad would probably be delighted by the scene taking place in my dining room today. I'm not sure he ever believed he'd see the day when I took an interest in this stuff again. It brings a smile to the corner of my mouth.

I save each of the articles, then dive into the PDF file of the first. I begin to read.

Oklahoma City, Oklahoma—This year's celebration at the Solomon house will be one for the ages, according to sources close to Mrs. Hattie Solomon, the hostess with a reputation that precedes her anywhere she goes. A private fireworks display is scheduled, as well as the annual party that everyone has come to expect. There are to be party favors ordered from Europe. For those with an invitation, the party is sure to be one to remember.

This article is dated in May 1917.

Apparently, the Solomons' annual Fourth of July party was such an event that it garnered press coverage two months prior to its scheduled appearance on the social calendars of those invited. It's hard to imagine a party so exclusive and exciting in Oklahoma City that it would make headlines. I can't fathom that now.

The only parties I ever hear about have to do with radio stations around Halloween or Valentine's Day. The exclusivity is gone. There's no dividing line, determining who can and can't go.

I dive into another article. The tone of this article is different. It's dated one month out from the Fourth of

July party. It seems that things took a turn for the worse within the walls of the Solomon house.

Oklahoma City, Oklahoma—The hostess responsible for the most elaborate party known to our great city has fallen ill. Mrs. Hattie Solomon has suffered a premature stroke. It is unknown what her condition is, though Mr. Andrew Solomon assures everyone the party will proceed as planned.

Reading those words sends a chill down my spine, knowing what I know about the ultimate outcome—the fact that Hattie drowned, and so did her young son. I think about Diana telling me that it was at the annual Fourth of July party that year that she met her untimely demise.

The writing's on the wall for anyone looking in with the advantage of history.

Finally, the third article isn't an article at all. It's an obituary. There is a picture of Hattie sitting next to a window, her hair down in a beautiful dress, a beautiful portrait of her.

Mrs. Hattie Solomon, beloved Oklahoma City hostess and philanthropist, has gone to be with our Lord and Savior. She departed this earth on July 4, 1917, at the very party where she made her mark on the Oklahoma City social scene. Mrs. Solomon was preceded in death by her parents, Michael and Angelina Forrester, accom-

panied in death by her son, Andrew Solomon, Jr., and her beloved canine companion Duke. She is survived by her husband, Andrew Solomon, and a host of friends and extended family.

Just like that, a life snuffed out.

I think about the woman I've seen in my visions and try to reconcile her with the idea that she had a stroke. She couldn't have been more than thirty when I saw her. What thirty-year-old has a stroke out of the blue?

She looks strong and full of life and fire. Her eyes danced with delight in the vision I had of her at one of the parties.

I reread the obituary and the other two articles. I comb them for any sliver of information I might have missed. I print them out and pass them over to Cash's station at the table. He grunts and mumbles his thanks as he mindlessly tucks them into the pile he's already got going.

"You find anything?" I finally ask.

He's staring at his computer screen hunched forward like if he leans close enough, the machine will whisper secrets to him that otherwise might remain concealed. He leans back and rubs his face. He looks tired.

"Some pictures," he says, and his eyes meet mine. "You find anything?"

I point at the top of the stack where he mindlessly tucked my printouts.

"Oh," he says, seeming to have forgotten they were there. He reaches for the papers, pulls them out of his little pile, and begins reading. I get up and go to the kitchen for another cup of coffee. As I'm pouring it, he calls out.

"Blair," he shouts.

I scurry around the corner back into the dining room.

"What?" I ask.

He gets up from the dining table without a word. He grabs another printed piece of paper. An image that I can't quite make out as he hurries to the staircase. I follow him as he takes them two and three at a time.

"Slow down!" I say, out of breath and trying to keep up with him.

He stops at the second story landing. He turns to face the portrait of the dog dressed in human clothes. He points at it.

"Look," he says as he holds up the black-and-white picture he just retrieved from the printer.

I stepped closer and look at the painting of the dog, then back at the black and white snapshot. Hattie Solomon, her hand resting on the head of a great black German Shepherd. He's massive, larger than any household pet I've ever seen. In the snapshot, she smiles, squinting her eyes into the sun. Duke stands steadfastly at her side, his tongue lolling, happy just to be next to her. I look at the portrait.

"Holy shit," I mutter.

"It's him," Cash says.

Mrs. Solomon was preceded in death by her parents, Michael and Angelina Forrester, accompanied in death by her son, Andrew Solomon, Jr., and her beloved canine companion Duke. She is survived by her husband, Andrew Solomon, and a host of friends and extended family.

The line from the obituary is burned in my mind. The words come back in an echo. Another chill descends the rungs of my ribcage. I tuck my arms around my body like I've just gotten cold.

"That's Duke," Cash says.

I stare at the dog in the portrait. The same one that was giving me the creeps when he was in my room. I look again at the picture in Cash's hands, trying to reconcile the happy-go-lucky animal with the one in that portrait. They're markedly different.

The two dogs seem to be two different specimens. The dog in the general's coat looks fierce. There's something about him that I find intimidating. The way you might find a guard dog intimidating. In the snapshot, he's gorgeous, full of life, and happy to be next to the girl that he loves. Hattie seems just as happy to be with him.

"It's him," Cash repeats. "The paw prints. The animal sound waking you up."

I stare at him. I hate this. I hate this. I fucking hate this.

"No," I laugh "No, Cash."

I stare at him, my mouth hanging open incredulously. That's just a painting of a dog. I point to the picture in his hand of Hattie Solomon with Duke. My finger shakes.

"That's just the girl and her dog."

"Take it off the wall," he orders when I laugh again.

"Take the painting off the wall," he says more clearly. Slower this time.

I don't want to. I'm afraid of what I'm going to see. I feel a hard lump in my throat. My hands tremble as I reached for the edges of the painting. I lift it from the nail and bring it to the floor. I hold it up, facing me and Cash.

"Look at the back."

"You need to turn it around," he says.

I swallow, spinning the portrait slowly on one corner. I look at the back of the canvas, covered in thin parchment style paper. Down next to my palm, I see something. I pull it up closer so that I can get a good look at what it says. Cash hovers over me, reading it at the same time.

And there it is, just as he predicted. In pencil.

It's been aged over a century.

Duke in oil for Mrs. Hattie Solomon 1917

TWENTY-SIX

CASH HANGS the portrait back up.

I descend the stairs wordlessly and find myself on the couch in the living room. Cash follows me in. He paces in front of the fireplace like someone that just found a clue as to who murdered who on the Orient Express.

I'm still in shock over the fact that the dog in the portrait is Duke, and that he might be the animal that's been stalking me at night.

"This doesn't mean anything," I say. I'm pretty sure this is the fourth or fifth time I've repeated the sentiment since examining the back of the dog portrait.

"Blair," Cash says. He stops pacing and makes direct eye contact with me.

"What?" I snap.

"What if it *is* him?"

I look up at him.

There's something in the timbre of his voice that causes me to pause on my unending quest to deny what's right in front of my face. He drops to a knee in front of me and grabs my hands. The gesture shocks me. His palms are warm.

I wonder if my hands are clammy and cold? Because that's how I feel right now.

"What if—," he begins. He trails off and looks back at the staircase, then back at me. "What if the thing that you've seen—"

"I haven't seen anything." I snatch my hands away from him, feeling like I'm a crazy person he's trying to reason with.

"Well, we both know that's a lie," he says evenly. "You saw the party. You saw the paw prints."

"Those were just dreams," I tell him, feeling a frantic desperation for this not to be real.

I fought so hard against this for so many years, to not become the person that I always thought my dad was. To not become someone that could so easily believe in such a thing. To not become the kind of person that I think he's taken advantage of.

Maybe he didn't take advantage of them. Maybe he really believed them, just like Cash.

He cocks his head, daring me to contradict him on things we both know I've admitted to.

"Just listen to me for five minutes without biting my head off, okay?" he pleads.

"Fine." I spit the word, crossing my arms and

making sure my hands aren't anywhere he can grab them. That was too uncomfortable, too intimate.

"Look," he says. "Did you ever have a dog as a kid?"

"No," I say. "Dad was never around and I don't think he thought it would be a good idea to leave two kids in charge of something they could actually kill by accident. It wouldn't be like having a fish."

"Okay," he looks around, realizing that I'm not going to just go with him hand-in-hand on this.

"Dogs are man's best friend. Right?" he asks.

"Supposedly," I tell him. "I wouldn't really know."

"Just entertain the thought for a second, Blair." He nods, trying to encourage me to go with him on this. I roll my eyes.

"What if that really is her dog?" he asks. "The one leaving the paw prints and making the noises to wake you up. What if he's trying to tell you something?"

I laugh. The whole thing is absurd.

The idea that this place can be haunted by a dog. I've never heard of such a thing.

"You cannot be serious right now," I say.

When his eyes meet mine, I realize that he is, in fact, quite serious.

"Oh," I say. "Oh, my God." I stand up, running my hands through my hair. "How many times have you found a place that was haunted by a dog?" I ask him.

"Not many," he admits. "Just hear me out."

"Oh, I hear you," I say, turning on my heel and pointing at him. "You sound exactly like my dad." He stares at me, and there's confusion in his eyes. It's obvious that he doesn't think this could be an insult. "Which isn't a good thing," I clarify. "You sound insane."

"You do realize that you let me set up cameras throughout your whole house because you do believe enough to know that something is going on here that goes beyond the scope of normal reality, right?" he asks. I feel my fight, flight, or freeze instinct begin to kick in.

I don't want to have this conversation. I don't want to go down this road. I want to go back in time. I want everything to be okay again. I want to be back in the old house, having a girls' night with Noelle, watching reality TV and making fun of the people on it.

I don't want to be here. I don't want to be doing this.

"I had no other choice!" I shout.

Cash looks at me, his eyes pleading. He wants me to give into this, but I can't.

"Because I know on some level," he says. "You know something is going on here that can't be explained by an exterminator or an intruder."

He's right. I know he's right.

There's no use fighting it.

But part of my brain tells me that I have to. That I can't give into this.

I bite my bottom lip, fighting back the urge to cry. I don't want to cry in front of Cash. I *will not* cry in front of Cash.

He steps forward, grabbing my shoulders and looking down at me.

"Blair," he says softly, and that's all it takes. The kindness in his voice. I think of how he took care of me during that anxiety attack. The thought of how much effort he's put into solving a problem for a total stranger.

Is he like my dad?

What if my dad was like him?

Maybe he was kind, really caring about the people that he gave a platform to.

And then I'm crying, sobbing, and shaking.

"Hey," he says. He pushes me over to the couch, once more making me sit down. He grabs a blanket and wraps his arms around my shoulders.

"This just can't happen," I choke out between sobs.

"Blair," he says. He reaches for my chin, turning my tear-streaked face toward him. "It's okay. It's okay to not always know."

"No, it's not," I say. "You say that, but I don't believe it at all."

"Why?" he pleads.

"Have you ever lost anyone?" I ask him. He's silent, suddenly clamming up. "Have you ever known anyone that went missing?" I probe further. "Besides my dad." I find the strength in my voice again.

He just stares at me, pain in his eyes.

"I would give anything to know where my dad's body is," I go on. "I know and you know, and my brother knows he's gone. Someone doesn't just disappear for seven years without a trace because they're on vacation in Maui."

"Blair—"

"No, let me finish," I say. This is the first time I've ever spoken any of this out loud. I realize then that if I don't finish this right now, I won't *ever* say it out loud. "You don't understand."

There's a look of pain on his face that makes me hesitate and makes me wonder how much he might understand.

"What do I not understand?" he asks.

He looks at me with pleading eyes.

"If this thing—" I point upstairs. "—is real..." I trail off, collecting my thoughts. "If it's real, that means that there might be other things that are real."

"That means your dad didn't waste his life chasing shadows," Cash mutters.

"Which means that maybe he found one of those shadows," I say.

"And he might not be dead," Cash finishes the thought for me.

"Which is worse," I say. "So, so, so much worse."

"But Blair, that means he might be alive," Cash says enthusiastically.

"No, you don't get it," I say. "If he's alive, something bad happened to him. He's somewhere bad."

He looks at me, his eyes searching my face. I see the gears in his mind turning, trying to find a solution to what I've laid out for him that will make me feel better. It's almost sweet. I smile sadly at him.

"This changes everything," I say with a gasp, trying to control my crying. He rubs his hand over my back. He whispers.

"It's okay. You're okay. You're safe. You're safe with me."

I can't control it any longer and I cry and cry.

———

"I'M SPENDING THE NIGHT," Cash says definitively.

We sit on the couch watching TV for a couple of hours after that.

I think he just doesn't want to leave knowing how upset I am, and maybe he feels partially responsible for that, even though it's not his responsibility to make sure that I'm okay.

I take a mug of hot chocolate in between my palms when Cash offers it, absorbing the heat. It's calming, soothing.

"You didn't need to do that," I tell him. "You don't need to stay."

"Not leaving," he says firmly.

"Is that supposed to make me feel better?" I ask with a small smirk.

It does make me feel better, but I don't want to admit it.

I don't want to admit to him that I'm afraid to spend the night in my own house alone at this point.

It's so silly. So absurd.

"That makes me feel like you think whatever's here is gonna kill me and you don't want to be liable with all your cables and cords running throughout my house," I tease him. He shoots me a fake, nasty look.

"That has nothing to do with it," he says, a little defensive.

"I'm teasing. Calm down."

"I'm just saying that I wouldn't want to be in a haunted house alone after realizing that the scope of reality expands a lot further than I thought it did while also dealing with some heavy shit concerning my father's death," he says.

My eyes widen at the bluntness of it all.

I feel like cold water has been splashed on my face, or like I've been slapped.

Somehow, hearing him say it makes me realize this might actually be the truth. That I'm stepping into a new reality.

I don't want to let on about anything.

"Suit yourself," I mutter. "You can sleep down here if you want." I just stare at the couch.

"That's fine," he says.

Cash looks around the house, reminding me of a guy trying to make sure a place is secure.

It actually makes me feel better for a second.

"Have you ever heard of someone being hurt by a

ghost?" I ask as I finish my hot chocolate. The thought has crept into my mind after he settled on the idea that he needed to stay here.

He looks up at me and stares, saying nothing.

And then he gives me a bit of a grimace.

"Yeah, not the answer I was hoping for," I admit, and laugh a little.

I stand from the couch and I take my mug back to the kitchen and go to the hall closet where I grab a couple of blankets for him. I deposit them on the couch and pat them.

"Here you go," I tell him.

"Thank you," he says and then he thinks about something, looking off into the distance. "I don't want to lie to you and tell you that never happens," he admits. It was better when he didn't say anything at all. "But it does. Sometimes there are cases of violent spirits or demons, even poltergeists."

"But this isn't a demon," I say, shaking my head as if that can't possibly be the case.

"Definitely not in this case." Cash looks away at the end of his statement. It makes me think there's always a level of uncertainty with this line of work. Frankly, an uncertainty that I'm not comfortable with quite yet.

"If you say so," I say. He nods.

"I do," he says. "You're dealing with a ghost. Totally different from a demon."

"What would you do if it were a demon?" I ask, a smirk curving my lip.

"We'd call an exorcist, of course," he says, as if only a *real* idiot wouldn't know that.

I just smile at him. The idea of an exorcist in my house performing rights and trying to rid me of some evil spirit. The thought is almost comical. Or it would be if I wasn't dealing with another sort of spirit right now.

"Thank you for staying," I say finally.

He shrugs his shoulders, dismissing the sentiment. He smiles and speaks.

"It's what your dad would have done."

TWENTY-SEVEN

WHEN I CRAWL INTO BED, I realize how much of a comfort it is to have another person inside the house with me at night. What kind of weak person needs a guy she barely knows to spend the night because she's starting to think her house is haunted? It's me. I'm the one who needs it.

I'm so very glad Cash is here and I feel safe. I feel like I can trust him. It's a sense of relief that I haven't felt in some time. Probably since everything started happening.

He feels like a good person.

I can't imagine doing something like this for someone I barely know. I think about his sentiment that this is what my father would have done, but I'm not sure that I agree. Then again, Cash can probably speak more to that than I can.

I think about Cash's words. I think about Hooper's. Both of them recounting a man that I didn't know.

I regret so much now.

How I treated my dad, for one. Maybe I should have tried to know him. Just like I think he should have tried to know me. Why didn't either of us do that?

The answer is obvious. One that plagues a lot of people's regrets. I think we always thought we'd have time. We get so caught up in the hamster wheel of our own bullshit that we forget time is making us all old. Our ability to be together is finite, numbered by years if we're lucky and moments if we're not.

Most of us won't realize any of that until it's far too late.

I lay there in my bed, the hallway door open. I glance at the light coming into the bedroom from the chandelier in the hallway. It casts a long, incandescent glow and I can see the portrait of Duke from here.

I roll over onto my elbow and stare out into the hallway. Something so eccentric wouldn't be such a big deal today. I'm sure there are plenty of wealthy people with portraits commissioned of their animals. It makes me smile because something my dad used to say pops into my head. *Only someone with more money than sense would do that.*

I'm not sure he really knew as much about having good sense.

Apparently, he thought he did.

The smile falters, replaced by a frown. God, I miss him.

I roll onto my back and stare up at the ceiling. I strain my ears trying to hear Cash downstairs. I wonder if he's asleep. Maybe he's lying awake on the couch thinking about the same things I am.

I think for a second about going downstairs to see if he's awake.

To maybe talk into the night.

I go back to the moment I asked if he'd lost someone. His hesitation told me everything.

He was too polite to cut me off, but he knows that dark, too. That thought circulates in my mind until I finally drift off to sleep.

CHUFF. *Chuff. Chuff.*

I wake to the sound like clockwork.

This time, my eyes open slowly, adjusting gradually to the brightness of the hallway light pouring into the bedroom, painting the ceiling orange. I've had my eyes closed long enough that the light seems too bright. I feel an ache in the back of my eye sockets.

I blink once, twice, three times, trying to acclimate myself to my surroundings. I'm in bed. I'm in the house that I bought. The Solomon house. Cash is downstairs. I'm not dreaming.

This is reality.

I hear it again.

Chuff.

Though, this time, much more insistent.

I cringe, not wanting to turn to face the direction it comes from. I'm afraid of what I'll see. That I'll see the dog I know shouldn't be there. That I'll see Duke. I'm afraid that everything Cash theorized will be confirmed. I'm afraid life, as I know it, is about to change.

I take a deep breath. My eyes open wide, my body fully awake. I'm fully aware that this is reality. That this isn't a dream.

Cash has been here all day, helping me with this.

This is real.

He does this for a living and I'm in need of his services.

I hold my breath and roll over, bracing myself for whatever comes next.

Standing there, solid as anything I've ever seen, is Duke.

He's enormous. Great, big, black Duke.

It's like he's in hyperreality, looking almost like an AI portrait. There's an uncanniness about his appearance. Maybe the edges are too detailed, too razor-sharp.

His tongue rolls out of his mouth and he pants, impatient with me. His tail wags and he *chuffs* one more time, adding a whine for good measure.

I lay there on my side, staring at him. The two of us nose-to-nose. I slowly push up onto my elbow. I glance over my shoulder, hoping that somehow Cash made it to the bedroom door in the last few seconds. I hope that he can see what I see.

Otherwise, I'm losing my damn mind.

Duke whines again. I feel something heavy on the bed next to me. I turned back to face him. A giant paw rests on the edge of the bed, his final polite plea for me to get up.

"Okay," I murmur to the dog.

I swing my legs out over the edge of the bed and place my feet on the floor. I stare at Duke, wondering if maybe this is a dream. But I know this is real. I keep my eyes on the dog and reach blindly for my cell phone on the nightstand.

Finally, my hand finds it. With my eyes glued to the dog, I use Siri to call Cash. I hear the phone ringing.

"What's wrong?" he asks. When he picks up, there's no sleep in his voice. He's been awake.

"Are you seeing this?" I demand. My voice comes out raspy. I hear him shuffling around, likely moving from the living room to the command center in the dining room. "Come upstairs," I whisper. I hear him moving more frantically. "Be quiet," I say, and his pace slows. Shortly after, I can hear his footsteps in the hallway and let the phone drop gently to the bed.

I don't take my eyes off of Duke. Finally, I stand from the bed and Duke follows me. Walking around to the other side facing the doorframe that Cash's giant statue fills almost entirely.

I look at him, hoping like hell I'm going to see confirmation in his eyes. That I'm not insane.

I'm rewarded tenfold. His face tells me everything.

"Do you see him?" I ask, just to make sure.

"Oh, my God," he says. He looks at me, unsure of what to do next. He kneels then, facing Duke. "Come here, Duke. Come here, boy," he says. Duke cocks his head to one side. I wonder how long it's been since he heard someone say his name.

The thought makes me so sad.

It's almost like I can feel what he feels. The loneliness of death.

The finality of it.

Eventually, someone says your name for the last time. Even if you're a dog.

I look from Cash to Duke and back again. Finally, I rest my eyes on the dog. He whimpers at Cash. Then, as if he hears something that neither of us does, he barks, loud and gruff.

Then he bolts from the bedroom, darting around Cash's legs and hitting the stairs at a breakneck pace. Cash looks at me and, in a split second, I'm throwing myself out of bed, following Duke and Cash down the stairs.

We're racing to keep up with the dog.

We take the stairs two at a time, Cash pulling far ahead of me with his much longer legs.

I try to keep up with the phantom canine in my bare feet. We round the corner at the bottom of the staircase and both of us end up in the doorway to the kitchen as we watch Duke sprint straight through the very solid door that leads out onto the back patio.

I look at Cash. He stares at the door.

He looks at me and we dash for it. He unlocks it, throws it open, and the two of us step into the frigid midnight winter night air.

Duke stands at the edge of the pool. He whimpers and begins to pace back and forth as he stares at the bottom of the empty structure.

Cash and I approach cautiously, one of us on either side of him.

He continues to pace and whimper.

He barks in frustration, first at the pool and then at the two of us. Like we're not seeing what he's seeing, and it's incredibly distressing to him. I look to Cash for guidance. He looks like a deer in the headlights. Shit.

Then, quicker than a bolt of lightning, Duke jumps straight into the pool.

"No!" I shout. My voice echoes our request over the vast backyard, bouncing off the tree line and returning to where we stand. I watch as Duke throws himself into the air, out over the middle of the empty pool. Even though it's empty, I hear the sound of a splash. I see the ripple of water cascade across the mostly invisible water's surface. In whatever reality we're in, it belongs to the dog. He's jumped into the pool.

Then he vanishes, swimming downward.

I look at Cash, his mouth open slightly. Like he's searching for what to say.

I want him to lend an expert opinion. I want him to solve this. But when his eyes meet mine, I realize that we're both at a loss and that this is above his pay grade.

And *that* is terrifying.

TWENTY-EIGHT

MY HEART COMES out of my chest.

I stare at the very empty pool in front of us. I glance over at Cash and see him standing just as close to the edge as I am. I feel a gravitational pull toward it. I wonder if he feels that, too. Like whatever is at the bottom of it is begging me to step through some portal and reach it on the other side.

He finally peels his eyes from the invisible surface of the water that we both heard break.

He looks at me, the expression on his face isn't what I'd hoped for. Because it tells me that he's at as much of a loss as I am.

"What now?" I croak. My voice is weak, and I'm about to break into tears.

"Well," Cash runs a hand through his blond hair. He rubs his neck and twists his head from side to side like he's working out some tension. He clears his throat.

He seems to be searching for the right words. "Blair, I don't know if you know this," he says. I brace myself for whatever he's about to say. "There are different kinds of sightings when it comes to hauntings," he says. His hands drop to his side. He stands there in his gray t-shirt, arms prickled with goosebumps from the frigid night air. "Like with EVPs," he says.

"You mean when you record yourself talking to a ghost?" I asked.

"Yeah," Cash says. "It's like you're recording a conversation with a ghost. You ask a question and wait for them to respond. You go back and listen. Kind of what I talked you through with the recorder settings when I first came here. Anyway, people always classify them as A, B, or C for quality. A is crystal clear, undeniably a voice, undeniably words."

"Why are you telling me this?" I ask.

"So, that's for auditory evidence," he goes on. "For visual evidence, a full-bodied apparition is the Holy Grail for any ghost hunter. A very tiny percentage of them ever get that experience. A tiny percent of regular people get that experience. It's highly sought after and it rarely occurs."

I clear my throat, trying to ground myself in my body. Trying not to get too swept up in the implications he's making.

"What we just saw," he begins. He gestures out at the pool. "What just disappeared—that was the Holy Grail."

I rub my temples as my head starts to pound

Cash steps up in front of me, grabbing me by the shoulders.

"Blair," he says, stooping down to look up into my eyes. "I saw it. You saw it. It was real."

"I cannot live in a world where ghost dogs are a thing, Cash," I blurt out, feeling panic swell in my chest. I let out a nervous laugh.

"Look," he says. "You already know this house is haunted. I get that admitting it to yourself opens a whole other can of worms that has to do with your dad, but—" he trails off and glances away from me. Without meeting my eyes, he speaks. "I'm here for you. We will get through this together."

He clears his throat and looks at me again.

The panic subsides, subdued only by the fantasy that this man in front of me has any intention of helping me through this. I'm not sure I've ever been able to trust anyone, especially men.

Every time I started talking to a guy, and he ghosted, it was like peeling back the scab left by the one my father gave me. It was like pouring salt into the wound and rubbing it, just to make sure that I knew men weren't promise keepers.

But the look in Cash's eyes makes me think that maybe he's different. A dangerous thing to think about, especially for me.

And it might be a fantasy.

But it's enough for now.

WE GO BACK INSIDE, and I make a pot of coffee. The caffeine consumption to the amount of sleep ratio in the house is getting a little out of control. I offer Cash a cup and he gratefully takes it. The two of us head straight for the dining room control center. We both have the same hope in mind.

"It might be on the video," he murmurs as we sit down, but when he pulls up the footage, it's disappointing. Duke doesn't show up. The best that we get is Cash sidestepping out of the dog's way. Sure, it looks like something is going on, but there's no objective proof that there was a dog in the house, let alone one that's from another world.

I sigh when he closes the video. I hang my head, my hand resting on the handle of my coffee cup. My forehead meets the edge of the table. I stare down at my bare feet.

"I'm not surprised," he says.

I bring my head back up.

"You didn't think it would be there?" I ask.

"You didn't either," he counters. "I mean, it's like you said to begin with. No one has ever caught something on camera that was definitive enough to take this from the realm of the paranormal to the realm of actual science."

He sighs and throws his head back, staring up at the dining room ceiling.

"I'm sorry," I tell him.

"What are you sorry about?" he tilts his head to look at me.

"I imagine you wanted there to be something. It's the Holy Grail. It could change your life," I tell him, leaving the monetary implications to his imagination. But Cash looks at me like I'm speaking Greek. "You know, like you'd be the first paranormal researcher to actually have something definitive," I prompt him.

He seems to roll this over in his mind for the first time. I'm shocked at the look of bafflement he gives me, like the idea hadn't crossed his mind at all. So much for being the businessman my dad was.

At that moment, his phone begins to vibrate with a call. I hear it buzzing against the back of the chair in his pocket. He fishes it out and glances at the screen.

"I have to take this, sorry," he mutters. He stands up, taking the phone with him out onto the front porch before answering. Maybe it's the fact that he spent the night in my house or that he's helping me with something this big, but I feel slightly affronted when he doesn't take the call in front of me.

A thought dances through my mind. It's unwanted, and it makes me feel uncomfortable. That maybe the phone call is coming from his girlfriend.

I wouldn't be too happy if my boyfriend was spending the night with some girl, especially if his reasoning was that she had a ghost living with her.

I hate how sad it makes me to think that he might

have someone. I strain my ears and hear him talking animatedly outside. I lean out into the hall, trying to see anything that might give me a glimpse into his personal life.

It's an invasion of privacy. I know that much.

But I want to know him as more than someone who's helping me with a problem. I want to know him as a friend. As someone that could be part of my life.

I quickly try to reposition myself at the table like I was when I see him stepping into the little entry alcove. By the time he opens the door into the house, I'm as I was. I glance up at him as he walks back to his station at the table. He puts his hands on the back of the dining room chair. I look at his face. He's troubled, his brow furrowing. After stepping outside to take the call, he seems then years older. He looks tired.

"I have to go," he says.

I fight the urge to tell him, *No, don't go*. I don't want to beg him to stay here. That's pathetic.

"Is everything okay?" I ask.

"Fine." He gives me the fakest smile I've ever seen.

And just like that, a wall comes up between us. A wall that makes me feel cold and renders hollow his promise from earlier. The one about going through this together. I feel myself stiffen in his presence, putting my own guard up.

"Will you be okay by yourself?" he asks.

"Fine." I give him an equally fake smile. Something

passes between us then. He knows I'm full of shit and I know the same thing about him.

He gathers his stuff and looks around, making sure he hasn't forgotten anything. I walk him to the door and he leaves, heading straight for his truck without turning around.

I guess we all have our secrets.

TWENTY-NINE

I SOMEHOW MANAGED to sneak in a nap after Cash leaves. I think it's the combination of how much adrenaline has dumped into my veins and the massive amount of sleep I've missed in the past couple of weeks. Finally, my body refuses to ask nicely for sleep, and I crash hard for a few hours.

I'm grateful when I wake that I have no memory of any dreams or nightmares. And I'm most grateful that my brain got the chance to fully rest without retaining any of the information from Dreamland to make this whole ordeal more stressful. The last thing I need is a nightmare where Duke turns on me.

So far, we've been on friendly terms and I see no reason for that to happen.

Even if I'm not sure what the hell he wants from me.

It occurs to me then that I'm analyzing what a ghost dog might or might not want from me.

This is insanity. The kind of insanity that my father grounded himself in. I groan and rub my face. I take in the surroundings of the bedroom. I keep hoping that, one day, I'll wake up and I'll be back in my dad's house. Even better still, I'll wake up and be a teenager again. And he'll be shuffling around the kitchen. I'll be able to tell him not to go on that business trip, saving him and thus saving me and Blake. I had no idea how comforting the sound of another human being just existing in the same space as you was until I lost it.

I wonder where Cash went.

The last thing I need in this weird time is to start feeling things that I really shouldn't for someone like him. I imagine he did go to his girlfriend. I wonder what she needed. Whatever it was, it was pressing. At least judging by the distress I could see on his face. Maybe they're getting back together after splitting up. Jesus, Blair, drop it.

I reach instinctively for my phone, telling myself that it's only so I can check my notifications. What I'm really hoping for is a message from Cash, an update or an estimation of when he'll be back over here so I can start counting down how much time alone I have left.

Alas, no dice.

I'm about to set the phone down when it rings. I almost jump out of my skin. I look at the caller ID and breathe a small sigh of relief. At least it isn't someone I don't want to talk to. It's Noelle.

"Hello," I answer.

"Hey," she says with more enthusiasm than necessary.

"I haven't heard from you in a while. I just wanted to make sure you're not dead," I say. "I was just about to call you."

"No, not dead," Noelle says more quickly than she needs to. It makes me smirk. "You thought I was dead?"

"No," I admit. "I think you're calling, though, because you're feeling super duper guilty because all you've been doing is screwing Hooper. You haven't had a spare minute to check on my welfare."

"Damn, Blair," she laughs. "I mean, to be fair, yes, there's been a lot of sex."

"I'm glad," I say. "You deserve all the good things, Noelle." She hesitates, and I know her well enough to know that she's skeptical about my statement. "Just let him be good to you, okay?" I say, my tone softer.

"Okay," she says. "I'll try."

"That's enough," I tell her.

"So, how are you?" she asks.

I debate telling her about everything.

If I didn't have my guard up so high all the time, I might, but as it is, I just can't yet.

"I'm fine," I say.

"You're full of shit," she says.

"Do you—" I try to find the right words. "Do you

remember the guy whose YouTube stuff we watched the night of the anniversary?"

"Oh, yeah. Cash Kelly. He's kind of the big deal, I guess." I hear her fumbling around with something while she talks to me.

"I guess he and I are kind of working on something together," I admit, the words coming out in a rush. The wrestling and fumbling on the other end stop.

"Blair," Noelle says. I'm silent, waiting for the hammer to come down. "I guarantee you that guy wants the scoop on your dad."

"It's actually not about that.," I say. "It's another thing," I lie, but not effortlessly. I pray Noelle doesn't detect it. I don't tell her that he already tried to get it.

The thought occurs to me that maybe that's why Cash has been so helpful and asking for nothing in return. Maybe he plans to ask for one very big thing when this is all over. The thought knots my stomach up.

"Just be careful. Okay?" Noelle says.

"I will," I promise her.

After a pause, she speaks.

"How are things with the house?"

"Fine." I lie again. "Just trying to get settled, you know? Old houses make a lot of weird noises."

"It probably doesn't help that the place has a long history." She's resumed whatever noisy task she was involved in before she cautioned me against trusting Cash.

"For sure," I say.

"Well, if you ever want company, you know my number," she says. "You know, if you get tired of looking at Cash Kelly." She says this part with a smirk in her voice. I find myself smirking on my end of the phone, though I do nothing to confirm her suspicions.

But that's not the point here.

"I'll be in touch," I tell her.

"Have your people call my people," she says and makes a kissy noise, then hangs up the phone.

I drop it beside me on the mattress and sigh, looking up at the ceiling. I cast my eyes out over the side of the bed, remembering Duke from last night. Did that really happen? It must have.

When I sit up and look around at the rest of the room, black cables are still running everywhere, which means that Cash Kelly has been here, which probably means that something weird is going on.

———————

I CURL up with a book around midday and settle in with a fire in the living room. For a little while, I'm able to be somewhere else, forgetting the shit show that has become my life. I get to live out an epic fantasy battle instead of dwelling on the fact that my brother forced me to sell the one and only house we ever knew so that he could pay off a gambling debt only for him to not return my calls afterward. I get to forget that now I'm living in a house that used to be a funeral home and has lots of sad and fucked up tragedies associated with it.

I get to forget that I saw a ghost dog last night.

I get to forget all of that for just a moment while I'm reading and that feels like a blessing.

Then I hear an engine rumbling in the driveway. I toss the book to the side and look at the windows. By the time I get up and make it to the front door, Cash is about to knock on the other side, hand raised mid-gesture. I catch him with the open door.

"Hi," he says.

"Have you slept at all?" I ask.

"I can sleep when I'm dead," he says as he pushes past me into the house.

"Wow," I remark, closing the door behind us and following him into the hallway. "Someone is remark-ably comfortable entering other people's houses without an invitation." I cross my arms and stare at him, but he completely ignores me.

Instead, he heads for our little command center.

"I've been doing some research," he says. "Using some of the sources I've gathered throughout the years doing what I do." He pulls a small notebook from his messenger bag. It's frayed with pieces of paper sticking out from it in every direction. The writings of a madman, no doubt.

"Yeah?" I ask, skeptical.

"You're going to want to sit down for this," he says. I furrow my brow and remain standing. "Suit yourself."

He opens his notebook and begins skimming, looking for the information he wants to share with me. "I talked to some old-timers. People whose grandparents might have been friends with the Solomons. And sure enough, a couple of them remembered stories passed down by their grandparents."

Okay, he has my attention now.

"And it seems that life wasn't a pleasure cruise for Hattie and Andrew," he goes on. Finally, he finds a place in the notebook he was looking for. "A woman named Alma Lewis—her family name told me that her great grandmother, Theodora Lewis, went to every single one of the Solomon family's Fourth of July parties. Says they were something else, according to her great grandma. So, I asked her if she ever said anything about that particular Fourth of July party. The one when Mrs. Solomon fell into the pool and drowned."

He leans forward. I can tell he's enjoying the fact that he's building suspense.

"It just so happens that Theodora Lewis's daughter was about the same age as Andrew Jr. at the time of the last party." Cash goes on.

"So Alma's grandmother?" I ask.

"The very one," he says and then continues. I stare at him as he sits there, drawing it out. "So, Theodora's daughter, Ella, came home from that party, the one where Mrs. Solomon fell into the pool, and wasn't ever the same according to her parents, and according to other relatives, their accounts passed down through the family. She eventually grew out of it and became a bubbly, talkative child and ultimately grew into a woman who married and continued the family line. Anyway, she suffered from dementia at the end of her life."

"Where are you going with this?" I ask, growing more irritated by the moment.

"Well, when Ella was beginning to experience the horror that is dementia, her family decided they would start making video diaries with her. They wanted to chronicle as many family stories as they could get before the lights went out, you know?" Cash gestures to his own head in a less-than-tasteful way.

"Okay," I say.

"So, in one of those videos toward the end, when things were getting harder and harder to draw out of her, Ella said some weird things, things that the family had never really thought anything about, other than the fact that they were slightly disturbing and likely the firing of random neurons in her brain. And of all those videos, she happened to know which video the weird stuff was on, and she gave it to me."

Cash pulls a VHS tape from his messenger bag.

"If your next question is whether I have a VCR or not, the answer is, *of course, not*," I say.

"Lucky for you," he says. "I do and I brought it."

"I hope you're prepared to do whatever technological gymnastics will be required to hook that up to a 4k television," I remark smartly.

"Worry not, little one," He says, giving me a smirk as he remarks on my stature. "I've got the goods."

Cash goes to his truck and retrieves a VHS player brought from home. He comes back inside and hooks it up with a series of cables to one of the monitors. Several adapters are required, but he makes it work, and when he pops the tape in, we can see the images clearly on the screen.

Fast forward, rewind, fast forward. He does this several times until he finds the section of the video he was looking for. In it Ella is lying in bed, on her deathbed, I presume, and someone is holding her hand just off camera. The person holding her hand asks a few questions, trying to get her to respond.

She says nothing. Then, suddenly, as if she sees someone in the room with her, she fixates on the space in front of her bed that's out of the view of the camera, and she begins to speak.

Cash and I stand side-by-side, staring at the screen.

"Here," he says quietly and points at it.

"Hat-hat. Hat-hat," the old woman says in the video.

She repeats it over and over. She raises a weak arm and points.

"The bad one helped them into the water."

The other person in the video tries to comfort the old woman as she grows more agitated.

"Hit him. My friend. Hit him hard, puppy dog."

She repeats the phrases over and over again. Then finally she says this.

"Always hated her."

Cash hits the pause button on the VCR.

"Okay," I try to puzzle together whatever it is Cash is trying to tell me.

"Blair," he says. "Ella was there that night and she saw Mrs. Solomon fall in the pool. Whatever she saw that night is why she got so weird as a kid. It took forever for her to act normal again, according to the family."

My eyes dart from the screen to Cash.

"Hat-hat," I say softly

"Hattie," Cash says.

"Puppy dog," I say.

"Duke."

I try to put it all together, reaching a conclusion before Cash.

"Whatever Ella saw, Duke was there, and Mrs. Solomon, obviously, but another person, too. The bad person. The one that hated Hattie and presumably pushed her into the pool." Something prickles on the back of my neck, like a realization just waiting to happen. I can't put my finger on it just yet. "So, whatever Ella saw must have been bad," I say.

"Couldn't a kid watching a woman in a wheelchair drown be bad enough?"

"Maybe it was worse than that."

"Are you suggesting—"

"I'm not suggesting anything, Cash. I'm saying quite plainly that Alma Lewis saw a woman murdered and not just a woman, a child too."

Revelation sends a chill down my spine. The two of us stand there staring at each other as the groaning walls of the house seem to press in around us.

What have I gotten myself into?

THIRTY

"YOU'RE SAYING that you think Hattie Solomon was murdered?" Cash asks for clarification.

I nod, sure of myself.

My head spins.

"I'm almost positive that someone did something to her that night."

There's an earnestness in Cash's eyes. He's pursuing this with the ferocity of a detective working on an active homicide investigation. There's something slightly charming about it.

"I think you're right," he says.

The fact that someone from our day and age would care so much about someone who died so long ago shows a level of empathy I hadn't expected from Cash. I hope that if I never figure out what happened to my dad, there will be someone who takes up the mantle just like this.

"What's wrong?" Cash asks.

Apparently, he catches the look that flits across my face.

"Nothing," I lie with a forced smile.

"I know I don't actually know you that well, Blair, but I'm pretty sure you're full of shit," he says with a little smirk, but there's a tenderness in his eyes.

"It's nothing. It's stupid." I wave it away. "Let's just keep working on this."

Cash stares at me like he's weighing his options. Like he's trying to figure out just how far he can push me before I snap shut like a Venus flytrap and keep him out permanently.

I want to tell him talking to him is the same game.

We're both keeping each other at bay. Both of us with our secrets. Him with his relationship he doesn't want to talk about and me with my own wounds. I'm not ready to be that open with another person besides Noelle. And even with her, it's hard.

But he tries his luck.

"It's about your dad, isn't it?" he probes.

"Why would you think that?" I snap. I cross my arms tightly over my chest and step back, slightly triggered by what he's saying.

I know that I have issues with that part of my life. But for someone who's a virtual stranger to call me out on it doesn't feel good.

It makes it seem like that's such an apparent thing that anyone would notice. I don't like that.

"Fair enough." He raises his hands in surrender.

Part of me wants to talk about it with him. To give in and let him have this little piece of me. To let him know me. The other part of me knows that opening up is just a one-way ticket to Brokenheartsville. In friendship and in romance, almost everyone is a leaver.

Look at my dad and my brother.

And my poor mother, who had no say in it, was dead before I was old enough to remember her.

"So, what now?" I ask him, trying to sound cheerful and redirecting our focus to the problem at hand.

"Well," he says. "We keep digging."

"Where?" I ask.

"Same places. We just have to get creative. Also, I think I want to try asking some more questions about it with all the inner family if they'll talk."

"Probably a good idea," I say.

"What about that lady that used to live here?" Cash asks. I draw a blank for a second. My mind is elsewhere. "The funeral home lady," he says, giving me a look like I'm crazy.

"Oh, Jean?" I ask. "Yeah, I mean, I could call her. I'm not sure if she'd have anything else to offer. She didn't seem eager to talk about much of it."

"Well, if she saw Hattie, do you think she ever saw Duke?"

"If she did, she didn't mention it. She only asked if I'd seen her. And I assume she was meaning Hattie," I say.

"Do you think she'd come here and let me talk to her?"

"I can't imagine why not. Other than not wanting to waste an afternoon."

"She retired?" Cash asks, as if she would have nothing better to do if that was the case. I laugh at him.

"You say that like retired people don't have lives," I remark.

"My mom's retired and her life consists of obsessing about whether I'm going to provide her with a grandson," he says.

"Are you trying?" I ask before I can filter myself and then realize how it sounds.

"I mean, I guess you could say that I practice," he says with a smirk and a quirk of an eyebrow as he looks at me.

My face flushes. I regret asking.

I walk out of the room and grab my phone to call Jean. As I do, Cash calls after me.

"I think maybe if you practiced a little, you'd be in a better mood," he says loudly.

"I'm going to pretend like I didn't hear that," I shout back.

I CALL Jean after Cash leaves. He makes plans to meet up once again with Alma Lewis. Jean agrees that she'll come by in the evening, which leaves me with an afternoon to fill without my new companion.

Staring out the front window as the fire blazes in the hearth, I realize just how nice it's been to have Cash's company throughout the last bit of time. Noelle is preoccupied with Hooper, and don't get me wrong, I'm thrilled for her. If anyone deserves a happy relationship, it's that girl. I know she said as much about me in the past, but I'm not sure if it'll ever happen.

I'm too closed off.

Sometimes it's hard to accept the idea that there's any sort of *meant to be* when you have a situation like I do.

People are fond of saying everything happens for a reason. I've always hated that.

I'm not sure I'm ready to put myself out there again for someone to stomp my heart into the dirt.

I sit down on the couch and grab my book again.

I read until evening falls and I see the beam of bright headlights hit the front of the house. Cash is back. I get up and unlock the doors, then sit back down. After a couple minutes he comes in, more comfortable entering my house than I think any well-adjusted person should be.

"I wanted to see if that's what you'd do," I say, looking up from my book.

"What?" He's oblivious.

"Enter without knocking," I say.

"You really have a hangup about that, don't you?"

he teases. "Who hurt you?" He walks over and sits down on one of the chairs opposite the couch.

"I don't think you have time for a list that long," I say, closing my book. "Well, what did you find out?"

"You'd be surprised," he mumbles. "And quite a bit, actually." He fishes his little notebook out of his messenger bag and I sit up straighter on the couch. "So, Alma's great grandmother, before she got sick, would talk a lot about these parties."

"Okay."

"Apparently, she was quite the high-society gal."

I smirk slyly at Cash's observation.

"Imagine what it would be like to live back then. The parties that the Solomons threw seem so glamorous. I'd have loved to have been a fly on the wall."

Cash considers this for a moment.

"Anyway, Theodora would tell stories about the good old days," Cash says. "You know, the way people do at family gatherings? Kids think it's a total snooze, but Alma liked to listen. She told me she always felt like an old soul. Like her great-grandmother understood her better than her own siblings." I nod, following along. "Anyway, one of the things that she seemed to always circle back to was the fact that Hattie fell ill early that summer. You remember how Ella called her Hat-Hat?"

"Yeah," I say.

"Theodora and Hattie were good friends. Ella played with Andrew Jr. A lot. Theodora couldn't quite ever reconcile how Mrs. Solomon got sick so quickly."

"Why? Isn't it pretty common for people to get sick early in life back then?" I ask, trying to poke a hole in whatever it is that Cash is about to tell me. I have a feeling we're veering into territory that I'd rather not get muddled in, paranormal or criminal, either way.

"That's true," Cash admits. "But according to Theodora, Hattie was the picture of health."

"They drank a lot, didn't they?" I shoot another bullet at his sails.

"They did," he admits. "But Theodora was apparently very adamant that Hattie was in good health. The way that Alma tells it, it's almost like Theodora became obsessed with how Hattie fell ill. She started changing her diet, exercise regimen, all of that. She saw snake oil salesmen and the like, trying to procure any miracle cure she could that might preserve her youth and health."

"I guess it really did a number on her," I say.

"Wouldn't it do the same thing to you?" Cash asks.

I think about what I might do if Noelle fell ill suddenly. At the very least, it would be a reminder of my own mortality right there in my face.

I can see how she got obsessed.

I say nothing. Instead, I let him follow his train of thought wherever it's leading.

"So, what now?" I ask.

"Well, I think we keep looking at Hattie's illness. I

find it sort of weird that Theodora became so obsessed with it. It must have made a huge impact on her, you know? It's like one day Hattie was fine. A week later, she's in a wheelchair, barely able to control her bowels and completely unable to hold a conversation or even answer a question."

"It was that bad?" I ask, not having realized it.

"Yeah," Cash says, his voice heavy. "It was really bad."

"A stroke can do that, though, can't it?" I ask.

"I have an aunt who's had five strokes," Cash says. "She's fine."

"Yeah, and I imagine she got to go to OU Medical Center to get help with it," I snap.

"I'm just saying, I think it's weird that a woman in her late twenties would be so adversely affected long term by a stroke when she was in otherwise perfect health by all accounts."

"You're the ghost hunter." I put my hands up in surrender.

Just then, another pair of headlights cut through the tree line and start down the gravel drive.

Jean.

I look at Cash.

"She's here. Are you ready?"

"Very," he says.

THIRTY-ONE

"THANK you so much for coming back over," I say to Jean as I hand her a mug of hot chocolate. "I know it wasn't on your list of preferred things to do."

"It's no trouble at all," she says, accepting the warm drink with a smile. But she looks around the room nervously, almost like she expects someone or something to jump out at any time.

It's clear that she doesn't want to be back here.

She wasn't kidding when she thought she wouldn't come back.

I feel a little guilty for asking her to, but I also think it's important, especially if I'm ever going to get my normal life back.

Cash sits opposite her in one of the chairs and I take my place at the other end of the couch.

I take a sip, raising an eyebrow and looking at Cash,

trying to give him his cue to go ahead with whatever it is he wants to ask her.

"I really appreciate it," he says.

"I've seen your videos," Jean says with a Cheshire cat smile at Cash.

"You have?" His voice is full of surprise.

"I imagine I'm not your typical audience demographic. Little old lady," she giggles.

Cash laughs despite himself. She's caught him off guard. I relish the vision of him trying to get back on his feet in the conversation.

"Well—" he rubs his neck. "You've got me there."

"So how can I help the two of you?" she asks.

"It's about the house, of course," I say.

"I had a suspicion," Jean says, looking now at me.

Cash clears his throat.

"Do you know anything about what happened to Hattie Solomon?" he asks.

Straight to the point.

I take another sip of my hot chocolate. Jean clutches hers with both hands atop her knees.

"It was quite the tragedy, wasn't it?" she asks, though the question isn't for us. Her eyes take on a far-off stare. "As I understand it, she was quite young when she had that stroke. It must have been massive. She was completely disabled. Couldn't take care of herself. Couldn't even speak," she says. She shakes her head. "Can you imagine?"

I glance at Cash. He cuts his eyes at me, then looks back to Jean.

"And it was such a different time," she goes on. "Medicine wasn't what it is today. Mental health, especially. I sometimes wonder if stress was what caused it."

"Why do you think that?" Cash asks.

"Oh, she and Mr. Solomon were never really happy, I don't think," Jean says. "According to all the rumors, he was quite the womanizer. Involved with one of the maids. Pretty sure that's who he married after Hattie's death."

Cash arches an eyebrow.

"Was he involved with the maid before Mrs. Solomon died?" he asks.

"Oh, yes," Jean says.

"Where did you hear that?" I ask.

"When I was a little girl, there were more things left behind by Mr. Solomon than not," she says. "Daddy bought the house, and it was full of relics. I found a diary. I read it like it was a salacious romance novel. And it read like one, too. I kept it. It belonged to one of the housekeepers here."

Cash moves to the edge of his seat.

"Do you still have it?" he asks.

I can hear in his voice how badly he wants her to say yes.

And then she does.

"I can do you one better," she says. "I brought it."

She digs into her purse and produces a worn, leather-bound notebook with yellowed pages.

"Where did you find it?" I ask.

"It was under a loose floorboard in the bedroom I shared with my sister. Upstairs," she points directly above us. "From what I learned, it was the maid's room."

Jean hands me the diary.

I roll it over in my hand, gingerly opening it to the flyleaf.

In a large, scrawling hand is a name.

Georgette.

"Thank you," I say, closing it.

"You can have it, dear," she says to me with a warm smile. She stands after finishing her hot chocolate. "I have a feeling that the two of you might find more use for it than I ever did. If that's all, I think I'll be going."

"Yes, that's it," Cash claps his hands onto his knees and stands, offering one to Jean. They shake. "Thank you so much for coming back over."

"Not a problem at all," she says.

As I walk Jean to the door, Cash heads to the dining room.

I let her out onto the porch and step out with her.

"Jean," I say.

She turns back to face me, her eyebrows raised in silent question.

"I remember when you left the last time you asked me if I'd seen her," I say.

She nods.

"Well, I have a question for you now," I say. "Did you ever see a dog?"

"A dog?" she asks.

"A big black German shepherd, to be specific," I go on, feeling stupid.

"Ah," Jean's face lights with recognition. "You've seen him, too, huh?"

I fight the urge to play the skeptic and simply nod, keeping my suspicions that we're all just living through a shared delusion to myself.

"Mrs. Solomon loved that dog," Jean says. "It's in the diary," she points at the little book I'm still clutching. "Duke was her favorite member of the household. Probably even more than little Andrew and definitely more than big Andrew," she says with a laugh.

"What happened to the dog?" I ask.

"Oh," she says. "You don't know?"

I shake my head.

"He drowned trying to save her," she says.

A chill runs through me and I tell myself it's the stiff north wind, nothing more.

"So, three souls were lost that night," Jean says. "Well, I'll be off."

She starts down the stairs.

"Thank you," I call after her.

And with this new knowledge, I return inside.

I CLOSE the door behind me and Cash comes walking out of the dining room.

"Hey," I say softly.

He looks up from his phone, and his eyes meet mine.

"You forgot to ask her something," I say.

He looks side to side, trying to figure out what I'm talking about.

"Duke," I say.

"Oh, shit," he says. "Call her, quick. Please."

"I asked her," I say, still leaning against the door.

"And?" Now it's him probing me to keep revealing detail after detail.

"He drowned that night in the pool with Hattie and little Andrew," I say. "I think he was trying to save one, if not both of them."

"Jesus," Cash says.

"You ever deal with a dog haunting a place?" I ask. I head for the living room.

"To be completely honest, no," Cash says. He follows me, speaking as we go. "Imagine what that dog must have seen."

"I think if we knew what Duke saw, we wouldn't be having to ask any of these other questions," I remark, plopping down on the couch.

He paces.

"Whatever that dog saw, it was enough to keep him in this house for a century," Cash says. "There's a theory that ghosts typically fall into a couple of categories. Either a sentient haunting or a residual one. Residual ones are the kind that repeat the same action again and again. Like when you hear about people always seeing a lady in white on the staircase of a bed-and-breakfast. But sentient ones are tied to a location by trauma or pain."

"So, you think this is a case of what the dog saw?" I ask.

He stops pacing and rubs his neck. He looks tired.

"It sounds like a cozy mystery," I say. "'What the Dog Saw' by Duke Solomon. I'd buy it."

Cash doesn't laugh.

"Whatever he saw is a big piece of it."

"So, what do you suggest? We play Ouija with a dog?"

Cash sighs, exasperated with me and my attitude.

"Let's fill the pool," he says. He turns to look me straight in the eye.

I make a face.

"Are you joking?" I ask.

"We have to fill it up," he says.

"What the hell good will that do?" I ask.

"I just have a gut feeling," he says. The pacing resumes.

"You want to fill up a pool with water in the dead of winter?" I ask.

"Just trust me," I say.

"The last time I trusted a man, he ran away and got declared legally dead seven years later," I snap.

It comes out before I can filter it. Before I can tell myself it's probably not the best thing to say. Especially if I don't want to talk about it further.

"Blair," Cash says. He kneels in front of me on the floor, looking up into my skeptical eyes. "Just go with me on this."

I sigh, completely exasperated and at the end of my rope. My nerves are shot, and I cannot fathom that filling up the pool is a good idea. But I also can't imagine it could hurt anything.

Except that I'll be left to deal with winterizing it in the middle of winter when this is over.

"Fine, whatever," I say.

And that's all it takes. He's headed for the back-yard before I can stop him.

THIRTY-TWO

"DO you have more than one hose?" Cash hollers back at me as I pull the patio door closed.

"Whatever I have is what I brought from my dad's house. It's in the shed," I gesture to the little storage structure that came with the property. "Why?" I ask.

He sighs, exasperated, kneeling next to the faucet in the back flowerbed.

"It'll go a lot faster with more than one hose," he stands and grabs his phone out of his back pocket. He starts typing, glued to the screen with fierce concentration.

I fold my arms over my chest and stare at the giant pool.

"Twenty-four hours," Cash says. I hear him lock his phone. I turn around in time to see him tuck it into his back pocket. "That the shed?" he points at the only structure in the backyard.

"It would appear so," I say smartly.

"Anyone ever tell you that you have a horribly bad attitude about life in general?" Cash asks without looking at me. He takes off for the shed.

I call after him.

"To be fair, no one would be at their best in this situation!"

"Noted," he calls back without turning around.

BEFORE LONG, Cash has dad's old hose hooked up to the back garden faucet. He runs it to the edge of the pool and cranks it wide open, getting as much water flow as possible going to the massive in-ground structure. I step to the edge and cringe. It's hardly clean. This is going to be a huge mess.

With a large cleanup after Cash Kelly is long gone.

It makes irritation flare in my chest, flushing my cheeks. I sigh and turn to see him messing with the faucet.

He finally stands.

"That's about as hard as I can get it to flow," he says. He wipes his hands on his jeans.

"So, what is this going to do, precisely?" I ask.

Cash is quiet for a moment.

"I'm not entirely sure," he admits.

"Oh, my God," I say, exasperated. "Do you realize what a mess—"

"Blair," he says. "I'll take care of it."

"Do you know how many fucking times I've had a man say that to me?" I snap. I poke him in the chest. He steps backwards.

Cash says nothing. But his features harden. He inhales. He seems to weigh his words.

"You're not the only one who's known a promise-breaker," he bites the words off individually, clearly pissed as hell.

He steps past me and goes to the edge of the pool. He stands there, arms crossed, surveying his handiwork.

"This is idiotic," I say, halfway to myself, but just loud enough that I'm sure Cash hears me.

If he does, though, he doesn't let on. He keeps staring into the slowly filling swimming pool.

I make a disgusted noise and go back inside, closing the door behind me as loudly as possible without slamming it.

Once inside, I try to find something to do.

I grab my book and sit down on the couch, irritation making it almost impossible to focus on a single word I see on the page. Finally, I slam the book closed.

I'm irritated with Cash.

What the fuck is he doing still outside in the freezing air?

Is the pool that interesting?

What's his fucking deal?

I don't even care about the diary at this point. Or the entire damn thing.

It's right about then that I get major ants in my pants. I can't sit still. Reading is impossible. I get up and find my jacket and purse. I hear the back door open and close. But before Cash can make it to the front of the house, I slam the front door behind me, and I head for my car.

STREETLIGHTS GLISTEN on the road in front of me. Puddles of water from recent rain look like mirages on a desert horizon. I plow through another puddle and splash water onto an empty sidewalk. I drive without a particular destination in mind, headed for the edge of town.

I fumble with my cell phone, finally getting it plugged into the stereo system. My music shuffles, playing random songs as I keep driving. I feel myself slowly calming down.

And then something strange happens.

I know exactly where I'm going, but I won't let myself think about it.

I take roads that I'm so familiar with. Turns that I know like the back of my hand.

Finally, I'm sitting with my headlights glaring against the wrought-iron gate of my father's house.

My house.

I clutch the steering wheel and stare at the property.

From here, all I can see is the gate and a slight bit of the driveway. Beyond that, the couple who bought the house from me are probably entertaining guests inside. Maybe someone stepped out to smoke in the frigid air, standing on the very patio where Noelle and I drank ourselves silly for the last time.

Profound loss settles over me.

Profound knowledge about the situation I'm in now comes next.

Grief clenches around my heart, making me feel like in just a moment, it will stop beating.

My chest aches, hollow and heavy.

And I scream.

As loud as I can. I slam my hands on the steering wheel.

"Fuck you!" I scream. "Fuck you for leaving! Fuck you for never being there! Fuck you, fuck you, fuck you!"

I scream the words over and over. Until I'm incoherent, sobbing, making animal noises with snot hanging from my nose. I pound the steering wheel over and over until all the strength from my body is gone.

I'm emotionally spent. Drained.

Living in a house that I never wanted.

With a brother who won't speak to me.

And my only company is a stranger that's probably

going to take every ounce of this experience and monetize it.

Just like you, Dad.

FUCK.

I sob, my chest heaving with each breath. I cry into the dashboard, screaming for a man that I never really knew. Screaming for a childhood that was stolen and relationships that I'll never get to experience.

I'll never have my dad walk me down the aisle.

I'll never get to introduce him to the man I'll marry.

I'll never get to ask him how to fix a broken ice maker. Or a washing machine. Or even learn how to change a tire from him. I'm in my thirties and have no idea how to change a flat tire.

The same echoing thought that I've had throughout this entire thing comes back to me, a chorus singing over and over in my mind.

I hate this.

I hate this.

I fucking hate this.

I PULL BACK UP outside the Solomon House.

Correction: the Graves House.

I don't even like the sound of it.

Exhausted from crying, my body feels the most relaxed it has in months. The anticipation of the day that my dad could be declared dead had been weighing on me without me ever acknowledging it. Then everything that came after. It was a whirlwind that I hardly had any time to process.

I'm not sure I realized how much I was carrying.

And for the first time—after sobbing my heart out—I feel a little lighter.

I park my car next to Cash's truck and head for the front door. Just as I reach for the handle, he opens it.

"Again," I say. "You really have no problem making yourself at home, do you?"

"I'm sorry, Blair," he says.

The words tumble out quickly, like he's been waiting this entire time to say them to me.

"For what?" I snap, pushing past him into the house.

Cash closes the door. As I walk into the living room, he grabs me by the shoulder and spins me around. I'm shocked at his strength, though I shouldn't be.

"I don't know what you're going through," he says.

I arch an eyebrow.

"I probably never will," he admits. He looks right into my eyes. "But I've known pain, too."

I watch as he seems to struggle with what he's going to tell me next. How much he wants to reveal.

And part of me wants him to tell me everything.

Another part of me knows that's a dangerous game. Getting to know someone.

Because eventually, they disappear.

Just then, his phone buzzes in his pocket. He groans, rolling his eyes.

"You better get that," I snark. "Your girlfriend might need you."

His eyes shoot daggers at me as he pulls the phone from his pocket. Pain flashes across his features as he reads the screen, just out of my view.

He steps back out onto the porch and takes the call.

I shed my jacket and go back to the couch. I'm not sure I'll be able to sleep yet again. I groan.

The door opens and Cash steps back inside.

"You might not want to take that coat off yet," he says.

I shoot him a weird look.

"Come on," he says. "I want to show you something."

He stares at me, waiting for me to comply. I look around the room. I have literally nothing better to do. Otherwise, I could just stay here and watch the pool fill up.

"Fine," I say.

And I grab my coat and follow him out the front door.

THIRTY-THREE

I CLIMB up into the cab of Cash's giant pickup. I don't think I realized just how big it was until this moment. My smart mouth can't help itself.

"Compensating much?" I snark.

"Wouldn't you like to know?" he replies with equal bite. He braces himself on the back of my seat as he turns around to back out. He turns us around and heads down my driveway and out onto the street.

"Where are we going?" I ask. "I doubt whatever girl you're going to rescue will appreciate me being here."

"Just shut up, okay?" Cash asks. Annoyance is clear in his tone.

So, I sit silently as we start heading north, towards downtown Oklahoma City. We exit the highway and end up in a portion of the city that's a little rougher. A lot of downtown OKC has been gentrified. Or, as some like to say, revitalized. But there's no question that the homeless population has been displaced.

We make a turn that puts us on a street I remember from high school. We would cruise around when a driver's license was our only permit to have fun. I remember this portion of town. The Jesus House looms ahead. Cash slows when we reach the stoplight just before it.

After it turns green, he pulls up outside the structure.

A man, probably early sixties, is standing outside in the darkness. He doesn't have a jacket. He wears a long-sleeved shirt that's clearly seen better days and his jeans are torn. He smokes a cigarette and stomps it out when Cash puts the truck in park.

Cash grabs something from behind my seat. I watch silently as he gets out of the truck with the bag in hand. He walks over to the guy and hands it to him. The guy immediately opens it, looking inside. He closes it and reaches out a hand to shake Cash's. Cash reluctantly does the same.

What kind of information could he be getting from this guy?

It makes me wonder about how Cash conducts his research. How many shady characters does he know?

Probably more than I'd care to be aware of.

My dad was always talking to people that I felt

were a little dangerous. But that's one of the hazards of living out an investigative journalism fantasy.

I sink into the seat, hoping I'm invisible as I stare at the pair of them.

They seem to be talking. Cash tucks his hands into his pockets. The guy seems to be trying to get out of the conversation. I can only imagine that Cash is questioning him ruthlessly, with no regard for what the guy might need to do.

I wonder if they chose this meeting place because it's so dimly lit.

Finally, the guy breaks away and Cash watches as he climbs the steps that lead into the homeless shelter.

So he actually lives here.

Puzzled, I watch as Cash finally turns and heads back to the truck.

He climbs in, silent as a stone, and sits behind the wheel for a moment without saying anything.

"He a source of yours?" I ask smartly.

Cash looks over at me without speaking. Pain is etched on his features. Finally, he speaks.

"He's the source of me. Or at least half of it," he says and shifts the truck into drive. He pulls back out onto the street and starts heading for the highway.

"That's your dad?" I ask, incredulous. I turn around in my seat like I'll catch another glimpse of the guy.

"The one and only," Cash says softly, somewhat sadly.

I turn back around in my seat without having seen anyone or anything. I stare at Cash.

"What's the matter?" he asks, dark humor in his voice. "You've never known someone who knew a homeless person? You've only ever seen them, far removed from you, begging at a stoplight?"

I'm left without much to say. I don't know how to respond.

"You grew up with money, right, Blair?" he asks. His voice is pointed.

I feel vastly uncomfortable.

"Yeah," I admit.

"I didn't," he says. His voice loses the edge. Now he just sounds sad. "My mom worked three jobs to keep us stocked with food and to keep the lights on. My dad was always into some shit he shouldn't be. Gambling, selling weed, other drugs. You know, the usual suspects."

I nod silently, still unsure of what to say.

"Where's your mom now?" I ask.

"Living in the suburbs. Single. She dates a little here and there, but never lets anyone get close."

I nod, knowing the feeling.

"Are you close with your dad?" I ask.

I see another flash of pain on his face in the glow from the dash.

"As close as we can be, I suppose," he says.

"When did he—" I struggle for the words.

"Become homeless?" Cash asks.

"Yeah," I admit, feeling awkward even asking these questions. It's like I'm peering in on a scene that I have no business watching.

"A few years ago," Cash says. "He was living with me. But I wouldn't let him do the shit he wanted to. You know, like hard drugs in the house."

"So, he chose to be homeless?" I ask gently.

"Bingo. He chose the Jesus House over my house."

His voice holds a note of bitterness.

"What I'm trying to tell you, Blair, is that I know what it's like to not have closure," Cash says. Now he looks over at me in the darkness.

"So, is this where you went the other night?" I ask. The question comes out gingerly, like I don't want to detonate a bomb. I want Cash to keep talking to me, even though I know that intimacy is where the danger lies.

"Yep," Cash says.

I nod in the darkness, not even sure that he sees it.

I feel the warmth of his hand on mine then.

It's an electric shock. I look down. His giant hand closes around mine. And I feel myself squeezing in return. I look up.

He smiles.

I smile.

We drive into the darkness.

BACK AT THE HOUSE, I shed my jacket. Cash does the same. He walks out back to check on the hose. I take a seat on the couch after grabbing my laptop. I pop it open and I'm busy searching for anything else I can find about Hattie and Andrew Solomon. My head is spinning with what I just experienced. At the revelation that Cash showed me a very delicate and intimate part of his life. Something that none of his followers know.

And somehow, that seems important.

Maybe it's just an effort to make me trust him so that he gets as close as possible to all of this. So that he can turn around and make money off of it. Maybe he'll offer me a share.

He comes back into the living room.

"Well, it's filling up," he says about the pool.

"Twenty-four hours, huh?" I ask, looking up from my laptop.

"That's the estimate I got from the pool fill calculator."

"The wonders of the internet never cease," I remark.

Cash offers me a wry smile. It's one of the first he's given me that didn't have a guard in front of it.

Something about it makes my chest flush.

I look back at my computer. Cash clears his throat.

"You want to take a look at this?" he asks.

I look up. In his hand is the diary that Jean left.

I had forgotten.

With everything that transpired, that one huge potential clue had slipped through the sieve of my mind.

I snap my laptop closed.

"Yeah," I say. "Yes. Of course."

I place the laptop on the end table and Cash takes a seat in the middle of the couch. I scoot closer to him as he opens the little leather diary. The pages snap and crackle. The spine gives slightly, and the flyleaf pops out.

"Shit," he mutters. "Old."

I make an affirmative sound, nearly holding my breath with the hope that we'll find something of substance here. On the flyleaf, there's that scrawling cursive name that we saw earlier. Georgette.

Somehow it feels wrong to read this. Even though the woman who wrote it is long dead.

It still feels vastly personal. Like what we're going to see are the inner workings of a woman's mind. And she never gave either of us permission to do so.

It reminds me of the age-old question about when it goes from grave-robbing to archaeology. What's the specific amount of time that has to pass?

But any hesitation I have is completely steamrolled by my desire to get my life back. To get this house back. I glance at the man beside me. He looks at me. Something electric passes between us at that moment. I swallow hard, my eyes not leaving his. Finally, he looks back at the little journal.

He clears his throat.

Cash turns the page.

And we begin to read.

THIRTY-FOUR

June 2, 1916

It's with great excitement that I accepted the position as head housekeeper for Mr. Andrew Solomon and his wife Hattie. They also have an adorable little boy, Andrew Junior. As well as a dog! A great black shepherd named Duke that Mrs. Solomon treats very well.

The Solomons were seeking help after the boy was able to walk. I suspect, like so many of the upper class, Mrs. Solomon would rather spend her days in other ways than rearing children.

I don't blame her.

Were I in her position—the hostess of

famous glamorous parties—I might feel the same way.

It's no secret that men have the easy role. Women have forever borne the brunt of the ugly parts of keeping society functioning. Even a maid such as myself is aware of this disparity in responsibility.

I'd much rather be in charge of bookkeeping than raising children.

But this is my lot. And I'm grateful, just as father always told me to be. A job is a job. And I'm glad to have secured one in such a beautiful house. The most beautiful in Oklahoma, if I'm being honest.

One of the responsibilities I've been shouldered with is helping Hattie in preparations for one of the lavish parties that the Solomons are known for: the Fourth of July party.

We have about a month until that time, so I'm going to do my very best in pleasing Mrs. Solomon and making the party a smashing success, even if I'm not an attendee other than as my position within the household.

Perhaps someday I'll be able to attend such a party in a glamorous dress.

But it won't be this day.

June 17, 1916

Almost all the decorations have arrived. There are exotic flowers that will arrive on the day of the party. Or so they're scheduled. It's a marvel to me that people can make such arrangements. It seems that absolutely nothing is out of reach for the rich in this country.

I don't begrudge them that.

But I wish that I had it for myself.

I'm sure that anyone who has worked in the capacity I now find myself in has felt much the same. It's not with envy that I look at Mrs. Solomon, but it is with a degree of sadness that I approach my own reflection after spending the day in her company.

So close to such glamorous things, but they're forever out of reach for me.

Today, Theodora Lewis brought her little one over to play with Andrew Junior. I watched from the hallway as the children played.

I can't help but feel that Mrs. Solomon bears some sort of resentment towards me. One of the other girls working in the house told me that it's because I'm younger than her. And that Mrs. Solomon is not oblivious to the way in which her husband steals glances at me.

I've never noticed such a thing and I wish that Hattie and I could be good friends.

But I'm not sure that a maid is ever in the position to have such a relationship with her employer.

At least being near her, I can experience this wonderful life that she's been granted through a voyeur's lens. And it's glorious. I wish that I could have been born into Hattie's family and she was born into mine. That perhaps we might switch places for only a day.

I'm afraid that's not to be, though.

July 5, 1916

The Fourth of July party. Oh! The Fourth of July party!

How do I even begin to describe the event? I'm not sure that a girl as simple as myself will ever find the right words to conjure images to a reader's mind of just how splendid the whole affair is. I've heard rumors of the Solomons' annual party and I must admit that those rumors were part of what drew me to the advertisement that Mrs. Solomon put in the paper when looking for a new head housekeeper.

But those fantasies I entertained before truly knowing the Solomons were nothing in comparison to what I found by being present for the event.

Car after car dropped people at the door where Henry, one of the staff, greeted them, taking their coats and storing them in the hall closet. I oversaw the food and made sure that all the guests were comfortable, well fed, and had a drink in their hand at all times. That was a specific instruction from Mr. Solomon.

"Georgette," he said. "Please make sure that all the guests are regularly refreshed on the drink of their choice." He offered me a wink that made me blush. A man like Mr. Solomon is hard to come by.

I envy Hattie for her choice. I wish that it was my fate to marry such a man, though I'm not sure in my position that I'll ever marry. It does happen sometimes, though.

In that interaction with Mr. Solomon, I did catch Hattie looking at me. I want to tell her that she has nothing to worry about. That I could never betray her. I want only to be her dearest friend. Nothing more.

The party was such a success. The house was filled to the brim with intoxicated partygoers. They reveled well into the night, even after the large fireworks display in the backyard. One of the hired help had to seek the doctor when he injured himself by setting off the pyrotechnics. But even blood couldn't dim the excitement of the Solomons' guests.

There is an ability in the upper class to seize with gluttony every ounce of hedonistic pleasure that they can from life. I think it comes from not having other responsibilities, perhaps. They have no worries. Not one of them.

Aside from being afraid their husband might steal away with the maid.

I imagine the human mind will find things to worry about when there are none.

Anyway, the party was glorious. I hope that next year I'll be able to leave some special mark on it that's particularly mine. Even if no one ever knows.

September 13, 1916

It's so strange to me how two people that have the world at their feet can be so damnably unhappy.

I must admit that it's frustrating to see as someone who would give anything to have the lifestyle that they so effortlessly take for granted. I bite my tongue many times when Mrs. Solomon complains about her husband. But today I could no more.

"I envy you, Georgette," Hattie said to me as she trimmed her roses. I stood by, helping her with the task.

"Why on earth would you envy me?" I barked with a laugh.

"You're not trapped in a loveless marriage, my dear," Hattie cast a sidelong glance at me with a smirk.

"Mrs. Solomon!" I gasped. "Don't say such things."

"Why shouldn't I, Hattie?" she turned on me sharply. "Why shouldn't I be able to say that I'm unhappy? Just because I'm rich? Hmm?"

"There are people who would die for your position in society," I said with an even tone, trying to bite back anything that might insult her.

"You mean die to be with my husband," she said.

"I meant no such thing," I said breathlessly.

"You might die to be with him, wouldn't

you, Georgette?" Hattie asked, her tone
sharp and her eyes sharper.

I flushed, flustered, and was unable
to speak anything reasonable.

"Perhaps if you paid him the attention
he so desperately craves, his eye would not
wander," I snapped.

I gasped.

Hattie looked as though I'd slapped
her.

"You're relieved for the day, Georgette,"
she said coldly.

"Mrs. Solomon, I—"

She turned to me, and with a calm,
even tone, she spoke.

"You will never speak to me like that
again," she said. "You are staff. You are
not my friend. Not even my companion."
She looked at me from head to toe with
disdain as she spit out the word. "You are
nothing, Georgette. And you are nothing to
my husband."

I swiped desperately as a tear fell
from my eye.

"Ma'am," I tried to say something

intelligent.

"Did you not hear me?" Mrs. Solomon asked with disgust. "Or are you deaf as well as dumb?"

Her words stung. I fled from the garden, dropping my shears at my feet.

As I passed back into the house, I saw the dog. Duke stood there, looking as though he was judging me. I could swear I heard him growl.

I have never cried so much in my life.

I don't know how much longer I want to stay here. Or if I even have a way to escape. Her cruelty knew no bounds today. And it makes me wonder if it ever has. Does it extend past me? Does it reach Mr. Solomon? Little Andrew?

I don't know the answers.

But I do know that I'm vastly unhappy here. More unhappy than I thought possible.

October 31, 1916

It surprises me that the Solomons do not celebrate Halloween with the same fervor they approach the Fourth of July. But things have been dismal in the house for the last month. Mr. Solomon seems to spend more time on his own and Hattie is leaving the house more and more. Coming home later and later.

Today Mr. Solomon expressed such kindness towards me that it almost made my heart burst.

"I know that my wife is unkind to you, Georgette," he said as I cleaned his study while he read.

"It's nothing to worry about," I assured him.

"She's jealous of you, you know?" he asked, closing his book.

"Jealous?" I asked with wide eyes.

"You're young and beautiful," he said matter-of-factly, straightening his pants leg. "And she knows that I'm aware of that. I'm a man, after all. Married, perhaps. But not dead."

He offered me a smirk.

I blushed furiously. Mr. Solomon is devastatingly handsome and for him to speak to me so openly felt like a slight against his wife. But I was happy to have it.

Mr. Solomon asked me to help him rearrange his books and so we spent the afternoon in such a fashion.

December 14, 1916

The tensions in the household are higher than ever. Mr. Solomon accused Hattie last night of seeing another man. She laughed at him. I could hear the entire thing from my room, only a few doors away from their chambers.

Doors were slammed. Shouting matches had.

The downstairs door slammed as well, one of them leaving the house.

And suddenly, there was a gentle knock on my door.

"Come in," I said.

Though I was only in my dressing

gown, something told me this was important.
That I shouldn't make the person on the
other side wait.

I gasped and clutched my covers close
to my neck when Mr. Solomon was the one
on the other side.

"Mr. Solomon!" I gasped.

"Andrew, please, Georgette."

He stepped into the room, closing the
door.

The inappropriateness of the position
he'd put me in rang clear as a bell in my
mind.

If Mrs. Solomon were ever to find
out, she'd die.

Or make sure that one of us did.

"What can I do for you?" I asked.

"Come here," he commanded, his voice
heavy.

"I'm undressed, sir," I said.

"I know," he said.

Something was in his eyes that I'd
never seen there before. Something I'd only
read about in novels. Novels too shameful
to ever let anyone know I'd read them.

I let the covers fall, standing up from the bed.

I felt the chill of the winter air permeate the house, making gooseflesh prickle my skin.

He reached for me in the darkness, his hands finding my upper arms.

And then, reader, I did something that can never be forgiven. Not by God or man.

I kissed Mr. Solomon.

I'm not sure if he leaned in first or if I did. I don't know anything other than it was wrong. Wrong. Wrong. Wrong.

And that I'm desperately in love with him.

THIRTY-FIVE

CASH FLIPS through the rest of the pages. They're blank.

"Fuck," he mutters.

I'm sitting so close to him, on the edge of my seat from what we've been reading, that I can feel the heat of his breath when he swears.

Cash closes the diary with a snap. He turns to face me and both of us realize exactly how close we are to each other. His eyes dart down to my mouth and quickly return to my eyes. I look away. He clears his throat and I scoot back into my corner of the couch, giving him space.

"So—"

"Well—"

We speak at the same time. Both of us stop awkwardly. I motion for him to go ahead.

"Well, I was just going to say that clearly, things weren't all sunshine and roses here a century ago."

"Clearly," I mutter.

"You know what..." Cash trails off. He stands from the couch faster than I can keep up with. He starts for the staircase.

"Where are you going?" I call.

I get up to follow him.

"Jean said she found this under the floorboard, right?" he asks over his shoulder, taking the stairs a couple at a time. I jog to keep up.

When we arrive on the landing, he looks back at me.

"Which room would have been hers?" he asks.

"That one, I think," I say, pointing at the room that Jean told me was hers as a girl.

Cash quickly enters the room. A room that I've used for makeshift storage of what I have left from my dad's office. He paces the floor, looking down at each board. He kneels. Knocks on several. He goes over the entire visible floor this way.

"Help me move that," he says, pointing at a filing cabinet in the corner.

I sigh, realizing that whenever this guy has an idea, there's no stopping him. He's like a dog with a bone. Good luck distracting him or getting him to forget his priorities.

I grunt as we move the heavy filing cabinet out of the corner. Immediately, Cash is on the floor.

And to my astonishment, when he knocks on the floorboard beneath the cabinet, it sounds hollow.

He looks up at me with a grin.

He reaches into the hollow bit of floor.

"Be careful," I advise him. "There was a raccoon living here not that long ago, and I imagine he had friends of all kinds."

"I've had rabies shots before," he says as he moves his arm around, searching below the floorboards. "Not a good time."

Finally, his face lights up. He's got something.

He pulls his arm out, now covered in dirt and dust. And in his hand is a large rusted ring with a key hanging from it. The key is rusted, too.

Cash turns it over in his hand.

"Any idea what this might be to?" he asks.

I reach out for the key, and he hands it to me. I roll it over in my own palm. Red rust pocks the surface. It's a skeleton key.

"I think I know what this goes to," I say.

Cash stands quickly.

"Really?" he asks breathlessly.

"Follow me," I say.

I FLIP the switch that lights the basement. I take the steps quickly, eager to get to the box.

Cash follows me as I snake around the embalming

tables and find the box that I found when I first moved in. The old wooden box sits just where I left it.

I take the key in my hand and put it to the padlock. Even with the rust and a century between them, they meet like two old lovers. A perfect match. And the padlock makes a clicking noise as it grudgingly gives to the key.

It comes open and I pull it from the box.

I look up at Cash. For encouragement, or something—I'm not entirely sure—but he nods, and that's enough for me. I crack the lid, letting the box yawn open wide.

Inside, a cloth seems to be wrapped around an object.

I reach into the box, gently grabbing the object wrapped in cloth. I take it out and sit down on the floor. Cash kneels beside me as I begin to unravel the wrappings.

Finally, the solid object inside reveals itself.

And when I unfurl the cloth completely, deep brown splotches color the cream cloth that's held the object for all these years. The object itself is stained with deep brown splotches, too.

"Is that a—" Cash wonders aloud.

"Rock," I finish for him.

"Jesus," he mutters.

The two of us sit there in the dim basement lighting, and I hold in my hand what I'm very concerned might have been used as a weapon.

"Hang on," Cash says.

He dashes upstairs, leaving me in the basement with the hefty rock and the unused embalming tables. I look over at one of them, seeing the hole where a drain used to be. It sends a shiver through me. And I can't help my poor brain for where it leaps.

The thought of death automatically brings me back to my dad.

And the implications of everything I'm living through.

That he might be out there somehow.

That there are things that I don't know anything about.

Things and beings.

A truth my father held as self-evident. A truth that I never, ever even gave half a chance in my mind.

"Here," Cash comes bouncing down the stairs. He holds a flashlight in his hands.

But when he turns it on, the light is bright blue. Like a forensic investigator's tool.

In his other hand is a tiny spray-bottle of something. Before I can object, Cash kneels beside me and squirts some of the mystery liquid onto the cloth and rock that I'm holding.

"Hey, isn't that a bad idea?" I ask.

He says nothing, completely engrossed in what he's doing.

After he sprays the liquid, he brings the blue light back over the cloth.

Every bit of the muddy brown stain lights up like a fucking Christmas tree.

I look at Cash.

He looks at me.

"I've watched enough Forensic Files to gather that you just sprayed luminol on this thing," I mutter.

Cash merely nods, still staring at the rock and the cloth it was contained in.

"Wait," I say. "How do you have luminol?"

"I'm good at making friends with the right people," Cash says.

I don't really want to push it further than that. It occurs to me that I never asked him what he gave his dad. Suddenly, I'm not sure that I want to know.

Apparently, Cash operates on the edge of propriety and potentially the law.

And my association with him has led to me holding a bloody hundred-year-old rock.

"What now?" I ask him.

But Cash's eyes are fixated somewhere else when I look at him. He's looking past me, past the rock, and down into the little wooden box I just opened. I slowly turn my head, matching his stare.

And looking back at me, illuminated in bright blue, written on the inside of the lid of the box is a sentence.

God forgive us.

"Blair," Cash says softly.

My heart is thundering in my chest. Somehow,

even with the players in this age-old mystery long dead, I feel like Cash and I aren't alone down here.

"Yeah?" I ask, almost breathless.

"Go get the diary."

I dash up the stairs, trying to take them quickly with my short legs. I stumble and scrape my palm as I do. I fumble back to my feet and up into the kitchen. I round the corner quickly and go to the living room where I find the diary just as we left it.

I grab it and head back to the kitchen. I jog down the stairs and find Cash looking the box over, presumably looking for more places where a message might be scrawled.

"Give me the diary," he says without looking up at me. He holds a hand out for it and I obey, handing it over quickly.

Cash puts his flashlight down for a moment and begins flipping the pages frantically. I'm not sure what he's looking for. I peer over his shoulder. Finally, he lands on the first blank page that we ran into when reading it earlier.

He grabs his blue light again and shines it on the page.

And just like that, the rest of the diary looks back at us in shining blue lettering.

"Invisible ink," Cash mutters.

"How did you know that?" I ask, partially in awe of his armchair detective skills and partially dreading what we're going to find in the rest of the diary.

"I've run into it a few times before," he says dismissively. Like it's the most normal thing in the world. Something about it makes me smirk. "Sometimes people used to use it on maps or letters when sensitive information was involved. Usually some acidic liquid, like lemon juice."

"Interesting work you must be doing," I mutter now.

"Sometimes a little too interesting," he says in return.

I sit down next to him, and we dive back in.

THIRTY-SIX

February 6, 1917

Andrew told me today that he loves me. That he is enamored of me. That he has never loved Hattie the way he loves me. But still, acting as her maid and watching the two of them take part in the daily rituals of a husband and wife—even a couple not in love—is more than I can bear.

I confessed as much to him this evening in the kitchen when he stepped inside from the patio.

Hattie was still out back with Andrew Jr., admiring the snow.

"I can't go on like this," I told him. "I have to leave you."

The look he gave me is one that will forever remain the most wounding glance any man has ever given me. The sorrow in his eyes at the thought of my departure was more than I could take. And even though the situation I find myself in is unbearable, his sorrow is worse.

The idea of leaving him here.

With her.

It's unthinkable.

So, I shall carry on as best I can until we find a solution.

April 23, 1917

Preparations for the annual Fourth of July party have already begun. Orders have been made to foreign countries for various bits and baubles that shall serve as decorations. Hattie is in good spirits and because of that has been nicer to me than she usually is.

That's a small mercy.

Although, I feel guilty every time she

speaks to me without a barbed tongue. I want to tell her that I deserve every slight she could deal me. That I am an adulterer. And so is her husband.

But my love for Andrew and hope for a different future stills my tongue and closes my throat tightly around the truth.

He told me that he has a plan. That he can get us out from under her. I have no idea what he has in mind, but I would do anything for him.

Anything.

June 1, 1917

Andrew had a doctor at the house yesterday. I've never heard his name before, but he was speaking to the man about Hattie. I overheard portions of the conversation. Most of it was just Andrew telling the doctor all the ways in which Hattie is difficult. Her mood swings. Her inability to be faithful. Her lack of maternal instinct.

I listened as the doctor told him it could be taken care of.

A simple procedure. Quite groundbreaking.

"She won't feel a thing," he said.

The words echoed in my mind as I went to bed last night.

June 20, 1917

Andrew has returned from the doctor with Hattie finally. She was taken two weeks ago to undergo this procedure. Though I'm not sure that's where Hattie believed she was going. As I packed for her, she told me that she was eager to see her sister for a few weeks.

She had no idea what waited for her outside the walls of this house.

When Hattie returned, she was markedly different.

Different in such a way that I feel like I might die of guilt.

She cannot walk. She cannot speak.

She has been rendered a child without

the ability to communicate or care for her own needs.

She has been stripped of dignity.

And a sense of dread is mounting in my stomach because Andrew told me that we must have the party, anyway. In Hattie's honor.

But I'm not sure it's a good idea.

July 5, 1917

It is done.

Mr. Solomon came to me before the party yesterday morning.

"She just needs to have an accident, Georgette."

The words came out of his mouth with a silkiness I never imagined a man could use to talk about his own wife's death. Her premeditated murder, to be precisely. My heart beat in the cage, my ribs held it in. I felt like it might fly away.

Different emotions mingled there.

Terror. Revulsion. Anger.

But bubbling beneath all of them was

the single most dangerous emotion a woman can feel.

Hope.

"Just a small push," he said.

And so I waited. I waited until Andrew brought her out to the patio to watch the fireworks display. Everyone else was around the front, watching from the yard. I brought her to the edge of the pool. That beautiful, pristine pool that I longed to swim in every time I passed it on summer nights.

I wheeled her to the edge.

She grunted. Some sort of recognition of what was happening.

No. God, no.

I prayed she had no idea what we were doing to her.

I waited for the biggest firework to blast into the sky. A huge echoing boom.

I pushed her. Wheelchair and all. She tumbled effortlessly into the pool. Her arms and legs moved slightly as I watched her drown.

"Mama?" Little Andrew's voice came out of nowhere.

I jumped like a ghost had snuck up on me.

"Oh, Andrew," I said.

"You hurt mama," he said. He stumbled backward.

The fireworks boomed overhead.

I reached for him. I only meant to hold him. To comfort him.

I grabbed him tightly, holding his face to my chest. Pressing him hard against my breast.

Until he quit moving.

I sobbed and let him fall in after her.

A whining growl came from behind me.

That damnable dog. Loyal to the last.

"Please, Duke, don't," I begged. I couldn't take anymore.

I couldn't kill anymore.

Just then, I heard a little cry from the house. I spun to see a small child running indoors. I prayed they had not seen everything.

Just then, Duke lunged. I grabbed a

stone from the garden next to me and I brought it home to his skull with a crunch. He yelped. He fell in as well.

The fireworks continued.

I sobbed.

I had done what was asked of me and I felt empty.

I still do.

I have no idea what to say other than I hope that God's mercy is infinite. I confess my sins here and I can only pray that I shall be absolved. For the only crime I committed at the beginning of this was falling in love with someone who did not belong to me.

To whoever shall find this: you are my witness.

And I assure you, my witness, that I shall never know peace. And that is my cross.

THIRTY-SEVEN

I HANG on every word of the diary. When Cash closes it and flips the light off, I crumple in a heap next to him, my body running out of adrenaline to dump into my veins.

"We just read a murder confession," I say, barely able to form the words.

"We did," Cash mutters. He seems equally spent.

"So, Andrew Solomon got his mistress to do his dirty work for him," I say.

"Disgusting," Cash says, his voice full of revulsion. He tosses the book into the chest. "According to other accounts I read, they thought Duke had injured himself by jumping into the pool. That he hit his head in a frantic attempt to save the person he cared about more than anything in this world."

"I'd like to think if I had a dog, he'd try to avenge my death, too," I say.

"Most dogs would," Cash says. "Cats, on the other hand. They'll just wait for you to die and then eat you. Eyeballs first."

"Is that true?"

"I have no idea. I just know they eat their dead owners if given half a chance."

"What do we do with all of this?" I ask him.

"Crazy isn't it?" Cash asks, not answering my question.

"What?" I ask him.

He scoots over to where his back is against the wall of the basement.

"How a creature can love someone unconditionally, even if that person isn't the best person in the world. To that dog, she was," he says.

"She might not have been faithful or have wanted to be a mother, but in that dream I had—that vision—she looked at little Andrew with love in her eyes."

"How much of the perception that she was a bad mother do you think was skewed by Mr. Solomon?" Cash asks. "Georgette was young. Barely twenty-one. Young enough to be snowed by a predatory millionaire, certainly."

I hadn't thought of it that way.

But the visions I had of Hattie didn't match with some of the things her husband and her former maid said about her.

"Dogs are generally right about people," Cash says.

He looks over at me.

"Why don't you have a dog, Blair?" he asks.

"My dad never wanted us to have dogs when we were kids because he didn't want another thing to take care of," I say, echoing what I told him earlier about my dogless situation. "But I guess, as an adult, I just never really thought about having one."

He seems to be digesting that.

"What about you?" I ask.

"I've never really been settled down enough to have a dog. But someday, you know? I think some people think settling down will mean a white picket fence, a wife, two-and-a-half kids. The works. But for me, I just want a dog. A lazy dog that doesn't like to do much more than sit on the couch and watch the backs of its eyelids."

"That sounds awfully nice," I remark.

It's strange. The two of us sitting down here in silence, absorbing what we've just borne witness to. A murder confession. A very tangled murder, at that.

Finally, I get up.

"Let's go back upstairs," I tell him.

I offer my hand and he takes it, standing from his spot on the floor.

"Leave all that. I'll deal with it later," I tell him, gesturing at the box and the rock.

He glances back at it.

"It hasn't gone anywhere in a hundred years, so I

imagine it'll still be there when I feel like dealing with it."

He seems happy with that explanation.

And we go upstairs.

———

ONCE THERE, I take up my spot on the couch. I'm sleepy and it's almost midnight.

Cash takes the spot next to me, sitting probably closer than absolutely necessary.

I don't mind though.

I don't mind being around him.

I stare at him as he pulls out his phone. I wonder if he's checking to see if his dad needs anything. I think about going with him downtown and seeing that. Seeing his father—a man I'm sure he looked up to at some point—reduced to begging his son for help. And then treating his son like an afterthought once he gets what he wants from him.

He finally puts his phone away.

"What did you give your dad the other night?" I ask him.

Cash tosses his head back in exasperation.

He brings it back to the center and looks at me. His face is tired. His eyes are sleepy.

"I don't want you to think less of me," he says quietly.

The words are barely a whisper. And they surprise me. Who knew that Cash Kelly could care what anyone thought of him?

"I won't," I promise him. I hope he hears the earnestness in my voice. "If my dad was here—or there —I'd take him anything just to get to talk to him again," I admit, the words coming out in a rush. The most I've spoken aloud about the pain I feel. Especially around Cash.

"I took him a bottle," he says.

I wait for him to elaborate, though I don't really need him to. But I want him to keep talking to me. I want this feeling of closeness to stay.

"Vodka," he says.

"Are they allowed to have liquor in the Jesus House?" I ask stupidly.

"My guess is going to be a hard no," Cash responds with a little laugh. "But he's good at hiding his addiction," he says. His voice grows somber. "Really good."

He sighs, as if thinking of something far away.

We sit there in companionable silence for a few moments. I feel myself getting more and more drowsy.

"Is it okay if I make a fire?" Cash asks.

He points at the unlit fireplace.

"Go for it," I say.

He busies himself, and I watch him.

There's something blissfully normal and domestic about the scene unfolding before my eyes. A handsome man in my house building me a fire. If someone were just looking in on this split second of my life, they'd think I had it all.

A beautiful old house. A handsome man. Money to spare.

They wouldn't know about the bloody rock used to bludgeon a dog to death in the basement.

Or the murder confession the two of us just read.

No. They wouldn't see any of that.

And I guess that's how it is for everyone. No one's life is perfect, even if it seems so in a snapshot sent out into the ether on Facebook.

Sometimes the mess goes deep. Snarling roots locked in at the base of your existence.

But for just a moment, I pretend that this little snapshot is my life.

And that's enough.

I WAKE, not to the sound of an animal chuffing at me, but to the sound of a dying fire.

I slowly open my eyes. I realize there's a blanket covering me. That I'm sitting up, leaning against Cash, and his arm is wrapped loosely around me. He's snoring lightly.

The fire is burning just embers now. An orange glow fans out across the flooring. I lean back into Cash, into the warmth of his body. Solid, strong, huge. And I place my head against his chest. I hear the sound of his heart beating.

Thud, thud, thud.

Slow. Peaceful. Easy.

The way everyone's hearts should always beat.

I begin to sink back into sleep, and then a sound startles me.

My eyes shoot open. I hear it again. Sharp. Loud.

A bark.

A dog's bark in the night.

Outside.

"Cash," I shake him gently, my hand on his chest. I force myself to sit up.

"Huh?" he jerks awake. He realizes how close we are and pushes himself up to a sitting position. "What is it?"

"Do you hear that?" I ask him.

Both of us quiet ourselves. We still our movements, straining our ears.

Woof!

The loud bark sounds again.

"That!" I say.

Cash stands immediately, having heard the same thing I did.

"Come on," he says.

I follow him to the backdoor. He glances quickly out the window and then throws it open.

The pool is full. I'd forgotten it entirely. Unnecessary in the long run.

But when we step out onto the patio, something happens. A glimmering shift in reality.

And it's a summer's day.

I feel the heat of the sun on my skin. I see the light glinting off the rippling water that fills the pool.

I hear that laugh. High, musical.

Duke nearly makes me jump out of my skin as he races past us. A ball flies through the air, over the pool. He jumps, seizing it in mid-air. Then crashes down into the water, sending it flying everywhere. When he pops back up, swimming for the shallow end, the ball is clutched tightly in his mouth. He gets out and runs back over to us. He drops the ball at Cash's feet.

He sits, happily panting at the two of us.

Duke is solid as a rock. As clear as day. I realize, when a figure walks right through me, that it's myself and Cash that are the specters in this scene. We're merely observing.

In a bathing suit appropriate for the times, Mrs. Hattie Solomon stoops down and grabs the ball. She tosses it again for Duke. He races for the pool again, making a gallant leap into the air to catch his prize.

"Mama!" I hear a voice. Not a toddler. A young man. A boy of about ten.

She looks over, and we follow her line of sight.

"Come here, Andy," she says.

Little Andrew. All grown up.

I look at Cash, but he's glued to the scene playing out in front of us.

"Toss it for him," Hattie says when Duke returns once more with the ball.

Ten-year-old Andrew tosses the ball. Duke once again goes after it, having the time of his life.

I'm puzzled by what I'm seeing.

Mrs. Solomon—Hattie—with her son. Both are well. Duke is there, too. Mr. Solomon and Georgette are nowhere to be found. Is this what might have been?

And at that moment, as I wonder what it is that I'm seeing, she turns as if she heard something. Her eyes look straight through Cash. She glances around, trying to find the source of the stimuli that caused her to turn away from her son and her dog.

And then, briefly, her eyes meet mine.

A calmness settles over her. I don't know if she sees me. I don't know if I even really see her or if this is some shared delusion Cash and I are experiencing. But at that moment, I swear to God that Hattie Solomon smiles at me.

A stiff winter wind blows the vision away, particle by particle until it's drifting up into the night sky like snowflakes. Cash and I are left standing on the patio, staring out at the pool, now full.

A shiver runs up my arm.

"Did you—" I start to ask. I don't know a lot about Cash Kelly or what kind of person he is. All I have to go on is what I've learned in the last few weeks.

"I saw it," he says.

But these things I've learned and the person I believe him to be are good. Good.

Maybe he's not like the others.

That thought dances through my mind.

And then he looks at me.

He smiles. And it feels safe.

THIRTY-EIGHT

"THANK YOU, OFFICER," Cash scribbles something on a piece of paper. Then he hangs up his cell phone. "Jesus Christ, they're useless."

"What's prompted this vote of confidence in the police force?" I ask.

Dawn is breaking, and Cash turned off the hose to the pool. Back inside, we decide to call the police about the rock and the diary.

"I don't really know how to put it other than I don't think they give too many shits about it," he says.

"What kind of cop doesn't want to solve a high society murder from a century ago?" I ask half-sarcastically.

"According to them, there was no murder. No evidence of there ever being a murder. And I don't know if you're aware of this, but Georgette and Andrew apparently propagated a whole line of

Solomons that live in Missouri now who seem to be extremely wealthy and not the kind of people who want the police digging into their family history." He finishes and takes a deep breath.

"So that's that, I guess," I say.

"Not quite," he says. "I got someone's number from the cop I talked to on the phone. So even though the police in Missouri aren't exactly faunching at the bit to pin a century-old murder on a rich-ass family, there is someone who would be more than happy to do that," he hands me the piece of paper he scribbled on.

I look at the name and number written on the piece of paper.

"Who is Nancy Miller?" I ask.

"Nancy Miller happens to be running for political office in Missouri," Cash says.

"What the hell does that have to do with anything?" I ask.

"She happens to be running against Andrew Solomon the fifteenth or fourth. Third? I'm not sure. Anyway, she's running against the original cocksucker's offspring."

"Could this help her?" I ask.

"Well, considering he's a direct descendant running on the platform of family values and he got caught having an affair recently on top of the fact that his great-great-great-grandaddy was basically a Charles Manson-type child-murderer," Cash bounces his head from side to side like he's calculating something. "I think it might be something she'd be interested in."

"Did the cop give you the info?" I ask, surprised.

"Turns out he and Andy the fifteenth went to high school together and old Andy stole the cop's girlfriend a week before prom," Cash says. "So, tonight, we count our blessings and be thankful that people have extraordinary capabilities when it comes to pettiness."

I smile at his words.

He smiles back at me.

"It's not much, but..." I start to trail off. Almost thinking better of what I'm about to say to him. "Do you think that somewhere—wherever she is—Hattie's happy about this?"

"I think you already know the answer to that," Cash says.

"I guess you'd better call Nancy, then," I tell him.

"I guess so," he says with a smirk.

***

AS CASH STARTS TEARING down his equipment in my dining room, I'm overcome by a feeling of loss. Also, the thought that I should tell him not to go occurs to me. Or that I should make some desperate beg for him to return under false pretenses.

I bite my tongue, though. He's already done enough for me.

I've made it through one night without any

unwanted dreams, vivid nightmares, or terrifying visions. And that seems to be proof enough for me that he did his job, and he did it well.

I watch him in his gray t-shirt and jeans, wondering what it would be like if he stayed.

It's an absurd thought.

Likely, what I feel for him is a transference of all the emotions I want to lay at my dad's feet, combined with gratitude to Cash for helping me out. And I've never known a man good at keeping his word.

Cash works methodically, boxing everything up in the cases he brought in at the beginning of this.

I stand in the doorway, having been instructed that he didn't need help and that tearing down was a more meticulous process than setting up. I was promptly dismissed.

"So, what's next for you?" I ask him.

He pauses as he's rolling cable.

"I have no idea," he says.

"I'm sorry we didn't get anything on camera," I admit. "I remember you saying a full-bodied apparition is the Holy Grail."

Cash seems to roll that over in his mind for a moment or two.

"It would kind of take the fun out of it, don't you think?" he asks. He looks up at me, a smirk on his face. "I mean, I'd have put myself out of a job."

I smile back at him.

"I guess that's the hazard you face in your particular occupation," I say.

"I bet your dad would have some thoughts about it," he says with a chuckle under his breath.

My heart hurts when he does that. When he talks about my dad so casually. The way that someone who is a permanent fixture in my life might talk about him.

"You ever find yourself wondering about stuff like that?" he asks me.

He keeps working on the teardown, moving on to the computer monitors.

"About what?" I ask.

"What your dad might think of this or that," he says.

"All the time," I admit. "Sometimes I just wish I could ask him how to change a tire."

"He never taught you?" Cash asks. He looks up from what he's doing.

"He didn't have time for stuff like that," I say.

Cash puts the monitor into its case and stands up.

"Come on," he says.

He heads out of the dining room, brushing past me in the doorframe.

"Where are we going?" I ask. "Don't you need to finish this?"

"It's not going anywhere," he says. "And I am about to teach you how to change a tire."

I stare at him, dumbfounded.

"Don't just stand there," he says. "Come on."

He heads for the front door.

"You really don't have—"

"I can't leave this house with a clear conscience if I don't," he says over his shoulder.

"It's not a big deal."

He turns and I run into him. I step back, flustered.

"How will I feel about myself when, months from now, I see a news story where some poor brown-haired, blue-eyed girl got dismembered by a long-haul truck-driving serial killer? All because she didn't know how to change her own flat tire," he looks off into the distance wistfully. "Tragic. And I'll feel terrible."

"So, this has less to do with me getting murdered and more to do with how you'll sleep at night after the fact?" I tease.

"Precisely. If you know how to change a tire and still end up in a ditch outside of a T&A truck stop, that's on you."

"Fine," I say. "Let's get this over with."

He winks at me, and I grab my jacket, following him outside.

"OKAY, so most cars—especially newer ones like yours —come with all the stuff you need. You can buy a few other items that make it slightly easier, but in a pinch, you're good with what came with the car," Cash says as he roots around in the back of my car. Finally, he upends the floorboard and reveals not only a spare tire but the tire tool as well.

I nod, standing next to him, surveying his handiwork.

"So, first things first," he says. "I would advise you to never stop on the side of the road. It's way better to find a safe place like a gas station or any other parking lot that's well-lit, if it's nighttime. Basically, pulling over on the side of the highway is a good way to get—"

"Abducted by a long-haul trucker?" I finish for him.

"I was going to say 'smashed like a bug into the grill of a Mac truck,' but suit yourself," he says.

"Ah, another legitimate threat," I remark.

"Anyway," he plows forward, gathering the cross-shaped wrench, a jack, and the spare tire all at once in his giant arms. He puts them all next to the rear driver's side tire. "Put your parking brake on. Also, your hazard lights."

"Do I really need to do that right now?" I ask.

"We're doing a drill, Blair," he says so seriously that it makes me smirk at him.

"Okay, fine," I hold my hands up and quickly busy myself in the driver's seat, turning on my hazard lights and activating the parking brake. I get back out. He's standing next to the tire.

"First, we're going to loosen the lug nuts," he says.

I nod as he hands me the cross-shaped wrench.

"Give it a try," he says.

I fumble with the wrench and struggle to get the lug nuts loosened.

"Here," he says.

He uses all his strength and the lug nuts come loose instantly. I try not to stare at his biceps.

"Now, we jack it up," he says after they're sufficiently loose.

He hands me the jack.

"What do I do with this?" I ask.

"Put it there," he instructs me. I follow his directions, placing the jack under the frame of the car in front of the pretend flat tire. He helps me jack the car up.

"Now," he goes on to instruct me to remove the lug nuts and I struggle to get the tire off the wheel. Finally, I drop it with a grunt onto the ground. He helps me place the spare tire onto my car and instructs me to tighten the lug nuts by hand before we let the car back down. Once on the ground, he helps me tighten them again with the wrench.

Cash laughs to himself.

"Good job," he says.

He reaches out and sweeps me into a sideways hug. My body stiffens instinctively, but the feeling of his broad chest against my shoulder softens my posture almost instantly.

"Thank you," I say.

"Everyone should know how to do that," he mutters. He lets go of me and clears his throat. "I'll put the real tire back on," he says, clearing his throat again. He doesn't look at me. "Go back inside."

I head back to the house and once I reach the porch, I turn around.

"Cash," I say, my voice carrying across the empty front yard.

He turns to look at me.

"Thank you," I say again.

We stand, both of us staring at the other.

Finally, he speaks.

"Anytime," he says.

THIRTY-NINE

THE HOUSE IS REMARKABLY QUIET.

The next couple of weeks come and go. Noelle and Hooper have become inseparable, and I'm glad for them. Especially glad for her. Glad that she gave him a chance.

I'm walking around the house one Saturday morning with a cup of coffee in hand. My sleep has returned to normal, and I don't wake up to the sounds of a dog's heavy breathing into the shell of my ear. Which is something that I think ninety-nine percent of people would agree is a very, very big improvement to my situation.

And still, somehow, I miss it.

I miss Duke.

Every morning I go out onto the second story landing and admire the portrait Hattie had made of him. A truly faithful companion. Sometimes I wonder just how alone and alienated she felt in her own home. And that leads me to think about every other woman in her position who likely felt the same way.

The heavy introspection leads me to grab my cell phone.

I want to call Cash; I realize it almost instantly when I pick it up.

What the hell for?

What would I say?

He helped me out so much and asking him to hang out would be idiotic. It would be asking way too much and pushing the boundary of our professional relationship.

In the last couple of weeks, he's checked on me a few times. He's sent memes, which leads me to believe he wanted to talk but didn't have anything specific to say.

But I'm far past analyzing what men mean through the written word.

If he wanted to hang out, he'd call.

My empty days and nights have led to a lot of thought about how I want to spend those days and nights going forward. I've piddled around so long just existing, using my dad's money to eke out something that can't really be called anything more than an existence. It's not a life.

And I need one.

But instead of trying to figure out just how I'm

going to go about creating one of those for myself, tonight I just want the company of my best friend.

And her boyfriend.

I smirk, realizing that Hooper won't want to miss out on whatever it is that we decide to do. There's something charming about it. He enjoys both of us as company. It's unusual, to say the least.

So I pick up the phone and call Noelle.

SHE AND HOOPER arrive in the evening. A flurry of snow follows them in. A post-Christmas semi-blizzard has plagued Oklahoma for the last few days. But it doesn't deter either of them from wanting to get out of the house. Plus, Hooper, like almost all men in Oklahoma, drives a truck that isn't intimidated by things like the weather.

Although, it's usually the guys who drive trucks that aren't deterred by the weather that end up driving into moving water in the spring and get made fun of big-time on the evening news.

That's a real thing. Our meteorologists make fun of them. There's very little patience extended in their cases. But I highly doubt—as cautiously as he approaches life—that Hooper would ever drive into moving water.

Cash, on the other hand...

"It's so good to see you!" Noelle squeals as she

wraps me in a tight hug. Cold flakes of snow stuck to the hood of her parka coat meet my cheek.

"Likewise," I say softly.

"Hey, Hooper," I greet him while still in Noelle's embrace. He raises a friendly wave in greeting.

"Hey, Blair," he says. "Mind if I help myself?" he gestures towards the kitchen.

I can't help but think of Cash. The way he let himself into the house like he belonged here. The confidence with which he wandered around my home. I smile slightly as Noelle and I pull away from each other.

"Knock yourself out," I tell Hooper. "Y'all get a drink."

The three of us go to the kitchen and Hooper grabs a beer. I get two hard seltzers for me and Noelle.

We head back to the living room.

"I see you put a television in here," Hooper remarks.

"That I did," I admit.

There's now an entertainment center situated in the living room, juxtaposed with the antique furniture and throwbacks from yesteryear.

Hooper grabs the remote and settles into one of the big chairs. Noelle curls up next to me on the couch.

"So," she says after taking a sip of her drink. "What ended up happening with that guy?"

"What guy?"

She rolls her eyes.

"Cash Kelly," she says, exasperated. "Weren't you guys spending a lot of time together working on a story for his channel or something?"

"Not exactly," I admit.

"What was he doing here?" she asks.

I hem and haw around the answer.

"It was nothing," I try to finish my incoherent rambling about what Cash was or wasn't doing here.

"Blair," Noelle touches my arm. "I've known you longer than anyone except your stupid brother."

I nod. She has a point. And he is stupid.

"I can tell when you're full of shit."

"You always had a gift for that," I mutter.

"What were you guys doing?" she prods.

"Okay, you're going to think I'm crazy," I tell her. I glance over at Hooper to make sure he's sufficiently engrossed in whatever he found to watch on the television. I look back at Noelle. "This is an old house, right?"

She looks around, then back at me.

"Yeah?" she says, her voice toning upward.

"Well, you know, sometimes old houses make weird noises and stuff like that, right?" I fiddle with a fraying stitch on the couch cushion beside me.

"Blair." She cocks her head to the side.

"Just let me finish," I say. "If I don't, I won't ever say it out loud."

"Oh, my God," Blair says, clapping a hand to her mouth.

"Hush," I gesture over at Hooper.

She looks at him and back at me, composing herself, realizing I don't want him to hear everything I'm about to tell her.

"Well, some weird shit was happening. Right around the time he asked to interview me. He ended up helping me check it all out," I say.

"He investigated your house for...?" She really wants me to spell it the fuck out.

"Anything...unusual," I say.

"Blair," she says. "'Ghosts' isn't a dirty word."

I sigh, not wanting to go down this road but realizing I've already bought a one-way ticket.

"Okay." I take a deep breath. "He was looking for ghosts."

Noelle smirks at me with a look fitting for a cat who ate the canary.

"Oh?" she asks casually. Like she's not relishing every minute of this.

"I don't want to talk any more about it," I tell her.

"Is he going to investigate your vagina for ghosts, because I imagine there are cobwebs up there with how long it's be—"

"Jesus Christ, Noelle!" I flush without any say in the matter. My cheeks turn red. I can feel the heat in the flesh that covers my collarbone.

"You do like him!" she squeals.

"Okay, you can leave right now," I say with a laugh.

"Why would I leave now that I'm all warm and

fuzzy inside about Blair Graves falling in love," she says with a giggle.

"No one is falling in love," I tell her firmly.

She glances back at Hooper.

"You will, Blair," she says softly when she looks back at me. "You will."

I shake my head.

"Let's just watch television with Hooper. He knows how to be quiet," I say.

She smirks into the can she's drinking out of.

"Fine," she says after a sip. "Whatever you say."

FORTY

IT'S LATER that week when my phone starts ringing off the hook. I'm in the shower when it starts.

"Just a minute!" I shout, rinsing the conditioner out of my hair.

But whoever's on the other end doesn't have the patience to wait until I'm done. The phone continues to ring. Finally, when I grab it with wet hands, fresh out of the shower, I see five missed calls from none other than Cash Kelly.

And I hate the way it makes my chest swell.

I call him back before I even put my hair up in a clip. Standing in nothing but a towel in my steamy bathroom, I listen to it ring. And it only rings once before he picks up.

"Blair," he says, almost breathless.

"What's up?" I ask, trying to sound casual.

"I'm coming over tonight. Clear your schedule. I

think there's something you're going to want to see," he says.

My brain races, trying to figure out if I have anything on my schedule to clear. Of course, I don't.

"Okay," I say. "What's going on?"

"Just trust me," he says.

"Okay," I say.

It wouldn't be the first time I put my faith in his hands.

"I'll see you tonight," he says.

Before I can agree to that, he hangs up. Gone just like that.

I bring the phone away from my face and stare at it, unsure of what's happening or what the hell this is about.

I look at myself in the foggy mirror. I wipe a streak to see my face.

"I guess you'll find out," I say to myself.

I FIND myself preparing an unusual amount for Cash's arrival. Trying to arrange things perfectly. Things that I haven't cared about before. I make sure there's coffee in the pot before he arrives. Then, right after sunset, I see those headlights pulling down my drive.

There's something in the sight that's so familiar and comforting.

A reminder of the weeks we spent trying to figure out what was going on inside this house.

My mouth feels dry as I see him approach the porch.

And then he does something I don't expect.

He knocks.

I chuckle and step out to the front door and open it for him.

"That's not your usual modus operandi," I remark.

Something is different. His hair looks like he put product in it rather than letting it be charmingly messy. He's also clean-shaven. And smells like heaven.

He clears his throat.

"There's a first time for everything," he says.

"I mean, I think you knocked the very first time," I say.

"Are we going to make an oral history of how many times I've entered your house without knocking, or are you going to let me in?" he asks with a snarky smile.

"That's entirely up to you," I tell him. But I step aside, and he walks into the house. He doesn't have his messenger bag, so I'm not entirely sure what he thinks he's going to show me.

He makes for the couch and grabs the remote, plopping down in the center of the couch, leaving me only one side or the other.

"Come here," he says.

He's already surfing through the offerings on my smart TV and settles on YouTube.

"What are we watching?" I ask.

"Sit down," he says.

I do as he says, taking my usual spot on the far end, next to him.

He navigates us to Nancy Miller's YouTube channel. The woman running against the Solomon guy in Missouri.

"What's going on?" I ask him.

"Well, let's just say that I've been on the phone with Nancy Miller a lot in the last couple of weeks," he says, smirking at me.

My eyes light up, eager to hear more.

"And apparently, Miss Miller is making a press conference tonight," he says.

"And it'll be live?" I ask.

"In living color, too," he says. "In about fifteen minutes, according to the timer here." He gestures at the television, and I look up to see the countdown to the live stream.

"I'm going to make popcorn," I say, and head for the kitchen.

I HEAD BACK to the living room and hand Cash the giant bowl of popcorn.

"Butter on top, just like the movie theater," he says, grabbing a handful and popping it into his mouth.

"I went all out," I say. "Microwaved the butter and everything."

"Let it never be said that you weren't domestic," Cash smirks.

I sit back down beside him. A few minutes remain before the live stream starts.

"Blair," Cash says after several more handfuls of popcorn.

"Hmm?" I ask in between bites.

"We made a good team, didn't we?" he asks.

I'm a little taken aback by the question. It's not what I was expecting.

I swallow and wipe my buttery fingers on my jeans.

"I mean—" I start.

"We did," he says conclusively. Then a little less sure, "Didn't we?"

"Yeah," I say. "I've never been great at teamwork, but yes. We made a great team, Cash."

I look over at him, and he's already looking at me. There's something soft in his eyes. The guard that's so often standing up in front of them has vanished. There's a vulnerability in the way he's looking at me that renders me entirely speechless. My heart thuds in my chest. My throat closes around any words I might offer.

Cash, without taking his eyes off me, put the popcorn bowl on the coffee table.

I inhale sharply. He leans close.

"Thank you all for waiting patiently for this press conference," a voice breaks into the moment. Cash swings his head to face the television. I do the same and suddenly want to curse Nancy Miller.

She stands front and center behind a podium, a slew of reporters eager for the bomb she's intending to drop, though most of them probably have zero idea what it has to do with.

My heart rate returns to normal as we watch the introductory remarks. She really knows how to draw this out and build tension.

"Here it is," I say, breathless, still reeling from whatever almost passed between us.

He clears his throat.

We both focus on the television.

"As many of you know, my opponent comes from a long line of wealthy and privileged individuals. You're also aware that he was caught having an affair this year. What you might not be aware of is the fact that less-than-upstanding behavior runs in his family. It has come to my attention recently that a very, very cold case surrounding the Solomon family has garnered some interest."

"I mean, technically, it's not a cold case," I mutter.

Cash shushes me.

Nancy Miller plows onward, outlining the murder that Cash and I bore witness to. She points out that the Solomon family has been less than forthcoming about a potential murder a century ago. She draws parallels between today and yesteryear. She expertly sews doubt into the integrity of the Solomon campaign for reelection. It's masterful. Watching this politician turn this into what very well may become the issue on which Solomon's reelection hinges is riveting.

"Wow," I mutter as she finishes.

"Wow, indeed," Cash remarks. "Remind me to never run for office."

"Why?" I ask as the feed cuts and YouTube starts playing random videos. "Have you got skeletons in your closet you don't want anyone to know about?"

"I feel like if I ran for office, I'd find out about skeletons I didn't even know were there," he says with a smirk.

"That was something," I say, referencing Nancy Miller's presentation. "Crazy how something like that could make the difference to her."

"Is it, though?" Cash asks.

"What do you mean?"

"People love a show," he says. "And that was a show. Eyes will be glued to her for her next move and eyes will be glued to Solomon, investigating the alleged affair. She's brilliant."

The way he talks about it, it reminds me of the fact that his livelihood is content creation.

"Are you one of those people that views everything you do as content?" I ask him.

I'm genuinely curious. Also, I still wonder if he

plans on doing anything with any of the stuff he got from our little project.

"Hell no," he says. There's disgust in his voice when he says it.

I'm a little surprised. When he looks at me, I think he sees that, because he elaborates.

"Some things are content, sure. B-roll, that sort of stuff. You can get that anytime, anywhere. But there are other things that aren't content. Things that are just for me."

He looks at me then.

I feel my heart thundering in my chest again.

"I didn't just come here to show you the press conference," he says.

I inhale, barely able to move and hating myself deeply for how I'm feeling.

Cash inhales deeply, like he's weighing what he's about to say.

I hold my breath.

"Remember when I said we make a good team?" he asks.

I nod, wordlessly.

"Well," he goes on. I can tell he's nervous. He wipes his palms on his jeans. "I was just wondering if, maybe, you know..." he clears his throat. "If you're not busy...maybe we could...do it again?"

His eyebrows go up. I see hope etched on his features.

A smile breaks across my face.

"Investigate another haunted house?" I ask.

"Not necessarily a haunted house," he says. "I mean—you know how I said I didn't know what was next for me?"

I nod.

"Well, I'm still not sure. But I did get an e-mail today about something that might be it. And I just wondered if maybe you'd want to help me out." He says it all quickly, then looks at me expectantly for an answer.

"What was the e-mail about?" I ask. "Am I going to regret this?"

"Almost certainly you will regret it. Every day. For the foreseeable future," he says. "And the e-mail," he clears his throat. I can tell this is going to be good. "There are a ton of Bigfoot sightings down in southeastern Oklahoma."

I bark out a laugh.

"I know how it sounds." Cash turns toward me on the couch, speaking with his hands, eager to get me on board. "But I've dealt with these people before. They're not attention seekers. At least most of them aren't. They're as level-headed as I am."

"That's saying a lot," I snark, leaning my head on my fist as I rest my arm on the back of the couch, facing him and enjoying every moment of this.

"Okay, maybe not the best way to qualify his credentials," he says.

"Almost certainly not," I correct.

"There's also a festival," he says.

"A festival?" I raise my eyebrows.

He clears his throat.

"A Bigfoot festival," he says.

I smirk.

"There will be a lot of good speakers there. It's not as weird as it sounds," he says, trying to reassure me.

"Weird?" I ask. "I'd never have conjured that word to mind when talking about a subject as serious as this one."

He reaches a point of exasperation with me.

"Look," he says. "What I'm trying to ask you is, do you want to go with me?"

"In what capacity?" I ask. "Am I an investigator?"

"In whatever capacity you want," Cash says. "Helping me make content, interviewing people, the whole thing. Or however little you want to be involved. I just—I want you to go with me."

There's something incredibly vulnerable about what he's asking me. Something swells in my chest. A dangerous thing that I try not to let myself feel too much of.

Hope.

"And you're welcome as long as you want to be," he goes on. "Or until you get tired of me."

"In that case, we'd better take two vehicles, because I'm pretty sure I'll be tired of you within the first two hours," I say.

"Do you want to go or not?" he asks.

I can't deny how much I'm enjoying watching him squirm. Seeing Cash Kelly thrown slightly off his game is probably my new favorite thing.

"I cannot believe what I'm about to say, but..." I inhale deeply. "Yes. I will go with you to investigate Bigfoot."

"And to a festival," he adds.

"And that," I agree.

"Good," he concludes. "Good."

"Good," I repeat. "That's that."

We sit there in silence for a few moments. The television plays in the background. Cash finally clears his throat and reaches for the remote.

"You want to watch something?" he asks.

"Sure," I say, nonchalantly as possible. Not like someone who desperately wants him to stay.

But when he surfs over to Netflix and chooses a four-part series about alien life forms on other planets, I smile to myself.

"You up for a binge-watch?" he asks. He looks over at me, that easy, charming smile on his face.

"Why not?" I ask. "Although I get to pick the subject next time."

"Fair enough," he says. "After deciding that ghosts are real, it's probably a stretch for me to want you to get on board with aliens just yet."

"Ever," I correct. "Ever."

He smiles at me.

"Do you believe in aliens?" I ask.

"I wouldn't want to scare you off," he says.

"Oh, Jesus," I mutter. "Have you been abducted?" I tease.

"Just the once. But when the alien queen discovered how high-maintenance I was, she sent me back to earth where I could find an earth woman who might put up with me."

"Is that so?" I ask. "I'm not sure she realized that earth women don't want to put up with your shit, either."

"Okay, now you have to be quiet," he says as the series credits end and the first episode of the documentary begins.

I smile to myself, sitting there with him. I'm glad he put on the series, even if the subject matter isn't my favorite or first choice. It's four hours long, and that makes me happy.

Because it means I'm not the only one who wants him to stay.

JOIN MY NEWSLETTER

Sign up now and get a free horror novella, The Body Snatchers. You'll also get updates, freebies, news about me and my dogs, plus book discounts and sales!

Sign up here:

https://BookHip.com/PZGBMZT

ALSO BY MARNIE VINGE

SHOP NOW

www.marniewritesthrillers.com

Psychological Thrillers

The Getaway

Swingers

For Rosie

I Remember Everything

Cold Blood

Women's Thrillers

The Way It Ends

What We Did That Night

Manspreader

The Blair Graves Files

The Haunting of Solomon House

The Holloway Hoax

The Vampire's Game

One Night in September

Short Horror Collections

Thicker Than Water

In Sheep's Clothing

The Reunion

Romance

Gunshy